Adrenaline

SPEED SERIES **BOOK 2**

KELLY ELLIOTT

ADRENALINE
Copyright © 2016 by Kelly Elliott
Published by K. Elliott Enterprises

Visit my website at *www.kellyelliottauthor.com*

Cover Designer:
Sara Eirew Photography and Design

Editing:
Nichole Strauss with Perfectly Publishable

Design and Formatting:
Christine Borgford with Perfectly Publishable

ISBN# 978-1-943633-03-6

Books by
KELLY ELLIOTT

SPEED
Ignite
Adrenaline (March 2016)

WANTED SERIES
Wanted
Saved
Faithful
Believe
Cherished
A Forever Love
The Wanted Short Stories

THE BROKEN SERIES
Broken
Broken Dreams
Broken Promises

JOURNEY OF LOVE SERIES
Unconditional Love
Undeniable Lov
Unforgettable Love

LOVE WANTED IN TEXAS SERIES
Without You
Saving You
Holding You
Finding You
Chasing You

Dedication

For my husband, Darrin, who gave me the idea to write a story about a NASCAR driver and helped me so much along the way.

I love you more.

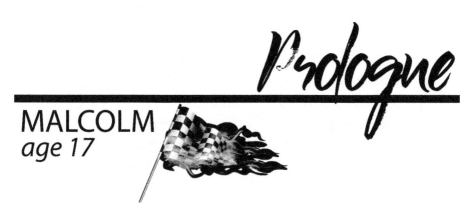

MALCOLM
age 17

S IRENS AND RED LIGHTS SURROUNDED me as I sat on the ground holding Casey in my arms. I looked at all the blood on her cheerleading uniform and cried out.

"This is not happening. Casey, please don't leave me! Baby, please don't do this to me. I'm so sorry!" I shouted as a paramedic rushed over to me.

Tears streamed down my cheeks as I looked up and begged God not to take her from me.

"Sir, you have to let her go. Sir! You have to let her go now!"

Reluctantly, I let go as I watched them perform CPR on the only girl I'd ever cared for . . . ever loved.

"I can't find a pulse!"

Burying my face in my hands, I felt my entire world come crashing down on me.

Nothing would ever be the same if I lost her.

Nothing.

NINE YEARS EARLIER

PAISLIE
age 8

I STOOD AND LOOKED UP at him as I asked, "Why are you leaving me here, Daddy? I don't want to stay here." My eyes looked everywhere as my tummy ached.

"Look at me, Paislie." His eyes were dark and cold, like when he was angry with me. "Don't cry, Paislie Lynn Pruitt. Pruitt's don't cry. You're almost nine years old, for Christ's sake."

My lips trembled as I fought to hold my tears back.

"Will you come back for me?" I asked.

He slowly shook his head. "No. I'm not coming back."

Taking a step back, he turned and walked away . . . leaving me all alone. The nun walked up and wrapped her arm around me. Bending down, she gave me a warm smile. I liked her right away. She looked like Momma. "Paislie, my name is Sister Elizabeth. Come with me and we'll get you settled in."

She guided me up the stairs as I lifted my head and read the sign, Saint Patrick's Orphanage.

Lifting my hand, I quickly wiped away my tear before Sister Elizabeth saw it.

One

MALCOLM
age 26

I PULLED BLACK JACK TO A stop as I looked out over the hill country. There was nothing like being back at home in Texas and on the ranch. No early morning strategizing meetings with Dalton. No pressure from the sponsors to be on my a-game. Nothing to worry about at all.

Just nature.

Pulling on the reigns, I turned Black Jack and headed back to the house. She'd be here soon and I still needed to take a shower. "Let's go, boy," I shouted as I gave Jack a bit of pressure to get him into a run.

Twenty minutes later and hot water was running over my body.

My hands were leaning against the travertine wall as I hung my head with my eyes closed.

"If that is not the best damn site I've seen in a while."

With a grin, I smiled as I felt her hands move across my wet body. "Did you miss me?" she whispered against my skin as she slowly moved her lips down my chest.

"Always, Ash."

With a snicker she took me in her mouth as my body jumped. My hands laced in her hair while I fucked her mouth. I knew it wouldn't take me long to come and soon I was spilling into her mouth.

Opening my eyes, I watched her wipe the cum from her mouth as she stood up with a frown, wrapping her hand around my still-hard dick. "Well damn, Malcolm. You could have at least fucked me first."

Laughing, I shook my head. "You're the one who went down on me, and it's been a while since I've had that beautiful mouth wrapped around my cock, baby."

Ashley rolled her eyes before inhaling a deep breath and blowing it out. "I'm going to go lay naked in your bed and wait for you." She raised an eyebrow and said, "Don't make me wait long or I'll get myself off."

And just like that, she was out of the shower and gone. I shook my head and quickly soaped up. That was one thing I liked about Ashley. She knew what she wanted, and what she usually wanted was a good, hard fucking. No games, no hugging afterward. Just sex.

I stepped out of the shower and wrapped a towel around my waist as I grabbed another towel and dried off my hair.

Taking a look in the mirror, I cursed when I saw the damn hickey on my chest that was left after my fling the other night.

"Fucking hell," I barely spoke. *This is why I don't fuck college girls.* I couldn't resist the beautiful blonde two nights ago though. It was my first night back in Texas and out with the boys. She eye fucked me the second I walked into the bar. An hour later we were in the bathroom and she was calling out the wrong damn name as I fucked her from behind.

I pushed out a frustrated sigh and headed into my bedroom where one very sexy woman waited naked on my bed. Pulling the towel from my waist, I crawled onto the bed and pressed my lips against her neck. Her hands grabbed onto my arms as she moaned.

"Condom," I panted as I reached over to the side table and grabbed one. Ripping the condom open with my teeth, I quickly sheathed my cock.

"I want on top," Ashley commanded.

Flipping her over, I smacked her ass as she yelped. "You got your way earlier; it's my turn to get mine."

Peeking over her shoulder, she smirked. "I want to finish you off on top."

"Deal," I said as I pushed into her. Once I got my fill of her from behind, I pulled out and let her take over.

Ashley liked it fast and hard, but tonight, I wanted it to last a little longer and I wasn't sure why.

"Slow down, Ash. I want to actually enjoy the feel of you."

Her hands were on her breasts as she dropped her head and smiled. "Can't . . . go . . . slow. Have a date."

Grabbing her hips, I stopped her movement. "What? A date? You're dating someone?"

Ashley shrugged her shoulders. "Not exclusively, we've gone out a few times. I have a phone date with him." She wiggled her eyebrows as my mouth dropped open.

"You whore!"

With a dry laugh, she began grinding on me as she raised a knowing eyebrow. "When was the last time you fucked a girl besides me?"

Without missing a beat, I replied, "Two nights ago."

"So why am I whore, but in your mind you're a stud?"

Shaking my head, I pushed my hips up, causing her to suck in a breath as she fucked me again.

She dropped her head and said, "Okay, you're a stud!"

I could feel her pussy getting tight. "Fucking hell, Ashley, I'm about to come."

"Not yet . . . oh God. Malcolm! Now!"

Her body trembled as her orgasm hit at the same moment I exploded into the condom.

She dropped to my chest as we both fought for air. Our bodies slowly came down from the euphoria.

"God, I love fucking you," Ashley panted out. She placed her hands on my chest and pushed herself up. "I swear to God, if you've ruined it for me with other men I'm going to kill you."

With a smirk and a wink, I replied, "I'm afraid once you've had a taste of the best, the rest will be a disappointment."

Rolling her eyes, she crawled off me and walked her naked ass back into my bathroom. As much as I enjoyed being with Ashley, I knew we were going to have to scale it back. Emmit was bound to find out, especially with his little sister flying in to my ranch in a damn helicopter. Someone with loose lips was going to talk.

Two minutes later she came walking out in jeans and T-shirt with her brother's car number on it.

"Seriously? You're going to fuck me and then come walking out with that asshole's car on your shirt."

With a wink, she grabbed her purse and phone and walked over to me. Sitting on the bed, she looked into my eyes. "Why do you think we do this, Malcolm?"

"Do what?" I asked.

She motioned between us with her hands. "This. The whole friends-with-benefits thing we have going on."

"Because you're good in bed, and I like the thrill of sneaking around behind your brother's back. It's a rush."

Ashley tilted her head. "It's a rush?"

"Hell yeah. It starts with that and top it off with hot sex, and it's fucking mind blowing."

Ashley's face dropped for one quick second before being replaced with a slight grin. "Yeah it is fun, but don't you ever get tired of this life? The constant rotation of girls?"

I laughed as I shook my head. "No, I don't. This is the life I want, Ash. I don't want to be tied down to one girl. Besides, I'm incapable of loving anyone."

Her eyes grew sad and I knew what she was thinking, but she was kind enough not to bring Casey up.

She looked down at her hands. "You remember Jon? The guy I was talking to? I kind of like this guy, Malcolm."

I sat up and leaned against the headrest. "What?" I chuckled. "You said you weren't looking for a relationship."

"I'm not! Well, at least I didn't think I was, but the whole time we were together tonight, I kept thinking about him."

Ouch. That hurt the ego a bit.

"Well fuck, Ashley, why didn't you just call out his name for fuck's sake?"

She shook her head and frowned. "That's not what I meant. As much as I like this thing we have, I think we need to take a step back from it. I'm feeling confused about my feelings for Jon, and as much as I love escaping reality and flying out to wherever you are for a fun roll around in the sack, I need to figure this out."

Pursing my lips together, I nodded. I'd been thinking the same damn thing earlier, but to hear it coming from her mouth hurt more than I thought it would. "Okay. Will I see you again or was this it?"

Ashley chewed on her lower lip before giving me a sexier-than-hell smile. "Oh Malcolm, you're not the type of guy a girl walks away from and never looks back."

Before she stood, she leaned over and gently kissed my lips. "Thanks for tonight. I had fun."

With a smile, I pulled her back to me and kissed her one more time. I never kissed the girls I fucked, but Ashley was different. As much as I didn't want to admit it, she woke something up inside of me and I needed to figure out what in the hell it was. "Let me at least walk you out."

Her eyes sparkled as she stood up. "Okay."

I quickly got dressed and placed my hand on her lower back as we made our way out and down to the helicopter pad. Ashley filled me in on the way about this Jon guy.

Stepping outside the door, I stopped and turned Ashley to me. "Hey, I know all of this has just been about having a good time, but I really do care about you, Ash. If this guy does anything to you, you'll tell me, right?"

With a tender smile, Ashley placed her hand on the side of my face and gently rubbed her thumb along my skin.

"Malcolm, one of these days you're going to meet someone who is going to make you want more. I know what we had was just the first step in moving on."

I swallowed hard and dropped my eyes.

"When you meet her you're going to know instantly. Don't push her away."

With a chuckle, I took her hand in mine and pushed one of her fingers inside my mouth. I slowly sucked on it while I pulled it out while her mouth parted open. If there was one thing I knew how to do, it was use sex to my advantage. Anytime a woman started to talk about feelings, all I had to do was give them a visual.

"I'm glad you found someone who makes you feel that way, Ashley. But I lost that privilege a long time ago and I have no interest in it anymore."

Ashley pulled a deep breath in through her nose and slowly blew it out. "I'll see you soon?"

"Is that a question or a statement?"

Giggling, she took a few steps back. "Bye, Malcolm."

She turned and headed over toward the helicopter pad as I shook my head and smiled. If finding love was what Ashley wanted, I wished her all the best. That shit was not in the cards for me.

Never has been . . . never will.

TWO

PAISLIE
age 26

T HE MOMENT I SMELLED THAT familiar cinnamon-apple scent, I smiled and instantly relaxed.

Home.

I dropped my keys on the antique table that sat in the entryway and kicked off the overly-expensive shoes my best friend, Annie, talked me into buying two weeks ago.

My hand went to the back of my neck where I massaged it while making my way into my modest two-bedroom apartment. Bending down, I held my hand out in hopes my bitch of a cat would at least welcome me home.

"Well hey there, sweet girl."

Princess was a gray and white cat who still looked like a kitten. She'd barely grown after I got her and every single one of my friends called her 'the kitten'. I was positive that was why she was such a little biotch. Her ego was bruised.

The cat stared at me like she couldn't have cared less that I was there. Standing, I blew out a frustrated breath and made my way over to the kitchen.

"I bet you'll love on me if I give you some food, won't you, girl?"

Sure enough, when I pulled the lid back on her cat food, Princess ran in between my legs.

"There ya go, girl; eat up while I look for something for me to eat."

My cell phone rang as I stood in front of the refrigerator and stared at nothing but almond milk, blueberries, and leftover Chinese food.

Annie's name moved across the screen as I swiped my finger. "Hello?"

Music blared from the other end of the phone. "Annie? Where are you?"

"Paislie! Oh my gawd! You have to come out tonight. I know you said you were tired, but the amount of hot guys at this new bar is insane!"

Rolling my eyes, I leaned against the counter. "I can't, Annie. I have a full day tomorrow at work."

"Why is it always about work with you?"

Annie grew up in a very privileged home, unlike me who bounced from foster home to foster home and always ended back at the orphanage.

With a dry laugh, I replied, "Um . . . because I need it to clothe and feed myself."

Annie huffed into the phone. "Paislie, you are the only person I know who puts a dedicated amount of money away in your savings. Girl, do you have any idea how fun shopping would be if you actually spent money?"

My eyes closed as I tried to keep my feelings in check. If she only knew how much I would love to go shopping and splurge on two hundred-dollar shoes and purses and go out every single weekend and party.

"Annie, you've never spent a day hungry in your life. If you had, you'd be more like me."

The music got louder as I heard Annie laugh and say something to someone. "I'm talking to my best friend, you'd love her!"

"What did you say, sweetie? I was flirting with this good-looking football player, who I'm pretty sure needs to be between you and your sheets."

A giggle slipped from my lips as I shook my head. "I don't remember the last time I had sex."

"Paislie, *please!*"

My eyes roamed my empty apartment. If I didn't go out, I would end up making a peanut butter and jelly sandwich and watching HGTV until I fell asleep.

"Fine. Where are you?"

"Oh. My. God! Did you say yes?"

Loosening my hair from the ponytail, I headed to my bedroom. "Yes, what should I wear?"

Annie screamed into the phone causing me to pull it from my ear. "Do you remember that little blue dress we bought a few months back?"

My eyebrows pinched together as I walked into my beautiful,

oversized, empty walk-in closet. I had three dresses hanging up on one side all by their lonesome. "Yep, I'm looking at it right now."

"Wear that, put your hair up, and wear those strappy heels we just bought."

I groaned at the idea of putting those bitches back on. "Fine."

"Sunset Row Bar! Hurry!"

The line went dead before I even had a chance to ask her if I should drive or not.

With a shrug, I called a car service and said I would be ready in fifteen minutes. Tossing my phone on the bed, I stripped my clothes off and walked over to my dresser. Pulling it open, I rummaged through my panties. I'd give anything to put on a pair of boy shorts, but the nude lace thong was picked instead.

"Where is that matching bra?" I spoke out loud. I'd gotten into the habit of talking to myself shortly after my father dropped me off at Saint Patrick's Orphanage. It was the only way to keep myself sane. Talking to God and myself.

Spotting the bra on the chair in my reading nook, I smiled. "There you are!"

Slipping the dress on, I pulled my hair up and applied a small amount of make-up before grabbing a clutch and heading back into the living room.

Princess was perched on her kitty condo cleaning herself. She barely acknowledged the fact that I walked by her.

I moaned as I slipped the Michael Kors shoes back on, that according to Annie, I got for a steal. "I'm going out, Princess. Be good while I'm gone!"

AFTER PAYING THE STUPID COVER to get into the Sunset Row Bar, I made my way over to the bar and waited in line for a drink.

Me: I'm here. At the bar getting a Bud Light.

It wasn't thirty seconds later and Annie was texting me back with my first mistake of the night.

> *The BFF: No! Don't order a beer. What is wrong with you? Get something fruity for Pete's sake!*

"What can I get you, pretty lady?"

My eyes looked up to find the handsome bartender smiling at me. Pushing a stray piece of brown hair behind my ear, I flashed him a smile and replied, "A Dos Equis with a lime please. Got to get my fruit in."

His eyes lit up as he gave me a quick once over. The sexy smile that spread wider across his face caused my chest to warm up. "I don't think I've ever seen you here before," he said as he opened the beer and pushed a lime on the rim.

Okay, Paislie, it's time to get your flirt on. "Never been here before."

When his eyes landed on my lips, I gave them a quick lick. "The name is Greg."

Reaching my hand across the bar, I replied, "Paislie, it's a pleasure meeting you, Greg."

"Oh, baby, I hope the pleasure will be mine by the end of the night."

Wow. Damn. Slow down there, boy.

Pushing a twenty his way, I winked and said, "Keep the change."

Before I even had a chance to turn around, I was grabbed and being drug out toward the dance floor.

"What have I told you? Never flirt with the bartenders and always order a fruity drink!"

I held my bottle of beer up in front of Annie's face. "It has a lime!"

She rolled her eyes and mumbled something I couldn't hear over the music.

Glancing over her shoulder, she gave me a naughty smile. "You are going to love Trey!"

"Who's Trey?" I shouted.

She scrunched up her nose and yelled, "You'll see."

We came to a stop in front of a large table filled with overly-beautiful people. "What is this, an audition table for The Bachelor?" I asked with a chuckle.

Annie hit me as I glanced around the table. My eyes stopped on one guy who had his face buried in his phone.

Oh holy hell. His body. His dark hair. His body.

My insides quivered at the thought of getting lost in him. A few forbidden moments of pleasure to forget everything else.

Yummy.

"That's who I was talking about on the phone. Come on," Annie said, leading me over to the hot guy on his phone.

"Trey, this is my friend, Paislie." Trey stood and I got a better look at his fit body. Okay, so my insides melted and my stomach was tugging with the idea of this guy on top of me.

Forgive me, Sister Elizabeth.

"Paislie, this is Trey. You're both workaholics in need of getting drunk and having some fun."

Trey laughed as he took my hand and gently kissed the back of it while my teeth sunk into my lip.

"Paislie, it's a pleasure meeting you."

Jesus . . . his voice melted my panties.

"Trey," I said. Then something happened and I forgot all my good sense. "Hopefully the pleasure will be mine by the end of the evening."

Annie's mouth dropped open as I tried to make it seem like I didn't just sound like a class-act whore. Worse yet . . . I took the damn bartender's pick-up line. How lame was I?

His dark-brown eyes lit up with a fire as he leaned in closer to me and placed his lips next to my ear. "I can make that happen."

Oh, hell yes. I was getting laid tonight.

Trey and I spent the next two hours dancing, talking, and drinking. Lots and lots of drinking. I wasn't surprised when we ended back at my apartment and Trey did indeed feel good between my sheets and me.

The moment his tongue dove deep inside of me, I gasped and grabbed his hair. "Forgive me, Sister Elizabeth," I mumbled as my body trembled.

I'd only let one other guy go down on me, and we dated for six months before he finally talked me into it.

Trey, however, was a one-night stand who I intended on having fun with. A lot of fun. If I was going to do this, I was going to do it the right way.

"Damn baby, I want to bury myself inside you."

My breathing was erratic as my brown eyes looked into his. "Do it!" I cried out as he ripped the condom open and rolled it on.

For one night I wanted to be naughty. I didn't want to think about clients, or money, or my worthless father who called again to ask for money. I didn't want to think how no guy ever made my insides all mushy or the fact that I was incapable of love.

Tonight I wanted to be fucked six ways to Sunday and I wouldn't feel guilty at all about it like I always did.

Wrapping my legs around Trey, I sucked in his lower lip while he slowly pushed in. "Oh God . . . I want it hard and fast."

He smiled and pushed in hard, causing me to let out a small yelp. I was going to feel that tomorrow.

"Fast and hard you say?"

Nodding my head, I held on while he gave me exactly what I wanted.

MALCOLM

I PUSHED THE DOOR OPEN and smiled when I saw Emmit sitting at the conference table. We'd become a lot closer the last few months and I was somewhat glad things had stopped with Ashley. As much as I loved the thrill of sneaking behind Emmit's back, I had to admit the guilt was getting to me.

Mr. Elliot had called a drivers' meeting and requested all three of his drivers be present. Something about an announcement being made before the start of the next season.

Walking up to my biggest rival and newly-made friend, I held my hand out. Emmit stood and shook it. "Malcolm, how's your break been?"

With a grin, I replied, "Good. Been doing a bit of traveling, working on the ranch. Shit like that. How about you? How is the domesticated life treating you?"

Emmit's face lit up and for a brief moment, my chest tightened. Once upon a time I dreamed of a life like Emmit's. A very long time ago.

"It's good."

"By the smile on your face, I'd say it's more than good."

Emmit let out a dry laugh. "Yeah, it's amazing. I wouldn't trade it for the world."

There went that tightness again. Turning my attention away from Emmit, I gave Doug a firm handshake. "Doug, enjoying your time off?"

"Yes, I am."

Mr. Elliot walked in with three suits following behind him. That was never a good sign.

"Gentlemen, thank you for joining me."

Out of the corner of my eye, I saw all three of our crew chiefs coming in and sitting down.

Mr. Elliot cleared his throat as he looked around the room. "I want to thank everyone for coming in for this meeting. It's hard to believe the season starts up in two months, but I wanted to bring everyone in before the holidays and before we made a public announcement."

I discretely took a look at both Emmit and Doug. Emmit didn't seem the least bit phased by this meeting, whereas Doug looked how I felt.

"After much debate and talking to his crew chief, myself and his family, Emmit has decided he is going to be stepping down as one of Elliot Racing's drivers."

My stomach dropped as I snapped my head over to Emmit. "Are you kidding me?" I busted out as Emmit turned my way. "Why? Emmit, you're at the top of your game. You just won the championship. You're not even old for fuck's sake!"

Laughter filled the room as Emmit smiled as he replied, "All the more reason to leave now."

I dropped back in my seat as I sat there in a state of shock and barely heard anything else Mr. Elliot had said. Something about a new driver being brought up from the Xfinity Series.

Before I knew it, the meeting was over and the suits were all shaking Emmit's hand and wishing him well. Once the room was cleared, it was just the two of us.

"Help me to understand this, Emmit. You're walking away from your dream career. For as long as I've known you, this has been the life you wanted."

His eyes turned soft as he walked up to me. He reached into his wallet and pulled out a picture and handed it to me. It was a picture of his son, Landon, and his wife, Adaline.

"Bullshit. You can't tell me you're quitting because of your family. Plenty of drivers have families, Emmit."

With a sigh, Emmit reached for the picture as I handed it to him. "I know it's hard for you to understand, but something in me has changed this last year or so. Don't get me wrong, I love racing and I always will. This isn't something Addie asked me to do either. She has been one-hundred-percent supportive." Emmit pushed his hand through his hair and let out a laugh. "I'm not retiring . . . I'm just taking a step back. Exploring different things. It wasn't an easy decision to make, trust me."

"I'm stunned, dude. I'm speechless and that never happens. Is this truly what you want, Emmit?"

His eyes lit up with a happiness I longed for as he placed his hand on my shoulder and squeezed it. "It really is. I'm honestly the happiest I have ever been in my life. I want to spend time with my family. I thought racing was my world; turns out it was a stepping block to the world I truly wanted."

I couldn't believe what I was hearing. If Emmit was happy though, then so was I. "I'm happy for you then. But fuck . . . who am I going to bump with out there and piss off?"

With his head thrown back, Emmit let out roar of laughter. "Oh trust me, you piss off plenty of drivers; you don't need me."

"WELCOME BACK HOME, MR. WALLACE."

I pulled Nancy into my arms and gave her a hug. She kept me sane, kept my house cleaned, and made sure I had food. "Hey, Nancy. I missed your beautiful face."

Her cheeks flushed as she lightly slapped me on the chest. "I'm old enough to be your mother, and trust me, you couldn't keep up with me."

And there was the other reason I loved her. She had a feisty spirit.

She took my coat from my hands and hung it up as I walked into the living room and headed to the kitchen. "I don't know, Nancy, I've been told I'm a pretty good lover."

"Pesh, stop talking nonsense. How was Texas?"

My heart ached at the mentioning of home. Sure, North Carolina was where I lived, but my true home was the three-thousand-acre ranch I owned in Crawford. This home was a four-thousand-square-foot museum for my mother to put shit in she bought while traveling.

"Texas was wonderful as always. The only reason I came back was for your chicken and dumplings."

"Uh-huh. I'm sure it was."

Nancy lived in the guesthouse behind the main house. There have been plenty of times she walked in on more than one naked girl in this house. And every single time she preached to them about walking around a man's home naked. She even brought one girl to tears. *Damn what was that chick's name?*

"Who's name?"

My head snapped over to look at her. "Huh?"

"You just asked, what was that chick's name. Girls are not chickens, Malcolm."

I grabbed a beer from the refrigerator and laughed. "I can't believe I said that out loud. I was trying to think of the name of the girl who you made cry when you basically called her a whore for walking around my house naked."

Nancy snarled her lip. "Oh. Her. Rhonda was her name I believe. Couldn't have been but twenty-one."

Placing the beer to my lips, I took a drink. "I like them young, Nancy. You should know that by now."

She rolled her eyes and said, "All I know is when you come home I need to make sure I have Lysol wipes for my poor kitchen island."

Laughing, I tried to remember the last time I fucked girl on my kitchen island. Oh yeah . . . Linda . . . the chick who does all the gardening.

"I ought to give Linda a call. See about some winter plants or something."

Nancy glared at me and shook her head. "Get out of my kitchen and let me think clearly so I can make you some dinner, or are you going out tonight?"

"Actually, Emmit invited me over to dinner."

Nancy's mouth dropped. "Emmit? Emmit Lewis? Is this a good idea?"

I downed the rest of my beer as I kissed Nancy on the forehead. "I think it will be fine. He wants to show me his blissfully happy life and all that shit."

"Or he found out you're having sex with his sister and he is going to poison you."

Tilting my head, I agreed. "There's that too."

My evening consisted of watching two people madly in love with each other exchange looks, kiss each other way more than needed and one over-the-top adorable baby who I couldn't seem to give back to his mother.

Adaline sat down next to me and gave me that smile of hers. The one where she thinks she is going to have this great heart to heart with me and all the problems in my world will be solved.

"So . . ."

I held Landon and continued to make goofy faces at him. As long as he kept laughing, I was going to keep doing it.

"So what?" I asked.

Adaline leaned over to see where Emmit was. "You and Ashley still . . . you know?"

I completely ignored her which pissed her off. It was fun making Adaline mad. I really needed to do it more often.

"Don't ignore me, Malcolm Wallace. I've carried your dirty little secret and I get to hear all the juicy details cause Ashley claims y'all are just . . . well you're um . . . how do I say this?"

"Fucking?"

Adaline made a dramatic gasping sound. "Not in front of the baby!"

"Oh yeah, cause he totally understands what fucking is."

"Oh my gawd! You did it again!" she cried out as Landon started laughing.

With a glance up toward the kitchen where Emmit still was, I shook my head. "I haven't seen her in a few weeks. We decided to call it quits."

Adaline fell back and clutched her chest. "Oh thank goodness. I was so afraid Emmit would find out."

"Yeah well, no need to worry anymore; she found Jon."

She leaned forward as she narrowed her eyes at me. "Does that bother you she found someone she likes?"

"No! I'm honestly happy for her. Surprised, but happy none the less."

"Are you sure? Maybe the old Malcolm is getting tired of all the sleeping with women."

Now it was my turn to gasp. Why did everyone think I was ready to settle down and be a one-woman kind of man? It was starting to piss me off. "Bite your tongue." I handed her Landon and stood. "Speaking of."

"Wait! Malcolm, seriously. You're not ready to start looking at maybe settling down? Find someone who will be there when you fall asleep *and* when you wake up?"

An image of Casey flashed through my head as I tried like hell to make it go away. "I've got to go. I'll show myself out. Tell Emmit I said thank you for dinner and I'll talk to him soon."

Her disappointed look made me feel guilty, but the last thing I wanted to talk about was my sex life.

"How about dinner on Sunday?" Adaline called out.

Lifting my hand, I gave her a wave. "I need to ease into this friendship thing with Emmit. Bye sweet, Addie. Thank you for dinner."

As I opened the door, I heard Adaline laugh. "Bye, Malcolm!"

I spent the rest of the night trying to forget how I felt being around Emmit and Adaline. Trying desperately to ignore the pain in my chest as I longed for what they had. Trying to forget as I fucked some girl in the back seat of my truck who I picked up at a bar.

Four

PAISLIE

TREY HAD SLIPPED OUT OF bed earlier and took a shower while I laid there and stared out my oversized window. The guilt of last night washed over me like a wave of nausea. I rolled over as the sheet slipped down, exposing me more than I wanted.

Trey turned and smiled. It was a beautiful smile and I wished like hell it did something more to me, but it didn't. I read in all those damn romance books how your heart is supposed to fall or stupid butterflies flutter in your stomach.

Bullshit.

None of that had ever happened to me.

When he dropped the towel he had wrapped around his waist, something did happen. My lower stomach pooled with heat as I licked my lips.

"Good morning," he softly spoke.

My eyes lit up at the sound of his voice as I pulled the sheet down, exposing my naked body to him. "Not yet it isn't."

His smile grew as he crawled onto the bed and kissed me sweetly. I wasn't used to guys hanging around the morning after. Not like I had a revolving door of men coming and going. I'd slept with about six different guys my entire life. None of them I shared any kind of relationship with.

All men wanted the same thing.

Sex.

Of course I had had plenty of fun with plenty of guys. If they were willing to get me off in the corner of a club, or in my car, I was more than up for it. Anything to numb the emptiness I felt in my heart. Sex was saved for when I really needed to forget life.

Wrapping my arms around him, I pulled him on me and quickly forgot about my guilt as my legs hooked around the back of his.

"Condom," I spoke against his lips as he grabbed one off the side table and sheathed himself.

He pushed in as we both let out a moan. Slowly he made love to me. It was different. It was nice. It was something I could learn to like. And that scared the hell out of me.

With his forehead leaning against mine, our breathing slowly returned to normal.

"I need to tell you I don't normally go home with women like this."

With a smile, I chewed on my lip. "I don't normally bring guys home like this either."

His amber eyes shinned a bit brighter as he kissed the tip of my nose; a sweet gesture that did nothing. I was positive it should have made me feel some kind of swoon moment.

Trey pulled out of me and removed the condom before lying down next to me. "Will you have breakfast with me?"

Pressing my lips together, I had to keep the panic feeling rising in my chest down as I rolled over on my side to face him. "Breakfast?" I asked with a smile.

"Yeah. And maybe after practice, dinner?"

My fingers moved lightly over his huge arm. Damn this guy was built like a rock. "What kind of practice?" His face pulled back in shock before it was replaced by a look of sheer bliss. His grin caused me to chuckle. "What's with that smile?"

"You don't know who I am?"

My heart dropped. *Oh shit. Am I supposed to know him? Oh hell. Shit. Shit. Shit. What have I got myself into?*

"Um . . . should I?"

He pulled my body closer to his as my hand went to his massive chest. "No. You have no idea how happy you just made with that simple answer, Paislie."

I liked how Trey made me feel. Not many men made me feel like I was wanted for something other than money or sex. "So are you going to tell me why you thought I knew you?"

His smile faded for a brief second. "Promise it won't change anything?"

Lifting my pinky finger up, I replied with, "I pinky promise."

"Trey Rogers. I play for the Dallas Cowboys."

My smile dropped and I pinched my eyebrows together as I let it sink in that I just had sex all night, and then again this morning, with the star running back of the Dallas Cowboys. "Does this mean I have to be a fan of the Cowboys now, 'cause I'm more of a Texan's fan," I said as Trey let out a roar of laughter and pulled me on top of him.

"I like you, Paislie."

As much as I didn't want to say it . . . I forced it out as to not hurt Trey's feelings. "I kind of like you too, Trey."

PUSHING THE LARGE DOORS OPEN, I made my way into the old church. Dipping my fingers in holy water, I made the sign of the cross. My heart felt light and free as I walked further in. Bending on one knee, I slid down the wooden pew and quickly went to my knees.

Crossing my hands, I rested my forehead.

Please forgive me father for my weakness. Forgive me for desiring the needs my body selfishly craves.

"I thought I saw you walking in."

Her voice pulled me from my prayer. Turning to look over my shoulder, I smiled when I saw Sister Elizabeth.

"Elizabeth," I said as I pushed myself up and made my way to her. Dropping to my knees, I let my head fall.

"Child, why are you dropping to your knees before me? Stand up, Paislie."

Doing as she said, I stood, took her hands in mine and kissed the back of them. "I've missed you, Sister Elizabeth."

My eyes took in the only woman I'd ever had in my life as a mother-figure. She was a young, beautiful twenty-year-old when she first held my eight-year-old hand in hers and led me into Saint Patrick's Orphanage. Now she stood before me as an even more beautiful thirty-seven-year-old woman, who also happened to be one of my best friends.

With a smile, I shook my head. "I'm not sure I'll ever get used to the fact you don't wear a habit anymore."

With a chuckle, she wrapped her arm with mine as we made our way to the front of the church.

"I see the heaviness in your eyes, Paislie. Do you want to talk?"

At one point in my life, I told this woman everything. Every hope, desire, and dream I had floating in my head, even my wish to follow in her footsteps and become a nun.

"I was asking for forgiveness."

"Hmm . . . for?"

My eyes closed as we sat in the front pew. "My ways."

"I see," she said as she looked at me. "Paislie, you're a young woman and your *ways* as you call them are normal feelings that every woman has. Even me."

Pressing my lips together, my chin trembled. "I'm not as strong as you, Elizabeth."

"Strength has nothing to do with it. I had a calling . . . your calling is not the same as mine."

"Do you ever wish your life was different?"

She lifted her brow as she stared intently at me. "Let's go for a walk outside. I need to check and see how my winter garden is doing today."

Lacing my arm with hers, we made our way out to the garden tucked behind the church.

I inhaled a deep breath of air as I let the familiar smells of this place fill my senses. After walking in silence for a few minutes, she finally spoke.

"Paislie, you let guilt fill your heart when you follow your human nature. Sex is not a bad thing and something you certainly shouldn't feel the need to drop to your knees and ask forgiveness for."

I swallowed hard. "What if I'm using it for all the wrong reasons?"

She lifted a brow. "You don't have feelings for him?"

I let out a gruff laugh. "No, Elizabeth. It's nothing like that." Anytime we were alone and just the two of us, I called her Elizabeth. Around others from the church, she was always Sister Elizabeth. Over the years we had grown very close. With just twelve years separating us, she was more like an older sibling to me. Almost a mother figure. "It's always been about the feeling I get out of sex. The desire to have a man want me for something . . . anything. The attention feels . . . good."

Motioning for me to sit on a bench, she softly replied, "Oh . . . I see."

"I'm making myself sound like a slut. Forgive my language. I haven't slept with that many men, but more than I should have at my age. I often wonder if I'm even capable of loving someone. If I let my heart open up to them, I have a fear they're going to leave me like my father did."

"Everyone is capable of loving, Paislie. Don't let what your father did to you lead you down a road you're not meant to travel."

I thought back to this morning with Trey. "I did meet a guy last night. We had a . . . um . . . well, we had a good time together." I felt the heat in my cheeks as Elizabeth covered her mouth to hide her smile.

"Do you like him?"

With a shrug of my shoulders I chewed on my lip. "I think I *could* possibly like him. He knows how to make me . . . well . . . gosh you know sometimes it would be so much easier if you weren't a catholic nun!"

With a giggle, she bumped my arm. "I am still a woman though. I have the same desires as you do."

"Oh, Elizabeth I'm pretty sure your desires are nothing like mine."

We both laughed as she nodded her head. "Most likely not. Paislie, do me one favor."

"Anything," I said with a smile.

"Open your heart and let your father leaving you go. You're going to meet someone who is going to love you and want to give you every bit of happiness he can."

Wringing my hands together, I pushed out a deep breath. "I sure hope God will let me know when I meet him. So far he has given me no clues."

Standing, she reached for my hand. "Trust me. He will. Now help me pick some of this squash. You can take some home with you."

My heart always felt so much lighter after visiting with Elizabeth. If only I thought the words she spoke were true.

MALCOLM

FEBRUARY

"**S**TAY CLEAR OF THAT DEBRIS around turn four," Dalton said as I focused on my line.

"Yep."

"Number eighteen is two car lengths ahead," Russ, my spotter said.

Gripping the steering wheel, I had four laps to try and pass the eighteen car to win the Daytona 500.

"Seventy-eight is coming up on your inside."

"The fuck he is," I said as I hit the gas more.

"We've only got three laps to go, Malcolm. Easy."

"Easy? It's the fucking Daytona 500, Dalton."

"Where is he?" I yelled out to Russ.

"Lap traffic has slowed him down; looks like you were half a second faster on that last lap."

Dalton calmly stated, "Keep doing what you're doing, buddy. We'll get him."

The next lap I focused on catching up to the number eighteen car.

"Bumper. Door. Door. Bumper. Clear! You cleared the eighteen," Russ shouted as I ran the line that had been working for me all day.

"Please tell me Emmit is watching this on TV and wishing his ass was back out here!" I said as I took the white flag.

"One to go. All clear."

My heart was pounding in my chest as I came around turn three.

"Where is he?"

Russ came over my headphones. "You're clear by at least two car lengths. Lap traffic coming up, go high."

Coming out of turn four, I took it high and passed the lap traffic and took the checkered flag.

"I can't believe it!" I shouted amongst all the whooping and hollering. "We fucking did it, boys! Yes!"

The Daytona 500. I just won the fucking Daytona 500.

BY THE TIME I MADE it back to my trailer, I was exhausted. Almost every other driver had pulled out already as I climbed up the steps and pulled the door open. Sitting on the sofa was a pretty brunette with her hair pulled up and piled on top of her head.

"Congrats on the big win," she said as she popped a giant pink bubble.

With a grin as wide as ever, I held my arms open as my baby sister bounced up and jumped into my arms. "What in the hell are you doing here, Autumn?"

"Surprising my big brother. Although there is one very pissed off girl who thought she was going to be getting lucky tonight until I had to send her away."

Laughing, I pulled her in tighter. "Please tell me Sophie is with you."

"Yep, she is crashed in your bed. Sorry. I know you're exhausted."

I held her out and took her in. "You look beautiful. Where's Jake?"

Her smile dropped and I instantly wanted to hurt the guy just from the look in her eyes. "He um . . . he told me he needed to take a break."

My head pulled back as I stared at her in disbelief. "Take a break from what?"

With a shrug, she said, "Our marriage. The life we made, the child we have together."

"That son-of-a-bitch. I'm going to fucking kill him. I told you something like this was going to happen. I never trusted that asshole!"

Autumn squeezed my arms. "Listen, Malcolm, it was a long shot that our marriage would even work, ya know? We got married way too young and had Sophie way *way* too young."

"How does he not want his own child?" I fumed.

"I didn't say he didn't want her. He doesn't want her full time."

My fingers laced through my hair as I paced back and forth. "That doesn't even make a fucking lick of sense, Autumn."

The door opened and Hank walked in. Since Emmit wasn't racing, Hank requested to drive for me. I welcomed him with open arms. The guy was easy going and one hell of a good poker player.

"Hey, Hank. This is my sister, Autumn. This is Hank, my driver."

Reaching his hand out, Hank gave Autumn a polite grin and said, "It's a pleasure to meet you."

"The pleasure is all mine. I hope you don't mind a few stowaways aboard the bus?"

Hank glanced around looking for someone else as he said, "Nope. No bother to me."

Motioning toward the back of the bus, I said, "My niece, Sophie, she's five and currently crashed on my bed."

Hank smiled. "Gotcha. The more the merrier."

Hank made his way to the driver's seat while I turned back to Autumn. "Listen, let me go shower and we'll talk okay?"

Her eyes filled with tears, but she quickly got herself under control. "Sounds good. Are you hungry? I can make you a sandwich or something?"

Pulling her toward me, I kissed her forehead. "Sounds good, sis."

Making my way to the bathroom, I snuck into the bedroom and grabbed sweats and a T-shirt. Glancing down at the princess sleeping on my bed, I felt that familiar tug on my heart. The same one I felt at Emmit and Adaline's place when I was playing with Landon.

"Jesus, I need to get laid," I whispered as I headed into the bathroom.

Fifteen minutes later I was sitting across from my sister, listening to her tell me how her husband decided their marriage was over.

"He bought plane tickets a few weeks ago for us to come and surprise you here for the race. Then, last night he decided was a good time to let me know he needed to take a step back and find himself."

My fists balled up as I said, "You realize I want to make him feel pain, right?"

With a lighthearted laugh, Autumn rolled her eyes. "I'm sure the punch on the jaw from me last night gave him a little dose of pain."

My eyes widened. "You punched him?"

She looked at me like I was insane. "Of course I did. I grew up with you; I know how to throw a good punch." Lifting her hand, it was swollen twice its size.

"Shit! Autumn, you should have ice on that."

Waving me off, she shook her head. "It's okay. It doesn't hurt nearly as much as it did last night."

I jumped up and walked into the kitchen area. Grabbing a hand towel, I put some ice in it and walked back over to her. "Here, put this on there, it will make me feel better."

With a huff, she took it and placed it on her hand. "Ice isn't really going to help it now, Malcolm."

I sat across from her, ignoring her last comment. "So did he move out?"

She looked down and stared at nothing as she said, "He works from home, so he asked if Sophie and I could move out."

"What the fuck?" I roared as her head snapped up.

"Malcolm! You'll wake up Sophie."

Leaning closer to her, I spoke softly. "He fucking expects you and the baby to move out? What kind of an asshole is this guy, Autumn? I mean, I never really liked him, but my God. What kind of man asks his wife and daughter to move out?"

"The kind who is currently only thinking of himself." She started chewing on her lip as she said, "I thought about moving back to Waco. Maybe I could stay with Mom and Pop for a bit. Get a job and get on my feet enough to rent a house for me and Sophie."

I laughed as I stared at her like she was insane. "Mom and Pop? You want to live with Mom and Pop?"

The look of despair was all over her face. I could hear the fear and uncertainty laced in her voice as she frowned and replied, "What else am I going to do?"

I pulled in a deep breath as I thought about how I could word this without it seeming like a hand out. I loved my sister very much and there wasn't anything I wouldn't do for her. "Is Waco where you want to be?"

"Kind of. I mean, Dallas is only an hour and a half from Waco, so if the asshole wants to see his daughter it's not that far. I don't think I can afford to stay in Dallas, plus Waco is home."

"North Carolina? You could stay at my place."

Autumn shook her head. "As much as I would love to take Sophie as far away from Jake as I could, I can't do that to his parents. They love her and she loves them."

If my sister moved in with our parents she'd surely lose her damn mind. "What about the ranch? Y'all could stay there. It's only thirty minutes outside of Waco. And for the time being, you could really help me out with some stuff."

Her eyebrows rose. "Wouldn't I need to be in North Carolina for that?"

"Nah. I've got plenty of shit and you'd take some heat off of Janet, my assistant. Meanwhile, how long are you planning on following me on the circuit?"

Autumn laughed before her smile faded. "I miss you," she whispered.

My throat had a huge lump in it as I replied, "I've missed you too. Please stay at the ranch, Autumn. The place is plenty big and no one is ever there when the season starts."

Fiddling with her hands, she asked, "Are you sure?"

Standing, I held my hand out for her. She placed her hand in mine as I pulled her up. "You're my sister. There isn't anything I wouldn't do for you or Sophie. As far as I'm concerned you can live there permanently if you want."

A tear rolled down her cheek as she fought to speak. "I don't want to depend on my family to help me raise my daughter. What if I can't do it? I'm so scared."

My heart ached for my sister, and if there was one thing I hated more than anything, it was seeing her cry. I lifted my hand and wiped her tear away. "Don't be. I'll always take care of you and Sophie. Always."

She practically threw herself against my body and sobbed. I closed my eyes and rested my chin on the top of her head as I plotted how to hurt that asshole husband of hers.

"Someday you're going to make someone so happy, Malcolm. She'll be the luckiest girl in the world."

Squeezing my eyes shut harder, I shook my head and confessed, "That dreamed died a long time ago."

PAISLIE

MARCH

"A NASCAR RACE?" I ASKED WITH my mouth dropped open in shock. "I hate racing."

Trey smiled as he held the door to the limo open for me. "Come on, baby. We're in Vegas, and I had tickets. I promise you'll love it."

I rolled my eyes as I slid into the car. As much as I hated Vegas, I desperately needed a vacation from work and when Trey offered up a trip to Vegas for the weekend, who was I to turn him down. Of course me being me, I paid for my flight and even booked my own hotel room. The last thing I wanted to do was make Trey think I was only with him for his money. Truth be told . . . I was about to break things off with him before he asked me to go. I didn't have the heart to do it, so I put it off . . . again. This was the fourth time I had tried to break it off and backed out. Trey was the first guy who ever really put any effort into a relationship with me, yet I still felt like something was off.

The sex was good. Not mind blowing, but good. I had hoped the longer we dated the more I would begin to feel something for him, but nothing happened.

"I seriously doubt I'm going to love watching cars race around a track as they are being driven by grown men who forgot to grow up."

Trey tossed his head back and laughed as he reached for my hand. "So, are you enjoying Vegas?"

With a fake smile, I nodded. "Yes. I'm having a really great time."

"So can I convince you to fly back to Texas on my plane?"

Why the idea of flying around in private planes with Trey made me feel like a paid whore, I'll never know. It didn't feel right.

"No, but I will let you give me one incredible orgasm before I leave for the airport tomorrow."

I could see the disappointment on his face before he flashed that brilliant smile of his. "It's a deal. But, in the meantime, I think we should have a warm up."

Before I could argue, his mouth was on mine and his hand went up my skirt. He pushed my panties out of the way while I opened wider, giving him access to ease the instant throbbing between my legs.

It didn't take long before Trey was swallowing up my moans as he finger fucked me to an orgasm.

Pulling his fingers out, he kissed me once more before pulling his phone out and making a call.

Frowning, I adjusted my panties and turned to look out the window, all of sudden feeling very uncomfortable in my own skin.

"Hey, it's me. Yeah, just checking in. That's great. Sounds good. Listen, got to run but I'll call you later, okay?"

I never knew who Trey was talking to half the time. I assumed it was his assistant. The only thing I thought was strange is how he always seemed to make a call after doing something like he just did. As if the guilt from doing something sexual with me made him feel bad. Every time the call was short and business-sounding, making me think it was his assistant.

"Who was that?" I asked. I never asked him before, but for some reason, I was bothered by the call.

"No one. Just an associate that's been blowing up my phone all morning."

For the first time since dating Trey, I got the feeling he had just told me his first lie. Plenty of guys have lied to me . . . practically my whole life. So when he didn't look me in the eyes and fumbled with his phone, I knew.

I wasn't the only woman in Trey's life.

I BLEW OUT A FRUSTRATED breath as I stood in the VIP-only area.

Trey was in heaven as he talked to a few NASCAR drivers and got his picture taken with them. When one asked if I wanted to get in the picture, Trey said no, which momentarily caught me off guard.

"I mean, let me get one alone, baby, then you jump in and you can get one."

Needless to say, his response only confirmed my suspicions that Trey was seeing someone else and couldn't risk a picture of the two of us together.

I slipped away when the photo was being taken and Trey wasn't paying attention. I wasn't sure where I was allowed and not allowed to go. All I knew was I needed fresh air.

Stepping outside the garage area, I turned the corner and ran right into someone.

"Shit! I'm so sorry," I blurted out as I looked up at the guy I ran into.

Strong hands took ahold of me, causing me to gasp at the zip of energy that rushed through my body as I stared into the bluest eyes I'd ever seen.

"I'm . . . I'm so . . . ahh . . . sorry," I said shaking my head to clear my thoughts as I stared at his features. He had a strong jaw line, perfect nose, eyelashes I'd kill for, and the most breathtaking smile I'd ever seen.

Down, Paislie. Settle down.

The man standing before me had to be the most handsome guy I'd ever laid eyes on. He was dressed in jeans and a white T-shirt that showed off his massive chest. He had tattoos all the way down his left arm that filled me with the urge to trace them with my fingers. No, with my tongue.

What in the hell is wrong with you, Paislie?

"Are you okay?" he asked.

Mother of all things good in this world. His voice sounded like God had opened the gates of heaven and sent an angel down. It vibrated through my entire body, and in a good way. A *very* good way. Was that a southern accent I heard?

Please let him be from the south.

"No," I mumbled.

His eyes filled with concern as they traveled over my body and I visibly trembled.

What in hell is happening to me?

He looked deeper into my eyes. "Did I hurt you?"

My mouth parted open and I tried like hell to talk.

"Paislie? Are you hurt?"

The second he said my name, I fantasized about him calling it out as he moved over my body with his lips and—

Closing my eyes, I pushed all those thoughts out and got control of myself. "I'm sorry. I think I was stunned for a moment." Pinching my brows together, I asked, "How do you know my name?"

His right hand dropped and my body instantly missed the contact. He lifted the VIP pass and smiled a crooked smile that honestly made my knees shake. "Oh," I said with a chuckle. "Duh."

Good lord. What are we, in middle school? Duh? That was the best I could come up with?

I couldn't help but notice his left hand was still holding onto my arm. I glanced down at it and he must have noticed too because he dropped it. "So . . . are you okay?"

With a wave of my hand, I let out a nervous laugh. "Totally. I'm sorry. I needed to get away from Trey . . ." I closed my eyes and cursed under my breath. "No, I mean I needed fresh air and I wasn't looking where I was going."

When I looked back up into his blue eyes, I couldn't help but notice the dimples on both sides of his cheeks. Jesus in heaven . . . *please give me the willpower to not jump this man right here and now.*

"You have a beautiful smile," I blurted out.

His eyes lit up with something I'd never before. "So do you, Paislie."

My cheeks flushed and I had to place my hands on them to cool my face. "Um . . . thank you. Again, I'm really sorry about bumping into you and acting like a crazy fool."

"We'll just call it a warm up, I'm sure I'll be doing lots of bumping out on the track."

All of a sudden I found myself very interested in racing. "You're a driver?"

With a cocky smile, he replied, "Yep."

I sunk my teeth down into my lip; clearly NASCAR drivers now turned me on as desire pooled in my lower stomach. "What number are you?"

It was then I heard a dog bark. Glancing down, a boxer was patiently standing at his hot owner's side. I instantly dropped to the ground as I cried out, "A boxer! I love boxers!"

The dog promptly licked and tried to climb up on me as his owner corrected him. "Sorry about that. He tends to lose focus when a pretty girl is around."

I peeked up through my eyelashes and tried hard to hold the eye roll back.

"Too cheesy?" he asked.

Standing, I held my thumb and index finger up. "Just a little."

"Told you it wouldn't work, Deuce."

"Deuce? Cute name."

Mr. Hotter-than-hot frowned. "Cute was not what I was going for with his name but . . . I'll take it."

Smiling like a schoolgirl, I tried to understand what it was about this guy that made me feel so . . . different. Giddy almost.

For Christ's sake. Get a grip, Paislie.

"Well, I should let you go. Good luck today and again, I'm sorry for bumping into you."

With a nod of his head, blue eyes and crazy sexy dimples leaned in closer and softly said, "I'm not."

My heart practically pounded out of my chest as I watched him walk off. "Wait!" I called out. "What's your number or your name or something for me to scream out when you drive by?"

With a wide grin, he said, "Malcolm Wallace."

Even if I wanted to, I couldn't stop the stupid look of happiness from spreading across my face. "Good luck, Malcolm Wallace."

His wink did me in and a moan slipped from my lips as he said, "Thanks, Paislie."

And just like that he walked around the corner and was gone.

I dropped back against the building and fought to get my breathing under control. My stomach dipped and my chest felt funny.

"What in the *hell* was that?" I mumbled.

"There you are."

I pushed off the wall and made my way over toward Trey. All the happiness and feelings I had just experienced vanished with the sound of his voice. "Sorry, I needed some fresh air."

"We should probably check out a few other things before heading up to the box seats."

Nodding in agreement, I said, "Sure."

Trey placed his hand on my lower back and guided me back past the open garage. Stealing a glance, my green eyes were caught by Malcolm's intense stare. Lifting my hand, I waved as he flashed me that crooked smile I was positive I would be dreaming about tonight and many future nights.

My heart felt heavy the further we walked away from the garage area. Once we were in our box seats, I searched the program until those blue eyes were staring up at me from the page.

Malcolm Wallace.

He raced for Elliot Racing and was twenty-six years old. He won the Daytona 500 last month and was ranked as one of the best drivers in NASCAR. The car he drove was number twenty-four. My new favorite number.

When they started their engines, I became an instant fan while the rumble from the sounds of the engines moved through my body. "Who you going for, babe?" Trey asked.

My eyes zoomed in on his car. The blue and white paint theme would be easy to keep track of as they raced around the track. "I think I'm going with my lucky number. Twenty-four."

"Ahh . . . Wallace. Good pick."

Keeping my eyes focused on the number twenty-four car, I took a sip of beer before saying, "I think so."

MALCOLM

WHAT. IN. THE. HELL. JUST. Happened?

My heart was racing as I tried to keep my breathing under control. Glancing up, I saw her again. This time some asshole had his hand on her, leading her away. When she lifted her hand to wave goodbye, my heart felt like it jumped to my throat.

"Dude, are you okay?"

Turning my attention to Dalton, I brushed the feelings away. I was probably just tired and it had been too long since I'd actually had sex.

"Yeah, Deuce and I ran into someone and . . . you know what. Never mind," I said, waving my hand to dismiss the conversation.

"How's the car looking?" I asked.

Dalton went into his normal spiel about how the car was and how he thought it would run. I watched him intently as he talked, but I didn't hear a damn word he said. My mind was thinking of a beautiful, dark-haired beauty with flawless skin, sensual lips, and emerald eyes. Damn, her smile about knocked me off my feet.

Deuce whined at my feet and I was wondering if he was missing her as well. The way her energy rushed through my body when I held her. I hadn't experienced anything like that before with anyone else since Casey.

My heart ached as I focused on the race and not Paislie.

Paislie. What a beautiful name. It suited her.

"Malcolm? Did you even hear what I just said?"

My eyes snapped up as I gave him a nod. "Sure I did, just trying to get in the right frame of mind."

His eyes narrowed as he looked at me. "You okay, dude? You seem like you're preoccupied with something."

Paislie. Her soft lips . . . a voice like an angel . . . and she fucking loves dogs. Lucky ass, Deuce, getting to lick her.

"Nope. I'm fine."

Dalton slapped me on the shoulder and gave it a squeeze. "Good. You know what you need?"

Lifting my brow, I asked, "What's that?"

"A good lay. When was the last time you were with anyone?"

"Too long."

Ashley popped into my head as I pulled my phone out and said, "I'm taking Deuce back to the bus."

"All right. Try going for a quick run. You've got to burn some energy."

With a wave of my hand, I started off toward my bus as I sent Ashley a text.

Me: How's it going?

It didn't take her long to reply.

Ashley: Good. You?

Me: Wondering if you're missing me yet.

Ashley: Awe. That's sweet. I am.

I wanted more than anything to tell her I wanted her . . . but I knew she was trying to move on and start a relationship with someone, and for some ungodly known reason I couldn't stop thinking about Paislie. I was using Ashley as a means to distract my thoughts.

Me: Miss you too, Ashley. How is the new relationship going?

Ashley: It's going good. Are you okay?

I clenched my jaw while I picked up my pace. I was happy for Ashley. I honestly was. At the same time I was jealous as hell that some fucker was getting her all to himself.

Me: Doing great. About to get focused. Was thinking about you.

Ashley: Good luck today, Malcolm.

Me: Thanks, Ash. Talk to you later.

I needed to clear my head. As I approached my bus, I saw a few girls hanging out talking to Tom, the rookie who took over Emmit's spot.

He glanced up and smiled as he motioned to the blonde with his head. "Malcolm, you've got a die-hard fan here who's been wanting to meet you."

With a smile, I walked up while she looked down at Deuce. "Oh my goodness! He's adorable." When she looked back up at me from a squatting position, she licked her lips.

"Why don't you come in and get to know him better," I said with a wink.

Her eyes lit up as Tom chuckled.

Five minutes later my jeans were down and she was sucking me off. My hands grabbed her head as I fucked her mouth, trying like hell to forget those green eyes haunting my every thought.

RUSS SPOKE IN MY EARS as I came into my pit box. "Five, four, three, two, one."

"Four tires and fuel. Make that track bar adjustment, go!" Dalton called out.

"Clear," Russ said.

"Go. Go. Go," Dalton said as I took off back onto the track. I was sitting in third place and my car was finally driving right.

"Where is Tom?" I asked.

"Running in tenth," Russ said.

I spent the next ten laps focusing on one thing. Winning.

"Bumper. Door. Door. Bumper. Clear!"

Passing the number eleven car pushed me into first place with six laps to go. *I fucking loved this feeling.* The feel of the car flying around the track, the power of controlling it was an adrenaline rush for sure.

"So, if I win . . . we're jumping, right?" I asked Dalton.

"Drive!" he replied with as I smiled.

Lap traffic was coming up as Russ guided me right along.

"Where is he?" I asked.

Russ came over the headphones. "Dropping back now at three car lengths back."

"Come on, baby . . . don't let me down," I said as I drove the fuck out of my car.

"Three to go."

My heart was racing as fast as my car as I thought about Paislie. She'd had a VIP pass and I prayed like hell I'd see her in victory lane. I also wanted to find out who the asshole was she was with. For some odd reason, guilt washed over me as I thought about the girl I let give me head before the race.

"Fucking hell," I whispered, trying to refocus. I had never let this kind of shit in when I raced. Never.

"White flag. One to go, Malcolm. Take it easy around the lap traffic. You've got this . . . plenty of room between you and the eleven car."

"Come on," I whispered as I held onto the steering wheel and took my last turn.

The moment I saw the checkered flag flying, I let out a holler. "Woo! We did it, boys!"

"Number two!" Dalton yelled out.

Pulling up to the finish line, I took the checkered flag and drove around the track. This feeling was unlike anything. Best damn feeling in the world.

"Coming in," I said as I brought the car up. Seeing my pit crew caused me to smile even bigger. These guys were like family. Slipping out of everything, I crawled out of the car and stood on the window.

"Yeah!" I shouted out as I got drenched in champagne. After being congratulated by the crew and Dalton, the media jumped in and started with all the interviews. I fucking loved it.

My heart was still pumping hard as we did all the press photos. I felt a slap on my back as I turned to see Mr. Elliot standing there. "Malcolm, I'd like to introduce you to Trey Rogers, he's a running back for the Dallas Cowboys and a huge fan of NASCAR. He'd love to meet you."

Ugh. I'd heard about this guy. He had a reputation for wanting drivers to take him out for runs. The guy was known as being a class-ass prick.

With a smile on my face, I turned and followed my boss. I froze in place when we walked up to a small group of VIP's. Those beautiful emerald eyes were all I could see.

"Paislie," I said a little too enthusiastically.

Her eyes lit up as she flashed me a huge grin. "Congratulations, Malcolm."

"Do you two know each other?" the oversized guy standing there asked. Not wanting to pull my eyes off Paislie, I smiled and said, "We're acquaintances."

Mr. Elliot cleared his throat and said, "Malcolm, this is Trey Rogers."

Moving my focus onto Trey, I reached my hand out and shook it.

"Running back for the Cowboys?"

His chest practically puffed out as he said, "That's right."

"Man, I like the Cowboys, but I'm more of Texans fan, though," I said with a laugh and slap on his arm.

The guy looked tense and a little pissed off. I couldn't decide if it was because my immediate attention was on Paislie, or the fact that I basically just told him his football team sucked.

"Great race, dude. My girl here had her money on you."

Snapping my eyes back over to Paislie, I couldn't help but notice the look she gave Trey. Either they weren't serious enough for him to be claiming her, or she was pissed about something else. I couldn't help the damn smile that spread over my face.

I bet this girl was pure spit and fire.

"You rooted for me, huh?"

Her gaze turned to me. "I did. It was fun watching you fight for first place."

With a quick scan of her body, I smirked. "I usually get what I want. One way or another."

Her lips parted as her eyes drifted to mine. I wondered if her attraction to me was as strong as mine was to her? With the way she was eye fucking me right now I'd say the answer was yes.

Mr. Elliot cleared his throat as he filled in the dead air space. "So, Ms.?"

"Paislie Pruitt," she replied with a polite smile.

"So, Paislie, do you work for the Cowboys as well? Is that how you met Trey?" Mr. Elliot asked.

Paislie about let out a roar of laughter. "Oh no! No sir, I don't work for the Cowboys. I work as a physical therapist in the Dallas area."

I lifted my eyes. "Really? Physical therapist?" And she lived in Dallas. Fucking hell yes. This was my lucky day.

With a nod, she replied, "Yep."

Trey was getting a bit upset the attention was not on him. "I thought there for a bit you weren't going to be able to pull off a win. You pulled through at the end, though. Of course I'm sure it's because the number seven's tire blew."

I slowly looked back at Trey.

Fucker. "That might have had something to do with it. I'd like to think it was my driving skills and the flawless car we had."

Trey stared me down for a good thirty seconds. "Oh, of course. Yeah."

Dalton walked over and bumped my arm. "Not to be rude, but it's time for the press conference."

I gave him a quick head nod before turning back to Trey. Reaching my hand out, I said, "It was a pleasure meeting you. We'll make sure you're taken care of in April when we hit Texas Motor Speedway."

"Yeah, same here. I'll be sure to hook you up with some tickets to a game, even if you are a Texans' fan."

I forced a smile as I shook his hand again. Before leaving, I reached for Paislie's hand. When her hand landed in mine, I was pretty sure we both felt the energy from that touch. Her mouth dropped open as she inhaled a quick breath. The feeling zipping through my body was a rush I'd never experienced before.

"Paislie, it was nice bumping into you."

She fought to hold back her laugh as she smiled the most brilliant smile I'd ever seen. It was then I noticed she had a dimple in her left cheek and one on her chin.

Fuck, that is cute as hell. Why was a girl like Paislie with a douche like Trey? It made no sense at all.

"It most certainly was. Congratulations again on your win."

With wink, I replied, "Thank you."

I followed Dalton toward the press house and took a chance at glancing over my shoulder. Trey was busy talking to Mr. Elliot, but Paislie was watching me walk off.

When she lifted her hand to wave goodbye, I lifted mine before turning back and looking straight ahead.

Why did it feel like I was fighting for oxygen to breathe?

One more look over my shoulder showed Paislie still watching me. My chest tightened and I wasn't sure how I should be feeling.

"You okay? You look like you've seen a ghost."

I ran my hand through my hair and tried to understand why, for the first time in years, the smile of one girl made my heart about jump out of my chest.

"I'm fine. Just tired," I mumbled.

Pulling my phone out, I texted myself a message.

Me: Paislie Pruitt—Dallas PT

Shoving the phone into my back pocket, I turned to Dalton. "There isn't anyone in my bus is there?"

Dalton frowned. "Yeah. A hot little number Tom said you had fun with earlier. You know I don't care what happens after the race, just not before it Malcolm. I need you to stay focused."

Before walking up to start the interview, I hit his chest and said, "It was a moment of weakness . . . I know your rule. Get rid of her, would you? I'm tired and just want to pull out after this."

Dalton pulled his head back in surprise. "Um . . . okay. You sure?"

With a pat on his shoulder, I grinned and said, "I've never been more sure."

S LIPPING INTO THE LIMO, I slid as far over to the other side as I could. Trey sat down and looked at me. "How in the fuck did you know Malcolm Wallace, and why didn't you tell me you knew him?"

Narrowing my eyes at him, I decided to turn this conversation around. "Who were you talking to earlier? Before we got to the track, after you gave me an orgasm?"

His eyes filled with something I was very used to seeing. Deceit.

"It was no one. I told you."

"Trey, as much as you probably don't believe this, I've got good intuition and I call bullshit. Who is she?"

He swallowed hard before laughing and trying to blow me off. "I have no idea what you're talking about, Paislie. You're being paranoid."

We sat in silence as the limo drove back to Caesar's Palace. When we pulled up to the front and the door opened, I stayed in my seat. Trey looked back at me with a confused expression.

"What are you doing?"

"I'm going to the airport."

His eyes grew angry. "Get the hell out of the car, Paislie. This is crazy."

Looking down, I took in a deep breath and slowly blew it out before glancing back up at him. "My father dropped me off at an orphanage when I was eight years old, and every time he came back into my life I hoped it was because he wanted me. It never was and I quickly learned in life to tell when a man was lying to me. You see, my father's been doing it for years. Please send my suitcase to my house."

Trey stood there staring at me with a stunned expression. "Paislie, please let me explain. She's just a girl I've been dating off and on and—"

Holding my hand up, I said, "Stop. I don't need your excuses, Trey. I need you to please make sure my stuff is sent to me."

He closed his eyes and nodded as he pushed the button to roll the privacy glass down. "Please take Ms. Pruitt to the airport."

Trey took one last look at me before taking a step back and shutting the door to the limo. He didn't even try. Just like that . . . he let me go. I tried to ignore the pain in my chest. Even if I didn't care for him, it still hurt.

He was found out and did what they all do. Walk away.

The moment the limo pulled away, I let my tears fall as I stared out at the Vegas lights zipping by.

I hate men.

THE KNOCK ON MY OFFICE door pulled me out of my thoughts. Turning from the window I was looking out, I called out, "Come in."

Stephanie, the receptionist, came walking in. "Your appointment at four canceled. And Trey called again."

I rolled my eyes and walked over to my desk. "Did you tell him to go fuck himself?"

Stephanie covered her mouth and giggled. "No! But if you really want me to, that might be kind of fun."

With a slight smile, I shook my head. "I don't think the other patients would take that very well if they heard you tell someone that."

She shrugged and silently agreed with her smile.

"So, what did he do? I kind of thought you liked this guy. You even went to Vegas with him."

Picking up a chart, I acted like I was looking through it. "It wasn't a good fit."

"Bummer. He was so cute. And that body!" She used her hand to fan herself. "Speaking of hot bodies, that hottie from SMU will be coming in tomorrow. Oh happy day!"

Chuckling, I dropped the file onto my desk and shook my head at her.

I worked for a large physical therapy clinic in Southlake Texas that I'd interned for and was hired on right after I finished school. It was a great place to work and I mostly dealt with athletes from Southern Methodist University.

"Okay, so if you're not going to give me the deets on Trey, I'll let it slide. I wonder if he had something to do with these, though?"

She handed me an envelope with my name written across it. "Please be Dallas tickets for this season. Oh please!" Stephanie chanted.

Hitting her with the large manila envelope, I snickered. "Stop it."

Stephanie stood there and stared at me. "Well, are you going to open it?"

With a frustrated sigh, I opened it up and dumped the contents out on my desk. Picking them up, I saw a VIP pass for Texas Motor Speedway. Smiling, I opened up the letter and read it. My mouth dropped as I sat down in my chair.

"Oh. My. God."

"What is it? Paislie! What's wrong?"

Slowly trying to clear my head, I looked up at her and said, "They're um . . . tickets for this weekend's race."

Her lip snarled as she looked at the tickets. "NASCAR? Do you even *like* racing?"

My heart felt as if it was about to burst from my chest as I looked back at the note and read it again.

Paislie,

Deuce requests your presence at a dinner function Thursday evening at Texas Motor Speedway.

Enclosed you will find one all-inclusive pass for this weekend. With this pass you are able to come and go as you wish. When arriving at the speedway, please use Gate One and show them the VIP pass and let them know you are a guest of Elliot Racing.

We really hope you can make it.

Deuce and Malcolm

Covering my mouth, I felt like a little girl in a candy store. "Paislie Pruitt. Are you blushing?"

I dropped my hand and pinched my eyebrows together as I gave her a huff. "No. I'm just really surprised. How in the world did he know where I worked?"

"Who?!" Stephanie exclaimed.

"Malcolm Wallace. He's a driver . . . a um . . . a NASCAR driver."

Crossing her arms over her chest she asked, "And how do you know a NASCAR driver? Oh my god . . . first a Dallas football player and now this! Where are you going to meet these guys?"

With a dry laugh, I stood and started to usher her out of my office. "We'll talk about it later. Right now I have a phone call to make."

She grabbed onto the door jam and held on for dear life. "With who? Him? The driver? Is he cute? Hotter than Trey?"

Placing my hand on her forehead, I pushed her out of the way and shut the door as she called out, "I'm googling him right now!"

I picked the letter back up and took in a deep breath while I reached for my cell phone. My hand was shaking as I dialed the number.

"Jesus H. Christ, what in the hell is wrong with me? He probably thinks he's going to get lucky or something. Like all of them."

The thought of Malcolm only wanting to see me for sex hurt more than it made me angry. I practically broke the glass on my phone hitting the numbers as I dialed him.

"This is, Malcolm."

My body melted as did all the anger I felt. *For Pete's sake, what is wrong with me?* Oh, I know what's wrong . . . I'd fuck this guy just to hear that voice whisper in my ear.

Looking upward, I mouthed, *forgive me father.*

"Hello?"

"Malcolm? Hi, it's um . . . it's Paislie. Paislie Pruitt."

"Paislie, how are you?"

I could hear the smile in his voice as I grinned from ear to ear. I felt like a teenage girl talking to her crush.

"Well, I'm a bit surprised by a package I received today. How in the world did you know where I worked?"

Malcolm let out a soft, yet deep laugh. "Let's just say I had to do my homework. And when I talked to Trey Rogers he happened to mention he was no longer seeing you and might have let it slip where you worked."

Rolling my eyes, I mumbled, "Figures."

"Sorry, what was that?"

I waved my hand as if he could see me. "Nothing, sorry."

"So?"

Chewing nervously on my lip, I replied back with my own, "So?"

He let out a small chuckle as he said, "Will you be able to make it at least for dinner?"

My finger moved over the handwritten note. "With Deuce? Your boxer, right?"

"That's right."

I wanted to giggle, but I stayed strong. "Is he looking for a casual evening or would I have to dress up? I'm not much of a formal kind of girl."

"Totally casual. He's super easy to please."

A thought occurred to me as my smile faded. "Um . . . will Trey be there as well?"

There was silence followed by, "Fuck no, that asshole isn't going to be there."

Oh God . . . why did that turn me on.

"Then count me in."

"Perfect! How about seven?"

I chewed on my thumbnail as I quickly thought this through. Hadn't I just given up on men again, and now I'm planning on meeting one for dinner? Of course, I'm really having dinner with his dog.

Frowning, I hit my palm on my forehead. Get it together, Paislie.

"Go to Gate One you said?"

"Yes. Show the security guard your pass and I'll be sure to let him know where to bring you."

Covering my mouth to hold my silly excitement in, I tried to respond like this was just another night and nothing special about it. "Sounds good. I'll see ya Thursday."

"Perfect! See ya then, Paislie."

My stomach jumped as I placed my hand on it. "Okay, see ya then."

Once I hit End, I dragged in a few deep breaths as I placed my hands on my desk.

"Holy hells bells," I said as I started laughing. I'd only talked to this man twice and yet each time he brought out emotions I'd never before experienced in my life. I wasn't sure if I should be thrilled beyond belief, or scared shitless.

Either way, I was counting down the hours until I got to see him again.

MALCOLM

W ITH A TOWEL WRAPPED AROUND my waist, I walked out of the bathroom only to find Ashley standing in my kitchen.

Fuck.

"Ash?"

She spun around and raked her eyes over my body before looking back up at me. "Hey. I see you're still looking fine as ever."

"Um . . . what are you doing here?"

She leaned back against the counter and looked at me with a serious look as she leaned in closer and stared hard. Her mouth dropped open as she gasped. "Oh my God. You met someone!"

My head pulled back in shock. "What?"

Pointing her finger at me, a huge smile moved over her face. "You. Met. Someone."

Right about that time, the door to the bus opened and Autumn came bouncing in. "Hey, big brother! Did we surprise you?"

I looked between Autumn and Ashley. "How . . . how did y'all meet up? I'm so damn confused."

Ashley laughed and said, "I left my little black dress at your ranch a few months back. Remember after that night of fun in Dallas and we went back to the ranch?"

I nodded my head. "Well, I needed it and I called the main number thinking Clarisse would answer, but Autumn did instead. We got to talking and found out we had a lot in common."

I wrinkled my forehead as I looked between them. "Okay, so you both decided to come to the race together?"

Autumn chuckled. "I've never missed one of your Texas races, and I don't plan on it now. I asked Ashley if I could stay at her place this weekend. Sophie is staying with Mom and Pop."

Ashely wiggled her eyebrows. "We're having a girls' weekend."

I raked my hand through my wet hair. "This is . . . weird."

"Why? Because we used to be fuck buddies and now I'm friends with your sister?"

Autumn set her bag on the counter and mumbled, "Gross, visual not needed."

"Wait!! Back to what we were talking about. You met someone didn't you?"

Autumn sucked in a breath. "W-what! You're dating someone?"

"No!" I said as I shook my head. "And no I haven't met anyone, Ash."

She walked closer to me and I wondered where that familiar pull was that I used to get around her. Any time I ever saw her I only had one thing on my mind. Sex. The only thing on my mind now was how to get her and my sister off of my bus.

Ashley smiled and slowly shook her head. "I see it in your eyes, Wallace. You met someone."

"Who is she?" Autumn said as she did a little hop and grabbed onto my arm.

With a huff, I turned and headed back to my room. "May I please change?"

They both started a laughing fit and said something about my manwhore days being over. "Never!" I yelled out as I shut the bedroom door behind me.

Reaching over, I grabbed my cell phone and pulled up Paislie's number and hit Call. I saved it when she called me the other day.

"Hello?"

I held the phone to Deuce who barked right on cue. "Deuce wanted to make sure y'all were still on for tonight."

"Where do you come up with this stuff? Do you always use your dog to pick up women?"

I thought about it for a second. I'd never really used him except when he was a puppy. He was a total pussy magnet then.

"Not since he was about six months old. Before that he was lining them up for me."

"Wow. Your sheer honesty was not expected. I don't know if I should turn around and go back home or floor it and get there faster."

The way my heart thumped in my chest had me holding my breath for a few seconds. Something about this girl did crazy ass things to me.

"My vote is to floor it."

With a chuckle, she responded, "I figured it would be."

Dropping my towel, I pulled on a pair of jeans and searched for a T-shirt. "I'm really looking forward to seeing you, Paislie."

"Same here," she barely spoke. "My GPS says I'll be there in thirty-seven minutes."

I glanced over to the clock and fist pumped. Perfect timing. "Perfect. I'll have Deuce ready."

When she laughed it did something to me I'd never experienced before. "Sounds good, see ya in a few."

"See ya," I said as I hit End and tried like hell to wipe the stupid grin off my face before facing my sister and Ashley.

The door to the bedroom opened and Ashley yelled out, "I knew it! Oh. My. Gawd! Who is she? Are you dating? What's her name? Where did you meet her?"

Autumn was behind Ashley jumping as she wore a huge smile.

"Stop it, both of you. I'm not dating her—I met her in Vegas at a race, she lives here in the Dallas area so I invited her for dinner tonight."

Ashley stumbled back. "Dinner? You invited her to dinner?" She spun around and grabbed onto Autumn's hands as they started screaming.

My hands went over my ears before I pushed them both out of the way. "What in the fuck is wrong with you two?"

I made my way into the kitchen and lit a candle that Adaline insisted I have. I'd never admit it to her, but I loved the damn thing. It reminded me of their house. I'd been back over for dinner almost half a dozen times.

Ashley stood on the other side of the bar in the living room and looked at me. "Malcolm, I'm the closest thing to any sort of relationship you've had in a long time and you never once took me to dinner."

I frowned. "That's not true. We went to dinner all the time."

She lifted her brow. "Yeah, after a roll in the sack and we were both hungry."

Autumn walked between us. "Again, can we not reference the fact that the two of you had sex. It really bothers me for some reason."

Ashley giggled. "It would my brother as well."

"Fine!" I said. "We never went out to dinner on a date before. This isn't a date. I mean at least not with me. Deuce invited her out to eat and she's coming to have dinner with him."

Oh shit. Why in the hell did I think that would be okay to say?

My sister looked at me like she really couldn't believe what she just heard.

"What in the hell did you just say?" Ashley asked while my sister still stared at me, but now with more of a concerned look.

"Did you wreck at practice?" Autumn asked.

I dropped my head back and moaned in frustration. "Please . . . will you both just leave? Paislie is going to be here soon."

Autumn and Ashley both said, "Paislie!"

"What an adorable name. What does she look like?" Ashley asked.

My hands came up and covered my face as I dragged them down slowly. "If I tell you, will you leave?"

"Yep!"

I closed my eyes and shook my head as I counted to ten and looked back at them both. "She is gorgeous. Dark hair, emerald eyes, a voice that sounds like an angel, a body that's sinfully perfect, and a smile that leaves me breathless."

Both of them stood there and stared at me. Autumn had tears in her eyes and Ashley looked stunned. "Where in the fuck was this Malcolm when we were—"

"Don't say it!" Autumn cried out.

Looking at Ashley, I tried to figure out where that came from. Even though I had spent more time with her than any other girl, I never had the feeling that it would have led us anywhere else and thought she felt the same. "Ash, I think you're amazing and . . ."

She placed her finger over my mouth and smiled. "Don't say anything. I was kidding. Malcolm, what we shared was fun, but that's all it was for either of us and we both knew it wasn't going anywhere outside of the bedroom. But this girl has changed something about you. I saw it in your eyes the moment I looked at you."

Autumn wiped a tear away as I looked at her with a confused look. "Why are you crying?" I asked and pulled her into my arms. She pulled back and looked into my eyes.

"This Paislie, she's brought a part of you back to life, Malcolm. I see it."

I shook my head and laughed. "I've only ever seen her twice and talked to her twice on the phone. The two of you need to slow your roll."

I lifted my hand and wiped my sister's tears away. "Now please, will you both go?"

I'd never seen either one of them move so fast. Ashley opened the door and screamed out when she ran into Janet, my assistant.

"Hey, Janet! Don't tell Emmit I was here!"

Autumn gave Janet a kiss on the cheek as she said, "Hey, Janet! See you later!"

Both girls walked off laughing and cackling about me finally meeting someone.

Janet turned to me and gave me a questioning look. "Do I want to know?"

I shook my head as Deuce ran up to his second-favorite person in the world. Janet was a retired fifty-nine-year-old teacher who lived her life for NASCAR. She had volunteered to help out in the office back in Charlotte and quickly started getting every single person organized. When I approached her about becoming my assistant, her husband had just retired so traveling for them was no problem. She gladly accepted and she has been covering my ass ever since.

"I have it all set up. I'm not asking questions, it's none of my business but I will say this, I smiled the entire time I was setting it up."

Walking up to her, I gave her a gentle hug. She was a tiny woman, five foot if that and thin. I was always afraid I would break her if I hugged her too tight.

Pulling back, I asked, "Wait. Who is there watching everything?"

She shot me a dirty look. "Are you saying I don't know how to do my job?"

I lifted my hands up in a defensive move. "No! I would never."

"Just know I had to pull some strings to get this done for you."

With a peck on her forehead, I said, "I owe you."

She patted me on the chest and winked. "I've always wanted to go to Aruba."

Before I could reply, she was out the door and gone. Glancing down to Deuce, I shrugged. "Are you ready for your dinner date?"

Deuce jumped up and barked as he wagged his tail. With a chuckle, I gave him a good pat and replied, "I feel the same way, boy."

PAISLIE

D RIVING UP TO THE SECURITY gate, I gripped the steering wheel harder.

What am I doing? I swore off all men and here I am again. Having dinner with Malcolm Wallace!

Stephanie and I had googled Malcolm after I accepted his invite. Needless to say, I wasn't surprised to find out he was quite the ladies' man. His reputation for being fast in and out of the racecar was evident.

Yet, here I am, about to have dinner with him. Maybe it's the idea of seeing him again that was the driving force behind me being here. I wasn't about to deny the strong attraction I felt for him. That's never happened to me before. Of course, it could be from all the stupid romance books I'd been reading nonstop. Did he really make my stomach drop or did I imagine that? Why was it so hard for me to catch my breath after speaking to him?

I needed answers to the questions floating around in my head. That was the reason I was here. That and I couldn't stop fantasizing what his lips would feel like on my skin.

My window rolled down as the security guard smiled. "May I help you?"

"Um . . . yes!" I exclaimed a little too excited. "Paislie Pruitt. I'm here to see Malcolm Wallace. He's expecting me."

"Oh yeah, yeah." Turning, he yelled for the other guy, who popped his head out.

"James! I'm taking Ms. Pruitt in to see Malcolm."

James gave a thumb's up to the other security guard who turned back to me. "Just follow me and I'll show you where to park. Malcolm is most likely waiting for you."

With a smile, I nodded and said, "Okay. I'll follow you."

Driving down the tunnel, I held my breath until we got to the other side. People were everywhere. I couldn't believe all the RV's set up and all the people hanging out and having a good time. I tried to do a bit of research before this dinner and I found out a little about this world. I knew they would be qualifying tomorrow, then the next level down from NASCAR, the Xfinity Series raced that Saturday and then the big race was on Sunday.

The security guard pulled down what I was guessing was Pit Road and parked. Parking next to him, I dragged in a deep breath before exhaling it. "Okay, it's not like it's your first date, Paislie. It's just dinner. Nothing else. Unless . . ." I shook my head to clear my thoughts. "No. No! Dinner only."

The knock on my window had me letting out a scream so toe-curling, I was positive the glass almost shattered.

Peeking through my half-closed eyes, I saw Malcolm standing on the other side of the window with his head cocked to the side and the most adorable smile I'd ever seen.

Damn, what is it about a crooked smile and dimples?

"God, be with me tonight and for once, keep me strong," I whispered before opening the door.

"Were you really in there just now talking to yourself?"

I let out a nervous giggle. "No, I was ah . . . praying."

His eyes widened as I cursed under my breath. *Way to scare him off, Paislie.*

"Praying? About what?"

"Strength." *No! No not strength!*

"For what?"

Shit!

"No . . . no wait. Okay, I wasn't *praying* praying . . . well I was . . . I um. Shit."

There went the stupid grin again. "You were talking to yourself," Malcolm said as my knees wobbled and my stomach felt as if I was on a thrill ride.

With a nervous laugh, I nodded my head. "Yes. I was talking to myself."

His eyes searched my face and I liked very much the way he was looking at me. My dark hair was pulled up into a simple ponytail. He had said to dress casual, so I did. Jeans and light-green shirt I knew popped the color of my eyes.

"You look even more beautiful than I remember."

I felt my cheeks warm. "Let's hope that trumps the talking to myself," I said with a wink.

Malcolm's smile grew bigger. "You hungry?"

Turning my gaze down to the ground, I found myself feeling something I'd never felt with a man before.

Excitement.

I was giddy to find out what he had planned and for once, I didn't feel like I was going to be let down.

That's when I noticed no Deuce.

"Hey. Where's my date?"

With a long dramatic sigh, Malcolm shook his head. "Deuce wasn't up for dinner tonight. Turns out he ate a little too much rawhide and isn't feeling like himself this evening."

With a pout I said, "Poor guy."

Malcolm tried to appear somber.

With a raised brow, I asked, "Are you his stand in?"

His hand went to his sculpted chest. "If you'll have me, I'd be honored."

I snarled my lip up and shrugged. "I guess," I sighed. "I was looking forward to that handsome boxer." My eyes traveled over Malcolm's body as I fought to keep the urge away to touch him. "I guess you'll do."

He tried to hide his amusement as he placed his arm out for me to take. "Let's get this party started."

The moment my body touched his, I felt it. Peeking up, I tried to see if Malcolm felt it too. If he did, he hid it well. We walked across the track as he helped me over the barrier and we started up the bleachers.

"Man, all I need to do is walk up and down these a few times a day and I'd be in great shape!" I said with a chortle.

We came out to where all the concession stands were and headed to another building with double doors.

"Where are we going?" I asked.

Malcolm opened the door for me and said, "Up."

"Up is always a good thing," I purred as I gave him a wicked smile and walked through the door. That time, I saw his reaction. Not only in his eyes, but in the way he attempted to hide the fact that he had to adjust himself.

He hit up as we stood there and waited for the elevator. "So, how long have you been turned on by racing cars?"

He looked at me with a somewhat surprised expression. "Turned on?"

The doors opened and we walked in. "Yeah. I'd have to think it was some kind of a rush that got you loving the need for speed. You must really enjoy it if you're as good as they say. You're turned on to the rush you get. Am I right?"

His eyes lit up and I wasn't sure why. Maybe because I used the words turned on. Lord knows I was already looking at his perfect body. Damn, his ass looked good in those jeans.

Paislie. Stop!

"I guess you could say racing is a turn on. It's more of an adrenaline rush than a sexual turn on, though."

I made a tsking sound and slowly shook my head. "That's not what Google says about you, Mr. Wallace."

His head dropped back as he let out a roar of laughter. I couldn't help but laugh along with him as the doors opened and we walked down a long hall to another set of elevators.

"Up again," I whispered.

He cleared his throat and placed his hand on my lower back, causing my entire body to tremble. I was almost positive he felt it.

I stole a glance at him as he stared straight ahead. As if he was concentrating on something very intently.

When the doors opened, he nudged me ever so slightly and led me out. I loved the feeling and had never had a man do that before. It was nice.

When his hand slipped down and took mine, I forced myself to hold back the moan.

One look around and I was even more confused. "We're on a roof?"

"Is that a question or a statement?"

"Both!" I said with a titter.

As we walked around a small building, I let out a gasp at the sight before me. "A picnic?" I whispered as I forced the tears down. I'd never been on a picnic before with a guy.

Three quilts were laid out on the roof along with three picnic baskets. "Do you like picnics?"

I walked up to the edge of the quilt and stared down at everything. A small bouquet of flowers was lying on the quilt. I swallowed hard and went to look at Malcolm when I noticed the view.

Covering my mouth, I sucked in a breath and stared out in disbelief. "It's amazing," I spoke into my hand. The view from up here was beyond anything I could have imagined.

"I take it you like it and you're not afraid of heights?"

Spinning back to face him, I smiled so big my cheeks hurt. "No! I'm not afraid of heights. Yes I love it, and I've never been on a picnic before."

His smile faded as he narrowed his eyes. "Really?"

I shook my head. "No. Never."

He took both my hands in his and guided me to the middle of the quilt. "Well then, I get to be the lucky guy to give you your first experience with it."

The lump in my throat was hard to ignore. When we sat down, he reached into one basket and took out two bottles of water, and then took out some plates. I couldn't help but wish that Malcolm had been the one to give me many of my first experiences.

Overcome suddenly with this strange emotion, I focused on anything other than the handsome guy who was making my heart pound so loudly in my ears I could barely hear.

I am so screwed with my vow of hating men.

So screwed.

MALCOLM

P AISLIE SEEMED TO BE OVERCOME with emotion for a quick moment before slipping back into her carefree mode.

"This really is amazing. Deuce is missing out."

I nodded in agreement. "His fault for eating that whole bone I gave him."

She flashed me a dazzling smile as she asked, "Are you sure he wasn't sabotaged? You know, by someone wanting to steal his date?"

I glanced over to Paislie. My blue eyes holding onto her green as we both got lost momentarily in each other. "I do believe there might have been a hidden agenda to that oversized bone," I softly spoke as she chuckled.

Reaching into the larger picnic basket, I smiled when I pulled out the chicken salad on croissants. Janet knew how much I loved her chicken salad.

"Hmm . . . I love chicken salad!" Paislie exclaimed.

"Then you will really love this chicken salad. My assistant, Janet, makes it all from scratch. I'm not even going to ask her how she pulled this off because I'm pretty sure I'd be buying her and her husband tickets to some fabulous hotel in Mexico somewhere."

Paislie chuckled as I made up each plate. "So tell me," she said as she pulled her knees up and rested her chin on them. I'd never seen anyone look so goddamn sexy yet cute as hell like she did that very moment. "How many girls have you done this with?"

Giving her a look of hurt, I asked, "Done what with?"

She motioned around with her hands and laughed. "This, Malcolm!

This is incredible, and not to be cheesy or make you think I'm looking for something more here, but this is the most romantic thing anyone has ever done for me."

When I looked back up at her, I couldn't help but be taken aback by the light in her eyes. I found myself wanting to make her this happy every day, but at the same time I was bothered by the fact no other guy had taken the time to romance her.

Jesus H. Christ. Where in the hell did that come from?

"How many girls have you taken up on a rooftop and swooned them like this?"

"That's easy to answer. None. Well, actually one. You."

Her smile faded slightly as her eyes turned darker and she wrapped her arms around her legs and whispered, "Oh."

"I'm not much of a romance kind of guy."

She lifted a single eyebrow and gave me a disbelieving look. "I would love to see what you think would be romantic."

Handing her the plate with the sandwich, homemade chips and fresh fruit, I looked up and thought about it.

"Holy crap. Did Janet make all of this?" She held up a chip.

"Yep."

Her mouth slacked open as she said, "You better give her a damn good thank you!"

I nodded. "Don't worry, I'm booking their trip Monday."

Paislie took a bite and practically melted on the spot. "Oh. My. Goodness. Oh yes. This is so much better than what I make."

"Told you it was good," I said as I took a bite.

Paislie popped a chip into her mouth and leaned back on one hand as she looked intently at me. "So tell me about yourself, Malcolm. From what I read on the internet, you're cocky, a manwhore, filthy rich, liked by a lot of people *off* the track, your nemesis retired this year opening it up for you to dominate each race, and you're from Texas."

"Looks like you covered it."

Shaking her head, she took another bite. "You're not even going to try and defend the manwhore thing?"

"Nope. Pretty much all of that was true." I looked up and thought for a second. "Yeah, no . . . all of it's true."

A look of disappointment washed over her face as she quietly took another bite. "I'm cocky when I need to be, I am rich, I hope like hell people do like me for me and not for my money, Emmit . . . my nemesis as you called him . . . did retire from racing, which still pisses me off."

"Why does that make you mad?"

With a shrug, I replied, "He's good. Damn good."

She leaned closer and asked, "Better than you?"

"If I'm being honest?"

Nodding her head, she gasped. "Always be honest, Malcolm. It's a very enduring quality about a person."

Her smile made my stomach drop. "Okay. Yes, he is better than me. Best driver I've ever raced against. He kept me on my toes. Made me strive to be the best I could be so I could take him down each week."

"Wow," Paislie said in a hushed tone.

With a dry laugh, I shook my head. "Trust me, I'm as surprised as you I admitted that out loud. If you ever repeat it, I'll deny it."

Holding up her hands, she locked her lips and pretended to throw the key away. "It's safe with me."

She looked down and asked, "What about the manwhore thing?"

I wanted to take every single moment back I shared with the endless amounts of women I had fucked so I could tell her that wasn't true.

"I've had my fair share of women and fun times."

Something moved across her face that I couldn't read and I wished like hell I had lied. But then again . . . there was something about Paislie that made me want to be honest with her. I never wanted to see her hurt or be the one to hurt her.

She took another bite and we finished the meal in silence. Paislie helped me pack the basket back up and looked out behind me as she jumped up. "The sun! Oh wow."

Standing, I took her hand and led her over to the other side where we stood and watched the most amazing sunset I'd ever seen. The orange and red colors were brilliant as they swept over the horizon. I felt as if I was seeing a real sunset for the first time in my life.

When the last part of the sun dipped below the skyline, Paislie turned to me. "I have to be honest with you, Malcolm."

"It's a good trait, remember?"

She let out a soft chuckle. "I can't get involved with a guy like you. No matter how attracted I am to you." My chest felt tight, but I wasn't sure if it was because she said she was attracted to me or couldn't get involved with a guy like me. "I didn't come on this date looking to spend the night in your bed, Malcolm."

"Why did you come then?"

Her mouth opened and she looked pissed, as if thinking that was my only reason for inviting her. "The small amount of time we've spoken, I've enjoyed it. I'm curious about you and you make me feel . . . um . . . I um—"

"I make you feel what?"

The night sky was starting to fight with daylight as her eyes turned dark. "Different."

"Good different or bad different?"

She lowered her head and looked down. Placing my finger under her chin, I lifted her eyes back to mine. "Paislie?"

"Good different, but I can't . . . I mean I've been hurt so many times by guys and you scare me, Malcolm."

Dropping my eyes to her lips, my dick jumped when she licked them. If I kept staring at them I'd say something I regretted. "Since I was in high school I haven't been on a date, Paislie."

Her brows pinched together. "What?"

"I didn't invite you here with hopes that I could fuck you. There are plenty of women out there that I could pick up and fuck." She swallowed hard as I kept her eyes trained on mine. "I invited you here because you make *me* feel different."

Pressing her lips together, she grinned and then asked, "Good different or bad different?"

I leaned over, closing the distance between us. My lips stopped short of hers as I noticed both our breathing pick up.

"Good," I whispered before pressing my lips to hers.

Her hands came up and gripped my arms. If there was anything I wanted more in this world, it was to kiss this girl. But I also wanted to kiss her so she knew that was all I wanted from her.

For now.

I gently rubbed my lips across hers as she squeezed onto my arms and moaned ever so slightly. When I pressed my lips to her it felt like a jolt of lightning. It was slow and soft. Nothing felt as if it needed to be rushed. When she opened her mouth to me, I swear I died and went to heaven. Our tongues moved slowly in perfect harmony with each other.

I fought the urge to pull her closer to me. To make her feel how badly I wanted her.

No. I needed to take things slow.

This was different.

Paislie was different.

Twelve

PAISLIE

M Y BODY WAS HUMMING AS Malcolm slowly kissed me. I'd never in my life experienced anything like this before. The urge to push him down and crawl on top of him was so overwhelming, yet, I longed to get to know him more. For the first time in my life, it wasn't about sex. It was about so much more.

When he finally broke the kiss, I opened my eyes. His beautiful blue eyes could still be seen by the fading glow of the sunset.

His stare was intense as he said, "Please tell me you felt that too."

My heart was pounding so hard in my chest I was sure he heard it. "I did," I softly spoke.

"Good," was all he said as his hands cupped my face and my arms moved to his chest. I needed to keep distance between us. If I felt him against me, I knew I'd lose all control.

I thought he was going to kiss me again, but he kissed my forehead and whispered my name against my skin.

My fingers flexed into his solid chest as a low growl came from the back of his throat. "I'm not so sure about my next set of plans."

I focused on my breathing so I could talk without seeming like I had just had a life-altering moment. "Why's that?"

"It involves lying down on the quilts."

I giggled as he moved his lips down my face, causing my entire body to spread with warmth. When he kissed my lips softly yet quickly, he took a step back.

I'd never had a man make me feel like this before. He oozed romance whether he thought he did or not. It was completely natural for him and that made all the difference in the world.

I placed my hands over my cheeks in an attempt to cool them. "We could . . . um . . . put the baskets between us? Although I would hope two grown, mature adults would have more self-control than that."

He nodded. "I agree."

"May I ask though why we're laying down on them?"

Malcolm twisted his head, wondering if I was being serious or not. "To look at the stars as they come out."

Oh. My. God. Is this guy for real?

I wanted desperately to pinch myself to make sure I wasn't dreaming. I did the next logical thing.

I spun around as I looked for the cameras. They had to be around there somewhere. *What sick fucker is playing this cruel joke on me?*

"Paislie, what are you doing?" Malcolm asked as I continued to look around.

"I'm looking around for the cameras. You know, for the people to jump out and yell something about how I'm on some reality show and I just got pranked."

His face softened as he reached for my hand. "Nope. But I will tell you you're giving my ego a huge boost."

I couldn't help but start laughing as he pulled me over to the quilts. "Lie down and look straight up."

Doing as he said, I started to see the stars. "How pretty."

Malcolm didn't try to hold my hand or even lay near me . . . much to my disappointment. "Look at all the stars coming out the darker it gets," I whispered. *Why had I never done anything like this before?*

"If you think this is amazing, you should see them at my ranch."

I turned my head and asked, "In North Carolina?"

"Nope. Here in Texas. Right now my sister, Autumn, and her young daughter, Sophie, are living there. Her rotten, asshole fucker husband told her he didn't want a family anymore and asked her leave."

My stomach felt sick as I thought about Autumn and Sophie and how I knew what they were feeling. "He doesn't want his daughter?"

"I said the same thing. What kind of fucker does that?"

I closed my eyes and barely said, "A monster."

Malcolm sighed but kept looking up. "Tell me about you, Paislie. I don't have the unfair advantage of Googling you and finding all the fun stuff out like you did."

I bit down on my lip and smiled. "I'm pretty boring. Nothing really to tell."

"Oh, no way. Spill it."

I slowly took in a deep breath. I'd never told anyone about my childhood or the fact that I was raised in an orphanage.

No. One.

But with Malcolm, I felt the need to share everything with him and I couldn't stop myself if I wanted to. "It's really kind of a depressing story. One I'm sure you could totally do without hearing."

He rolled over on his side and rested his head on his hand. When I glanced his way, I couldn't help but notice how built he was. Damn. I bet he had rock-solid abs and a chest that would make me—

"I don't think so. I want to hear it. Please."

Dear God. Please give me the ability to not give in to my desires.

I looked back up at the sky and fixed my eyes on one single star and started talking before my brain could catch up with my silly heart.

"I was eight years old when my father left me at St. Patrick's Orphanage. I wanted so badly for him to want me, but he never did."

Malcolm's hand took mine as I kept my eyes focused on the stars. "Your mom?"

Tears pooled in my eyes as I bit down hard on my inside cheek before speaking again. "She died when I was five."

His hand squeezed mine. "I'm so sorry. Do you remember her?" A slow smile spread across my face as I thought of my only memory of her.

"I remember standing on a chair at the counter. It must have been Christmas because we were making cookies, and I remember pressing the cookie cutters into the dough. I can't for the life of me remember what shape they were though."

Malcolm ran his thumb over my hand and I couldn't ignore the way it caused my skin to tingle. "Tell me what she looked like."

I took in a shaky breath and I blew it out slowly as I grinned. "She was beautiful. I remember her smile the most. It was a happy smile. That's the only way I know how to describe it. Her dark hair was pulled back into a low ponytail and I remember how it swung over her shoulders as she turned her head. That's the only memory of I have of her. No pictures. Nothing. I hold that memory close to my heart."

Malcolm didn't say a word as he patiently waited for me to continue. "Anyway, the day my father dropped me off I met Sister Elizabeth. She was twelve years older than me and had always been more like an older sister. She still is," I said with a chuckle as I continued to stare up.

"At one point in my life I thought I wanted to give my life over to God and join the sisterhood, but Elizabeth talked me out of it. She knew I was using it as an escape from reality. I of course turned to guys as my escape, went to college, and decided physical therapy was for me."

"What made you pick that career?"

Moving my head to look directly at him, I laughed. "Football players."

He lifted his eyes and chuckled. "Do tell."

"St. Pat's had a football team I used to help out with. Kind of like the manager I guess. Anytime the guys would get hurt, I'd watch Sister Mary tend to them. She had started nursing school before becoming a nun. The older I got, the more I did." I wiggled my eyebrows and said, "Of course it didn't hurt that I got to touch all the boys when that was very frowned upon. I lost my virginity to one of them after a game in the girl's locker room. That is not a pleasant memory."

Malcolm laughed and I loved how it vibrated through my body and settled deep into my lower stomach, pulling out the desire I had to touch him even more.

"Once I got to college I knew why Sister Elizabeth steered me away from becoming a nun. I wouldn't have lasted a year."

His hand squeezed mine as I shook my head and looked back up. "I worked my ass off in college, made good grades, did God's work whenever I could and never forgot my roots at St. Patrick's. I got hired on with one of the best physical therapy practices in the Dallas area. And guess what?" I asked as I dropped my head back to the side.

"What?"

I bit down on my lip as I stared at him before speaking again. "I still get to touch football players."

Malcolm closed his eyes and said, "Tell me they're pro players and not high school."

I rolled over and slapped his chest as I laughed. "Mostly college. Some pro."

I couldn't help but notice he still had a hold of my hand. "Is that how you met asshole Trey?"

I jerked my head back. "You didn't like Trey?"

"No. Mostly because he had his hands on you."

My stomach fluttered. "Oh." Rolling back over, I sighed. "We met at a bar. He was the first guy I'd dated in a long time. That day in Vegas, the same day we met, it hit me. He was cheating on me. I went to the airport and flew home after we left the race."

"Really? How did you know he was cheating?"

I sat up and quickly wiped the tear away before Malcolm could see it. He followed my lead and sat up. Trying to keep my breathing steady, I turned to Malcolm. "When you've been lied to your whole life by people, especially men, you learn how to read when people are telling the truth and when they're not. Like when you go to a foster home and after a few weeks they tell you things aren't working out and you have to go back to the orphanage, but not because they don't love you . . . but because the sisters are so lonely without you."

I could see the look of pity in Malcolm's eyes and I hated it. I quickly turned away and stood up. "Anyway, like I said, it's all very depressing, but I am who I am because of it."

"You never got adopted?" Malcolm asked as he stood.

Shaking my head, I said, "Nope," as I popped the p loudly. "After I turned fourteen, I started working around the orphanage. It worked out perfectly. I got to stay in the wing where the sisters all slept and I earned money for college."

"So, the reason you didn't become a nun is because you were too horny? You slut."

My mouth dropped open as my eyes about popped out of my head. I knew what he was doing and I appreciated it more than he knew.

"What?" I gasped. His face was deadpan as he stared at me. "I wasn't . . . I'm not a slut!"

His arms wrapped around my waist as he pulled me to him. "Thank the fuck you're not a nun, 'cause if you were I would surely be going to Hell with all the things I've thought about doing to you in the last hour."

"Oh," was all I could manage to say as I felt Malcolm's dick pressed against my stomach. My body trembled slightly and I was positive he noticed.

"We better get going. You have to work tomorrow and I have qualifying."

He leaned over and folded up a quilt as I did the same. My mind was spinning around in my head as I tried to figure out why in the hell I just told my life story to him.

Needing to forget the last few minutes, I asked, "What's qualifying?"

"We get time to race around the track some, and whoever has the best time gets the pole position."

I pinched my eyebrows together. I knew nothing about racecar driving. "Pole position?"

"Basically you start up front."

I nodded my head. "Oh, I see. So um, does this little nifty pass I have get me into the race Sunday?" I asked as I tucked a quilt under my arm and picked up a basket.

We made our way toward the elevator as Malcolm said with a hint of naughty in his voice, "That pass gets you everywhere, including on my bus."

I wiggled my eyebrows and stepped into the elevator. "Yes!" I said with as much enthusiasm as I could. "I'll finally get my date with Deuce. I think we'll make popcorn and watch HGTV while you drive around the track."

For as long as I live, I will never forget the look on Malcolm Wallace's face as I declared I would watch HGTV on his bus . . . with his dog.

"It's called racing, Paislie. It's full of strategy and talent."

I nodded as I said, "Uh-huh. Oh, I'm sure it is." I shrugged and said, "I think Deuce and I would prefer something more entertaining and exciting like *Flip or Flop.*"

As I headed down the bleachers with a huge grin on my face, little did I know Malcolm Wallace and this track would change my life forever.

MALCOLM

OPENING THE DOOR TO THE bus, I couldn't help but feel my heart do another fucking skip. The last few days I'd called myself pansy-ass I don't know how many times and it was because of the girl standing in front of me. The sound of her voice, her name across my phone; each and every time my heart jumped or my stomach dropped. *What in the fuck was happening to me?* And I didn't have the urge to fuck her. Well, that's not true . . . I did want to fuck her, but I wanted to get to know her first. Kiss her while I held her firmly in my arms. Slowly make love to her while I whispered her name against her soft skin.

I closed my eyes and pushed my wayward thoughts away.

"I believe Deuce and I have a date with *Fixer Upper.*"

With a dry laugh, I motioned for her to come in. "You found the bus okay I see."

Paislie rolled her eyes. "After I got hit on by at least ten guys all promising to rock my world in some way or another. A couple of them were kind of tempting."

Pulling her to me, I quickly kissed her lips. I wanted to move slow with Paislie. It meant a lot to me that she knew I wanted to get to know her before we jumped into bed. Although seeing her again had me fighting the urge.

"I'm glad you weren't too tempted."

She grinned and replied, "Me too."

"I missed your smile," I whispered.

She took in a breath as her eyes lit up. "This from the man who claims he doesn't do romance."

"I don't."

Her arms wrapped around my neck while her eyes landed on my lips. "What a shame. I'd be tempted by a romantic, handsome guy who doesn't get his kicks from driving around a track at a gazillion miles an hour."

"Shit! I forgot I need to make the reservations for the jump."

Paislie dropped her hands and tilted her head. "The jump?"

"Yeah, I won Daytona so Dalton has to jump with me."

"Jump what?"

Damn, I love how clueless she is. "Dalton, my crew chief, said he would jump out of a plane with me if I won. I won. So we're going sky diving."

Jerking her head back, she gave me a dazed look. Stammering over her words, she asked, "Wait . . . what? You're jumping . . . out of . . . a plane? W-why?"

I quickly kissed her lips as I hit Tom's number. He owned a sky diving operation back in Charlotte.

"It's amazing. Bigger adrenaline rush than driving a gazillion miles an hour around a track."

Something passed over Paislie's face quickly before I could fully read it. Turning, she dropped to the floor and Deuce was all over her. "You're the only sane one of the bunch, buddy."

Deuce barked and licked Paislie across the face as she let out the cutest giggle I'd ever heard.

I shook my head and turned away from her. I needed to keep my head in the game, and being around Paislie only made me want to devote all my attention to her.

The knock on the bus door had me walking over and pushing it open. Tom wasn't answering, so I sent him a quick text asking to call me back.

Dalton walked in and came to an abrupt stop when he saw Paislie. He looked between us and narrowed his eyes at me.

Paislie stood up and flashed that beautiful smile. "Hey, I'm Paislie."

Dalton eyed her up and down like she was a bug that needed to be stomped on. "What are you doing here?" he asked as I punched him on the arm.

"What the fuck, Dalton."

He turned and looked at me. "I need to talk to you now. Outside."

Paislie made a face like I was in deep trouble as she took a few steps away and sat on the sofa. Deuce jumped up and sat next to her as she reached for the remote.

"Let's find HGTV, shall we, buddy?"

I rolled my eyes as I followed Dalton out of the bus. He spun around and held up his index finger. "One rule. We had one fucking rule about the women. No fucking them on race day *before* a race. I walk in and see some knock out sitting on your damn floor. Are you kidding me?"

Right on cue, Autumn and Ashley walked up. Both of them looked between us as I pushed my hand through my hair.

"She's not some girl I'm fucking. She's a . . . a um . . . well she's . . . ah."

All three of them leaned in closer to me. "She's what?" Dalton asked.

"More than that."

Autumn and Ashley screamed as they raced past me and onto the bus.

"Great," I whispered as I turned back to Dalton. "At least she was before those two showed up. Now she'll be running away from them for her dear life."

Dalton held up his hands and motioned for me to stop talking. "Wait. She's more than that? Are you dating this girl?"

"No."

He gave me a hard stare. "No?"

"No," I repeated.

"Sleeping with her?"

I crossed my arms over my chest. "No."

His eyes widened. "What's wrong with her?"

"Nothing," I said with a chuckle.

"So, let me get this straight. You're not dating nor are you fucking her and all because she is . . . more. You're doing exactly what with her then?"

I shrugged. "I have no fucking clue. I've only seen her four times since I've met her, and all I know is I want to see her more."

Putting his hand to his chest, Dalton acted as if he was dragging in air. "Oh. My. Fucking. Hell. You finally fell for someone?"

"No, I didn't say I was falling for her. I said I wanted to get to know her. She's not like all the other girls I've met. She's . . ."

"Different," Dalton said with a smile. Pushing out a fast breath, he waved his hands around. "Fine, whatever. I just need your head in the game. Is your head in the game?"

I nodded. "It is."

"All the way? Dude, I can't have you day dreaming about Presley."

"Paislie."

"Whatever. I think I liked it better when you fucked them and didn't know their names." I glared at him as he turned and headed back to the garages. "Head in the game and get your ass down to the garage. Now! And leave Preston with your sister and Ashley."

Laughing, I called out, "Paislie!"

"What the fuck ever!"

Fourteen

PAISLIE

T HE DOOR TO THE BUS flew open and two women came rushing in. Standing, I watched as Deuce jumped up and made a beeline straight to them. They each pushed one another out of the way as they walked up to me.

"I'm Autumn, Malcolm's sister."

Feeling slightly at ease, I reached my hand out for hers. "Oh, it's a pleasure to meet you. I'm Paislie . . . a friend of Malcolm's."

His sister looked me over quickly. "Uh-huh," she said with a wink.

Okay. That's awkward. Did she assume every female around Malcolm was someone he is sleeping with?

I turned my attention to the other girl. "Hey, I'm Ashley. Malcolm's recent fuck buddy."

My smiled dropped and Autumn jerked her head to look at her. "Ashley!"

She shrugged and said, "Well I am, I mean we've know each other for a while, but then we . . ." She looked back at me and smiled. "I mean we're not anymore! I met someone and we started dating." She frowned as if regretting her loose lips. "Anyway, my brother is also Emmit Lewis."

"The driver who retired," I absentmindedly said while I tried to process everything that just came out of her mouth.

She pointed to me and said, "Yep! You know your NASCAR."

A part of me instantly didn't like Ashley. I wasn't sure if it was because she made it very clear from the get-go she'd slept with Malcolm, or if it was because she was so amazingly beautiful. Why wouldn't Malcolm be attracted to her? From the sounds of it she was more than a one-night stand. How much did this Ashley mean to Malcolm? Did he have feelings for her?

I shook my head. "No, I know nothing about NASCAR. Malcolm told me about him."

"Oh." She waved her hand as if to dismiss my lack of racing knowledge. "Don't worry if you don't know anything. Malcolm won't care about that. I mean, even though it's a huge part of his life, you can pick it up easily."

My lack of NASCAR knowledge hadn't even fazed me until she pointed it out. Autumn cleared her throat as my attention fell back on her. "So, this is kind of exciting. Malcolm hasn't really had a *friend* since Cas . . . well I mean since high school he hasn't really been with the same girl. Oh gosh."

The air quotes around friend made me smile. It was obvious Autumn was younger than Malcolm. I wanted to ask her how old she was. She must have had her daughter young and most likely missed out on a lot of things girls her age did. My heart hurt for her knowing her husband up and left her and her daughter.

Ashley turned to Autumn and said, "Well besides me, but we weren't dating."

My eyes snapped back over to Ashley. This time I think it clicked to her what she had said because her face turned red. "Right. Because you were just fuck buddies," I sneered.

"Um, I wasn't meaning anything when I said that. I'm not used to someone being in his life seriously or at all really, and oh my God. I'm making this so much worse."

I plastered on a fake smile. "No worries at all. Like I said, we're just friends." I reached down for my purse and placed it over my shoulder. "If you'll excuse me, I need to take off."

Autumn reached out and gently touched my arm. "You're not staying for the race? We usually hang out in here and watch it."

I looked between both girls. As much as I wanted to pretend like I didn't want anything serious with Malcolm, the idea of sitting next to the girl he had been recently fucking didn't seem like a good time to me.

"Thanks, but I don't think so."

Both girls stepped out of my way as I made my way to the door;

opening it, I ran into Malcolm. "Hey. Where are you going?"

I felt like an idiot for how I was acting, but I couldn't help it. For once in my life I felt something stronger than just a sexual attraction for a man, and I wasn't sure I could do this. At least not right now. "I'm going to take off."

Malcolm's eyes immediately went to his sister and Ashley. "What happened?"

I placed my hands on his chest and quickly pulled them back when I felt the jolt of energy. He turned back to me and gave me a confused look. "Good luck on the race, Malcolm."

Pushing my way past him, I quickly walked to where I had parked my car.

Ugh! I can't believe I'm letting this bother me! What, am I sixteen again?

I picked up my pace, angry that I was letting something like this get to me. I didn't even know Malcolm when he and Ashley were together. And what did it matter?

I shook my head to clear my thoughts.

"Paislie!"

The sound of Malcolm's voice caused me to stop on a dime.

I plastered on my famously-practiced smile and turned to face him. He was jogging up and stopped right in front of me. "I'm sorry about Ashley. I have no idea what in the hell she said to you, but I can see it made you feel uneasy."

"It's okay. Honestly. Deuce and I will just have to hang out another time. I'll talk to you later?"

His eyes filled with hurt as I tried to take a step away, but was frozen in place by his words. "Please don't go. I won't be able to stop thinking about you if you leave."

My mind was racing as I tried to come up with a single reason why I didn't want to stay. Only for the fact that I was letting petty jealousy in the way, I really was interested in what Malcolm was doing.

It was then I noticed all the people around us and I became completely aware that almost all of them were drivers. And they were all staring at us.

I took a step closer to him, trying to make light of the situation. "I'm not upset, I promise."

"Then stay and watch the race. You'll have a front row seat to the whole show."

I was touched Malcolm asked me to watch the race. I'd never had a man treat me the way Malcolm did and it was refreshing. Lifting my eyebrows I asked, "Will it be loud?"

"Very."

"Will I have to wear those ear things that go over my hair?"

"Headphones? Yes."

I contemplated for a few seconds and looked around. "I'm not sure. I don't like loud places."

Malcolm reached for my hands. "I'd love to know you were sitting there watching me. It would mean a lot."

I pressed my lips together as I took in his beautiful blue eyes. "I'm still not sure I'm looking for anything serious, Malcolm."

His hand came up to the side of my face as I found myself leaning into it. "I'm not asking you to date me. I'm asking you stay and watch me race."

Oh lord. There went my heart.

Before my brain could catch up with my heart, I replied, "Okay."

The smile that spread over his face caused me to giggle like a little girl.

"You're going to love it!" he said enthusiastically as he practically pulled my arm out while leading me back toward the track.

I rolled my eyes and let out a sarcastic groan. "Don't get your hopes up."

"HOPE YOU'RE NOT AFRAID OF heights," Malcolm said as he pointed up to scaffolding holding a few chairs and a bunch of equipment.

With a stunned and somewhat frightened expression, I asked, "That's where you want me to sit?"

The evil sexy grin on his face had me searching for my next breath. "Yep," he replied.

He was now dressed in his racing gear and I had to admit he looked hot as hell.

The amount of activity going on had my head spinning. The cars were all lined up with Malcolm's being in the second row. He qualified third, which I thought was good, but according to him he could have done better.

Malcolm's arm was wrapped around my waist while he talked to two of the guys on his pit crew. People walked by snapping pictures, but pretty much left him and the other drivers alone. Every now and then someone would ask for a picture or for something signed, and Malcolm would comply with that southern charm he had.

Of course, I'd seen the cocky side of him earlier when he was talking shit with another driver.

Men.

This was nothing like when I had been with Trey. If cameras were around, I was not anywhere near him. Looking back, I wanted to smack myself for being so stupid.

Malcolm's warm breath hit my neck as he softly spoke in my ear.

"Is this too much? If you want to go sit with Dalton you can."

With a grin, I shook my head. "No, I'm good. It's all very exciting."

His smile spoke volumes. I enjoyed being in his company as much as he enjoyed mine.

After driver introductions and the singing of the "Star Spangled Banner," Malcolm crawled into his car. Panic filled my entire body as I watched them help him get strapped in. It took everything in me not to beg him not to do this, but I knew how unfair that would be. This was his life. I imagined it was his everything.

Malcolm said something to the guys and they stepped aside while he motioned for me to walk up. With a nervous smile, I leaned over and said the only stupid thing that came to mind.

"Hey."

He grinned so big I couldn't help but laugh. "I've never had a girl down here with me before."

I raised my eyebrows and asked, "Really? Does this mean I get to kiss you before you take off a gazillion miles an hour in a circle?"

His hand came up to my neck as he pulled me closer. "Yes," he spoke against my lips as my body caught on fire when he kissed me.

I pulled back and licked my lips as I gazed into his eyes. "Be careful, Malcolm."

With a wink, he said, "I'm always careful, baby."

I stepped back and watched as he put his helmet on.

Oh. My.

Why did that look hot as hell on him? Shit. Everything looked hot as hell on him. But when he turned and looked at me and all I saw were those blue eyes, I had to force my legs not to go out on me.

Malcolm lifted his hand and I lifted mine. I was well aware of the cameras and I'm sure everyone was dying to know who the girl with Malcolm Wallace was.

"Come on, Paislie, I'll help you up there with Dalton," Justin, one of the pit crew guys, said.

It didn't take long for me to chew half my thumbnail off as I watched Malcolm do what he did as he raced at almost two hundred miles an hour around the stupid track. I could hear everything he was saying as well as his spotter and Dalton. I quickly found out Malcolm Wallace doesn't like to be pushed around and he had a temper.

Russ came on the headphones and said, "Go the high line in turn four, looks like the number seven might be loose."

"Fuck, she's slipping all over the goddamn place. Dalton, we need to adjust the pressure. I can't drive her."

Dalton nudged my shoulder, causing me to turn my head. He winked and said, "Paislie, you're going to bite your lip off. Stop being so worried."

I nodded my head and let out the breath I hadn't even noticed I was holding.

"Trouble in turn three. Here it comes! We're in it."

"I'm going in blind," Malcolm said as I dug my fingers into my jeans. I had a terrible feeling something bad was about to happen.

"High! Go high, high, high!"

When I saw his car emerge from the cloud of smoke, I pushed out a relieved sigh. Then another car shot up the track and clipped the back of Malcolm's car, causing it to start spinning.

I quickly stood as did Dalton. It happened right in front of us. His car flew in the air and proceeded to flip end over end before hitting hard and being hit on the driver's side by another car and driven up into the wall.

That did not just happen. Please God, no.

Every ounce of air was sucked out of me as I covered my mouth and I fought to hold back my tears. It wasn't lost on me that a camera had been pointed up to me numerous times since the race started. The last thing I wanted to do was something wrong. This world was so new to me and I was the gossip talk of the track today.

Grabbing onto Dalton's arm, I turned to him as he spoke. "Malcolm. Talk to me."

Silence filled the air. I couldn't hear anything else. Not the crowd, the sirens, the yelling. Nothing.

"Malcolm," I whispered as fear gripped my chest.

"Russ? Movement?"

Russ didn't respond and I found myself glancing up to all the spotters. It wasn't but a few nights ago we were up on that roof, and one single kiss from Malcolm had brought to life a part of me I never knew existed.

I slowly sat down as I focused on Malcolm's car.

"No," was all Russ said.

Dalton shot a quick look my way before saying Malcolm's name again.

Sitting motionless, I watched as emergency crews rushed to Malcolm's car.

Closing my eyes, I prayed like I had never prayed before.

Please God. Please don't take him from me.

Not him, I beg of you.

Please.

MALCOLM

T HE PAIN IN MY RIGHT leg was like nothing I'd ever experienced before in my life.

"Don't move, Malcolm!" the emergency crew guy called out.

"Fuck!" I cried out as they helped me out of the car. The smell of burning rubber and gas filled my senses and made my eyes water. Or maybe it was the pain making my eyes water.

"Your leg is broken," someone said as I shut my eyes.

"No fuck," I said, squeezing my fists together.

People were surrounding the car and me as I fought to keep from crying out.

Son-of-a-bitch. I can't believe this.

"Keep still, we've got to stabilize your leg," one of the guys said.

Paislie.

Shit. She's probably scared shitless.

"Who has a phone?" I called out as they all looked at me like I was insane.

By the time I was being put in the ambulance, I was practically on the verge of begging them to knock me out. The ambulance stopped and the doors opened. The moment I saw her, the pain vanished.

Okay maybe didn't vanish, but damn near did.

Her brows were pinched together as she narrowed in on my leg. When her green eyes looked up, I was stunned to see the tears in them. She quickly got her composure and started asking the medic if they did certain things to which he said yes to everything. She moved and sat next me while reaching for my hand.

"Hey," I said as she closed her eyes and sighed loudly before looking back at me.

"Malcolm Wallace, you scared the piss out of me!"

"Were you a little bit impressed, though?"

Her mouth dropped before snapping shut as she glared at me. "Are you insane? You're completely insane."

"It was pretty bad ass how that car was flipping, though, admit it."

She held up her hand and looked away. "I need a minute."

Everything started to go blurry as the medic's voice seemed to be talking in slow motion.

Trying to talk, my mouth felt dry and my eyelids heavy.

Before I knew it, there was nothing but darkness.

OPENING MY EYES, I LOOKED around the room. Why was I not surprised it was empty?

I heard a door open and turned to see an adorable Paislie yawning as she stretched her arms over her head.

When she looked over to me, her smile melted my heart. "Malcolm," she mumbled as she came to my side. "How's the pain?"

"Hurts like a motherfucker."

She lifted her brow and gave me a look that only a mom should be giving.

"Your sister and parents are here. I also got to meet one very adorable little girl who sure loves her Uncle Malcolm."

My heart filled with warmth as I thought about Sophie. "Sophie."

I tried to adjust myself but had a hard time with practically my entire leg in a cast and held up. "Fuck, I thought they only did this shit in the movies."

Paislie helped me get more comfortable as I dropped my head back and let out a moan. "So . . . my mom and pop haven't scared you off yet?"

She giggled and said, "Nope. I've only talked to them once. Autumn introduced me to them. I've kind of kept out of the way. You passed out in the ambulance, and once they brought you into surgery I hung out with my friend Karrie who's a nurse. She kept me updated on your surgery."

I wasn't sure why it bothered me that Paislie felt like she couldn't be with my family.

"Where are they now?"

"Um, they ran back to their hotel for a bit. Sophie was cranky and tired. I think Autumn said she was going to stay at the hotel while your mother and father came back to the hospital. She asked if I would stay with you until you woke up."

I closed my eyes and shook my head before looking up at her. "So, tell me . . . who's gonna be the most honest with me about this?"

Her teeth sunk down into her lip as she stole a peek at my leg and then back to me.

"You want honest?"

"Always."

Something moved over her face as she cleared her throat. "You're going to need extensive rehabilitation. You not only had a compound fracture of your leg, you broke your patella."

My heart dropped. "What about racing?" Paislie's eyes looked away. "Paislie . . . please."

She pulled and pushed her lip in and out of her mouth nervously. "Your doctor should be the one to talk to you, Malcolm."

"Paislie!" I said louder than I wanted to.

She jumped and took a step back before standing up straighter. "You'll be in the cast for at least six weeks and then you'll have to do physical therapy. Your mobility in your leg might be . . . compromised."

I swallowed hard. "Meaning?"

"I'm guessing you use your left leg to push in the clutch. Your strength in that leg could be affected by the break. If you have good physical therapy, there's a chance you'll have full use and can build it back up."

"Then that's what will happen," I said, matter-of-factly.

She smiled. "Positive thinking is a great way to be."

"How often will I need the physical therapy?"

She shook her head. "I'm not sure. You'll need another surgery to remove the pins. I'm more concerned about your knee than your leg. The doctors will give you more of an idea as you begin to heal."

For the first time in my life, I was unsure about my future and that scared the piss out of me. Racing was my life. I needed the rush. I craved it. I had to have it to keep all my other demons away.

There was nothing in this world that could ever replace the feeling I had when I was behind the wheel.

Nothing.

"Nothing in my life matters besides racing."

Paislie looked at me with a confused look. "So you're tell me your life is over if you can't get into a racecar again? Seriously, Malcolm? You're lucky to be alive."

The whole reason I raced the way I did was because I never cared about life. I lived it from day to day.

"I race the way I do because I don't give a fuck about life."

She sucked in a sharp breath. "How can you say that?"

With a gruff laugh, I shook my head. "Why do you think I'm the way I am?" My leg was throbbing as the pain built. "I like the rush from the adrenaline. I don't fucking jump out of planes or rock climb because it's a fun sport. It gives me a thrill and makes me forget."

Her head tilted as she stared at me. "Forget what?"

I closed my eyes and saw Casey's smile. Popping my eyes back open, I shook my head. "You wouldn't understand."

Her eyes grew angry as she shook her head. "Oh yeah, because I've never wanted to escape life before," she said sarcastically. "I don't try to kill myself while doing it, though."

I laughed as I looked into her eyes. "No you only try to escape by fucking guys. I do it with living my life on the edge."

Her mouth parted open and I saw the hurt move across her face. Pressing her lips together, she shot me a dirty look.

Fuck. *Why did I say that?*

I needed her to leave before I said something else I would be regretting.

"Paislie, would you mind leaving me alone for a bit, please?"

A look moved over Paislie's face before she took a few steps back. She reached for her purse and headed to the door.

"Wait. I didn't mean what I said, I—"

Paislie turned back and glared at me. "I've never told anyone the things I shared with you on that roof. But thank you for letting me know what you think about me, Malcolm. It was very enlightening."

"No. Paislie, I'm just angry and I need some time to process all this bullshit and I can't do it right now."

She let out a huff. "Don't worry, I'm sure you'll have plenty of people to help you process . . . including Ashley."

Before I could even think of something to say in response, she opened the door and walked out.

Leaving me in the silence I asked for.

Sixteen

PAISLIE

TWO MONTHS HAD PASSED SINCE I walked out of Malcolm's hospital room. It took him two days before he called and left a message saying he really wanted to see me. When I didn't answer, he kept calling and sending text messages.

I changed my number two weeks later. The only good thing was he at least had the decency not to bother me at work. He probably met some nurse who was taking care of him.

Letting out a frustrated sigh, I dropped my pen onto my desk and buried my face in my hands. Was it time to go home yet?

My phone buzzed as I picked it up. "Hey, Stephanie, what's up?"

"Tyler wants you to come to his office."

I closed my eyes and shook my head. Tyler was the owner of Southlake Physical Therapy and if you did your job, he left you alone. I could only imagine why he was calling me in. The last time it was to work on a patient no one else could handle. He was cranky, mean, and never wanted to do what you asked him to do. Unfortunately, Tyler felt like I was the right person for the job. It took three months to finally break the guy's mold. It took tough love and me telling him to piss off a time or two. I had a strange feeling I was about to be tested again.

"I'll be right there."

I pushed my chair back and stood as I pulled a deep cleansing breath through my nose and blew it out through my mouth. Elizabeth had decided I needed to do yoga with her. After telling her what happened with Malcolm, she declared a no-guy zone for six months and I agreed to it. I was getting my inner-nun on.

Knocking lightly on Tyler's door, I heard him say to come in. When the door opened, I smiled and walked in, taking a seat in one of the chairs facing his large oak desk.

He had multiple awards on the wall behind him as well as pictures of his family.

He looked at me intently for a few moments before saying, "Paislie, you know you've become one of my top physical therapists."

I moved about nervously in my seat. I was never one to take compliments well.

"Thank you, Tyler."

"You've been a huge part of the growing of this practice. But I need to know how far you'll go to help it grow even more."

A sick feeling moved over me as I raised my eyebrow at him.

"Are you willing to travel for a job?"

My body relaxed and I almost sighed with relief. I shrugged and said, "By travel, what do you mean? Like drive somewhere each day?"

"No, I mean travel to a client's house and pretty much live-in with them during their recovery. They are willing to double your salary, take care of your room and board and pay your current monthly rent in return for PT four times a week."

My eyes widened in shock. "Wow. That seems pretty excessive to have a physical therapist at their beck and call.

Tyler nodded. "I admit, it was a shock to me at first and he offered a rather hefty bonus for taking you away from the practice, but this client is not hurting for money."

"Clearly," I mumbled. "I mean . . . well, I have my cat. What would I do with her?"

"Take her."

This time my mouth fell open. "W-what?"

"They were very specific on this. If you had any pets, you were free to bring them."

I furrowed my eyebrows and gave Tyler a dazed look before laughing. "Wait. Is this some kind of joke?"

He slowly shook his head. "No. I'm being one-hundred-percent serious. The client has had two other physical therapists and fired them both."

Oh great. Another asshole is exactly what I need in my life right now. The last thing I wanted to deal with was a guy with a big ego and even bigger pocketbook. Those were the kind who usually thought they owned you.

My father had shown up on my doorstep two weeks after seeing my picture in the paper with Malcolm. He figured I had landed a rich boyfriend and was seeing what he could get out of me. The minute he found out I was no longer in contact with Malcolm, he took off again. Never mind the fact I agreed to have lunch with him and he never showed up.

Someday I'll learn.

I brought my fingers up to my temples as I chuckled and said, "Okay, so let me get this straight." Dropping my hands back down, I looked directly at my boss. "I have to travel to this person and live with them?"

"Yes, here in Texas."

I shook my head in a very confused manner. "And they're willing to pay twice my salary plus room and board, plus pay my current apartment's rent, *and* I can bring my cat?"

"Yep."

"Are they are a hermit or something? Have you checked them out? Will I be held captive and chopped up into a million pieces?"

Tyler smirked along with giving me a shrug. "I hope not, because like I said, you're one of my best."

I rolled my eyes. I knew Tyler would have done his research before sending me off to live with a hermit. "Do I have set days off?"

Tyler handed me a piece of paper that listed me working Monday, Tuesday, Wednesday and Friday. Thursday, Saturday, and Sunday I had off.

Shit. Tyler had me at twice my salary, but something didn't feel right with this, but I let the money override my good sense.

"I'll do it."

With a sigh of relief, his body relaxed. "Thank God, I already said you would."

"Tyler!" I cried out as he picked up the phone and hit the button for Stephanie.

"Stephanie, please let Mrs. Moss know Paislie will be there first thing Monday morning."

"Yes, sir."

Tyler and I both stood up as he gave me a warm smile. "Paislie, it means a lot to me that you're such a team player and don't worry, I had the guy checked out with a full background check and all. It's because of people like you that our practice has such an amazing reputation. Matter of fact, this client requested you personally so he'd already heard about how great you were. You're going to love Crawford, Texas. The guy owns a huge ranch and said you'll have access to all of it."

My heart fell to my stomach. "Crawford, Texas?" My breathing picked up. There is no fucking way. "You said he owns a ranch . . . in Crawford?"

"Yep."

A sick feeling moved over my body as I asked, "W-what's the client's name?"

"Malcolm. Malcolm Wallace. He's a NASCAR driver, so I'm hoping this will open the door for us even more."

The room spun as I reached for something to hold me up.

"That asshole," I whispered under my breath. I was going to break his other leg the second I saw him.

I SAT IN MY CAR and stared at the mansion of a house. "Holy. Shit."

Never mind it felt like I drove forever down the long-ass driveway, but now I stared at a ranch-style house that looked like it was the size of the White House.

Okay, that's a stretch. It was big, though.

Huge.

Frowning, I shook my head. "Guess Malcolm has a size issue."

With a frustrated huff, I opened the door to my car and got out as I took a better look at the house.

It was a sandstone two-story house with a metal roof. All the windows were framed in black shutters with a black iron railing running across the porch. The front door was a massive double wood door.

"Pompous ass."

Maybe I should have talked to Elizabeth about this. I had a feeling I made a very poor decision. But the money would help me in so many ways. Depending on how much time I'd be here, I could make enough money to buy the house I'd always dreamed of.

The front door open and an older woman and Sophie came running out. Her pigtails bounced as she raced toward me. She was the cutest five-year-old I'd ever seen.

"Paislie!"

My eyes widened in shock. She remembered my name?

She stopped just short of me and stared up at me with huge, bright blue eyes. She resembled Malcolm so much, it made my chest feel tight.

"Hello there, Sophie!" I said as I bent down to get at her level. I'd worked with enough little ones at the orphanage to know how to talk and interact with kids.

"You look like a princess! I hope I'm as pretty as you when I grow up."

Either she was the sweetest child on earth . . . or Malcolm bribed her to say that.

"That is the sweetest thing anyone has ever said to me. Thank you, Sophie. But I think you're very pretty and surely you *must* be a princess for you live in this grand castle!"

She smiled and looked down as she kicked at the ground nervously. With a giggle she shook her head. "Uncle Malcolm says I am. He said I was the prettiest girl in the whole world."

My heart melted. "He's right."

Her little smile caused an ache in my chest. I'd never before in my life longed for a child, until that very moment.

"Well guess what, Sophie, I brought along a real princess!"

She gasped. "You did?"

I scrunched up my noise and said, "Well, her name is Princess, but *she* thinks she is a queen."

Standing, I opened the back door and pulled the cat carrier out as Princess started making it very clear how pissed off she really was.

Sophie let out a scream that had my toes curling and Princess freezing in place.

"A kitty!"

I had to admit, the torment that Princess was fixin' to go through made me smile internally a bit.

"Can I help you with your bags, Ms. Pruitt?"

I glanced up to see an older gentleman standing before me along with an older woman. Reaching my hand out, I introduced myself.

"Hello, Paislie Pruitt."

His smile was so kind as he shook my hand. "Mr. Moss and this is my wife, Janet."

Janet shook my hand and said, "I'm Malcolm's assistant."

With a smile, I nodded. "Oh, yes. Malcolm has spoken very highly of you, Mrs. Moss."

"Janet, please call me Janet. And he better have." Her wink caused me to chuckle.

Before I knew it two younger guys had my two suitcases and Princess and headed toward the house. When I finally looked back toward the front door, my breath caught in my throat. Malcolm was standing there on crutches.

O sweet Mary mother of Jesus. He looked so good. He clearly hadn't shaved in a few days and the scruff on his face suited him. He wore light-weight sweatpants and a blue T-shirt that I was positive would make his eyes pop the closer you got to him. The thing that got me though was his smile. I didn't want to like seeing it . . . but I did.

Pulling my eyes from him, I glanced back down to Sophie. At some point in time, she had taken my hand in hers. "I want to show you my room Uncle Malcolm made for me."

Turning to Janet, she nodded. "Malcolm would like to have lunch with you and talk about everything, if you're not too tired of course."

Did this woman know I was the girl Malcolm took up to the rooftop? Surely she didn't. She did know we knew each other though. I wondered if she knew he practically bribed my boss and me to be here?

"No, of course, that's fine," I said as my voice cracked. The thought of being alone with Malcolm scared the hell out of me.

"Come on, Paislie! I'll show you all around."

And just like that, a sweet little girl who clearly was excited about the prospect of having a new friend here was dragging me up the steps.

She stopped and looked up at Malcolm. "Uncle Malcolm! She's here! Paislie's here!"

The way he smiled down at her with such love in his eyes had my low-er stomach pooling with heat. It had to have been the sexiest damn thing I'd ever seen.

"I know she is, princess. Are you going to show her all around for me since I can't?"

She nodded her head and looked back at me. "Uncle Malcolm hurt himself really bad. But you're going to fix him so he can drive his fast cars again!" she shouted as she jumped. My heart slammed against my chest while my head snapped up to look at Malcolm. The sadness in his eyes gutted me as I quickly got lost in the sea of blue.

"I hope so, Sophie," I said softly. *I sure as hell hope so.*

Seventeen

MALCOLM

HER GREEN EYES WERE HOLDING me captive as she stared at me. My heart had been pounding so hard in my chest as I watched her with Sophie. I wasn't sure what these feelings were I was feeling, but I knew I needed more of it. These last two months had been fucking hell. There were so many times I longed to see her. Craved to see her. To taste her lips.

Paislie was unlike anything I had ever experienced. For the little amount of time I had spent with her, I had become addicted. It was as if she was a drug, and I needed a fix every single day.

Seeing her here now was almost too much.

"You look good, Paislie."

My voice seemed to pull her out of her trance. Her eyes were soft but quickly turned dark as she opened her mouth to say something but quickly shut it.

Sophie tugged on Paislie's arm. "Come on! We're wastin' time!"

Paislie's eyes softened as she looked down at my niece. "Okay, let's go."

I watched them as they hurried off into the house. I could hear sweet Sophie talking a mile a minute.

Janet walked up next to me and chuckled. "She's certainly excited, isn't she?"

"Yeah, she thinks she scored a playmate."

"I'm thinking she's not the only one who thinks that."

I did a double take over at my assistant. "What?"

Janet gave me a look like I knew exactly what she was talking about. "Please, you don't think I know? Paislie was at the hospital, remember?

She was the girl you spent the weekend with before the accident. I also know you're not stupid enough to pay someone twice their salary and room and board to come and be your personal physical therapist. I may be old, but I'm not stupid. You don't pay me to be stupid."

Shit. I totally forgot about Paislie being at the hospital.

"No ma'am, I do not."

Janet held the front door open for me as I used the crutches to walk into the house. I'd gotten my cast off and had begun therapy a few weeks back. The first two physical therapists were idiots. The first one seemed to be more interested in my cock than she was getting my leg back in working order. The other one was so old, I was sure he was about to fall asleep during our first session.

Paislie was my only hope at returning back to racing. A heavy feeling rolled through my stomach as I remembered why she walked away from me in the first place.

The first thing I needed to do was tell her I was sorry for what I said to her.

"Come on, you need to do some walking. Help me make lunch."

I followed Janet through the house and into the kitchen. When I bought this house, everything needed updating. Janet was in charge of all of it. The kitchen was her biggest project and I had to admit she did a great job.

Cream cabinets with black granite countertops were her first pick. I moaned internally as I thought about the hours upon hours she had me looking at backsplashes. I finally pointed to a random picture just to get her to stop. Tumbled stone she called it. It now graced the walls in the kitchen and I had to admit it looked damn good.

I perched my crutches up against the wall as I helped her get everything ready for lunch.

"Malcolm, I've never asked questions because honestly it's none of my business, but I have to ask you something."

As I picked grapes and set them in a bowl, I replied, "Go for it, Janet."

"What happened to you that makes you push love away?"

My body froze. "What makes you think I push love away?"

Her eyes were on me and I could feel the intensity of her stare.

"You seem to forget I know everything that goes on in your

life . . . probably better than you. I also hear things."

I turned to her and raised an eyebrow. "You hear things? What kind of things?"

She smirked as she went back to making the sandwiches. "Oh you know, Dalton making arrangements for . . . *visitors*. Ashley, Emmit's sister, and her *visits* to you. Those kinds of things."

"You knew about Ashley?"

Janet let out a dry laugh. "What do you pay me for, Malcolm? Do you know how many times I had to cover for you? Like the one time you flew Ashley in for a . . . *visit* . . . and Emmit almost walked onto your bus with his little sister in there. I intercepted him, because if he ever found out, you'd have gotten two broken legs at the hands of one very pissed off brother."

My mouth fell open. "Wow. Janet, you're like Super Woman."

She nodded. "Yes, I am."

I wrapped my arms around her and kissed the top of her brown hair that was sprinkled with bits of grey throughout. "I love you like you're my mother. Thank you for always taking care of me."

"Don't change the subject," she barked as I dropped my arms to my side.

With a shrug, I said, "I'm not interested in love. It's not something I want."

"Really?" she questioned as she sliced avocado and placed it next to the lettuce. "Pop that bread down in the toaster, will you?"

Doing as she asked, I nodded. "Yep."

She wiped her hands on a dishrag and turned to face me. "What was her name?"

The heaviness in my heart came back as I lifted my head and looked out the massive floor-to-ceiling windows.

"Casey was her name. We started dating our freshman year of high school." My hand came up to the back of my neck as I tried to rub the immediate tension out. The memory came back as if it had just happened. I could smell her perfume, like she was standing right next to me. "She had been at a football game and I just found out I was being moved up to the Xfinity Series. I couldn't wait to tell her. After the game, I pulled her under the bleachers and told her. I always knew a part of her hated I did it because she was always afraid I would get hurt. But she knew how much I loved it." I smiled as I remembered her launching her body against mine as she hugged me.

"Oh my gosh! Malcolm, this is the best news ever!"

I held onto her tightly as she hugged me for what seemed like forever.

When she stepped back, she shook her head. "You're going to become so famous. People will go crazy when you drive around those tracks."

I laughed as I took her hands in mine. "Let's hope. I'm not starting out driving full time. I have to work my way up and earn that, but this is a great move. I'm one down from the big times, Casey. This could change our future."

She nodded enthusiastically. "I know." With a huge smile on her face, she pulled me closer to her. "Let's go to the cabin. I want to be with you. Let's celebrate by making love."

I placed my hand on the side of her face. "Sounds like a fucking amazing idea."

Our cabin was six miles outside of Waco and was on the old dairy farm that was my grandfather's. The cabin Casey and I would go to was the old original cabin. It was our spot and the place where we made love for the first time over a year ago.

Casey grabbed my hand and pulled it to her lips. "Malcolm, do you see us getting married someday?"

I turned to look at her quickly before looking back at the road. My heart felt as if it froze. Casey mentioning marrying her had me a bit freaked out, but I knew I cared about her. Hell, she was the only girl I'd ever loved. "Yeah, I see us getting married someday."

"Tell me I'll be the only girl you'll ever love. Promise me that."

I hesitated for a moment and I wasn't sure why. With a smile on my face, I squeezed her hand and went to tell her just that when all I heard were tires skidding. The lights from another car shined into my truck as I felt the force of their vehicle slam into the passenger side.

After my truck stopped spinning, I called out Casey's name when I saw her lifeless body. The whole side of her face was bleeding. Another driver helped me pull her from the car as I checked to see if she was breathing.

Nothing.

I started CPR on her as I heard someone behind me crying.

I didn't answer her. Shit! I didn't answer her.

"Please don't leave me! You'll always be the only girl I'll ever love. Baby, don't leave me! I swear to you, Casey!"

"By the time the ambulance got there, she hadn't been breathing for over ten minutes. She was gone."

I fought to hold my tears in. "I never got to answer her. She died before I had a chance to tell her what she wanted to hear. Since that day, I never took another moment for granted. Life can be stripped from us like that," I said as I snapped my fingers. "I was living life for her. Every time I got behind the wheel of a racecar, I raced for her. Every time I jumped out of a plane, I did it for her. That rush I got out of it only reminds me that each day is a gift and how her life was stripped of that gift."

Janet placed her hand on my shoulder and squeezed it. "Oh darling, what a terrible thing to happen to you at such a young age." She paused for a moment and then shook her head. "You can't not ever love again, Malcolm. You need to open your heart and let love in. Casey would not have wanted you to go through life not loving someone."

I looked down at my hands. "I know, Janet. I know. The thought of opening my heart to someone else is frightening, though." I exhaled a deep breath as my cheeks blew out. The only woman who ever made me feel alive other than Casey had been Paislie. And the fact that I'd only been around her a few times and she brought out more feelings in me than even Casey did scared the ever-living fuck out of me. I was positive Janet saw it in my eyes.

"You'll never know unless you go for it. Life is messy, you know that. But wouldn't you have rather have loved and lost, than to have never known what that feeling of love was like?"

"Considering the hell I went through after her death, I'm not sure how to answer that."

Janet's eyes pooled with tears as I heard little feet running down the hall. Janet stepped away and headed over to the sink when Sophie ran into the kitchen.

"I showed Paislie my room and she said she would have loved to have had a room like mine when she was little!"

My eyes peeked over to Paislie who stood awkwardly in the doorway to the kitchen. "Did you show her where her room was?"

Sophie shook her head. "Nope. I thought you wanted to show her."

Sophie skipped over to Janet. "Am I eating lunch with Uncle Malcolm and Paislie?"

With a laugh, Janet said, "Oh no! We're having a picnic outside in the backyard under your favorite oak tree." She reached for a basket and showed it to Sophie. "See! I packed us a lunch."

"Oh yay! Let's go, Ms. Janet! Let's go!"

Paislie and I both chuckled as Sophie pulled Janet out the back door and down the path to Sophie's favorite spot.

"She has a ton of energy; I don't know how my sister does it," I said as I watched them through the glass window as they walked away.

I needed to clear my head after talking about Casey. I stood slowly and pointed to the plates. "Would you mind bringing these over to the table? I'll grab the grapes."

Paislie stood there and looked at me with a blank expression for a few moments before walking over and balancing both plates on her arm while grabbing the grapes. "You'll want to make sure you use the crutches; don't try to put too much weight on your leg and knee. You'll only do more harm than good."

I didn't say a word as I did what she said. Her tone was cold and distant.

Janet had already placed glasses of iced tea on the table.

"Hope you like BLTA's. The A is for the avocado Janet insists putting on."

She slid down into her seat and bowed her head. I was guessing she was saying a quick prayer. She'd done it that night on the roof as well.

"It's fine, thank you."

We ate for a few minutes in silence before I couldn't take it any longer. "You changed your number, why?"

Without looking at me she answered, "You wouldn't stop calling."

"Paislie, you didn't even give me a chance to explain."

Her head jerked up. "Explain what, Malcolm? Why you called me a whore?"

Anger flowed through my veins as I shook my head. "I didn't call you a whore."

Her eyes glassed over as she softly spoke. "You might as well have because that's how you made me feel."

My breathing slowed and my body felt heavy. "I never meant to make you feel like that. I was angry and I'm so sorry I took it out on you. Especially with something you confided in me with. I have no room to judge anything you've done. Please forgive me, Paislie. Please."

She cleared her throat and sat up straighter. "It's fine, Malcolm. Let's move on and concentrate on your recovery. I'll stay for as long as it takes for you to find another physical therapist you like. We'll figure out why you haven't liked the others you had and find the right fit for you."

My stomach dropped. "I don't want another physical therapist. I want you."

Her eyes lit up for a quick moment before she looked away. "This is crazy for you to be paying me this much. You're very capable of going into an office for therapy. I've already looked into it and there are plenty of very good therapists in the Waco area."

I wasn't sure if I should be angry or upset that she didn't want to help me. Not uttering a word, Paislie's eyes grew wider. "Malcolm! Don't you see how insane this is?"

Pushing my plate back, I slowly stood. "I'll show you to your room. There is a copy of my medical records there for you to look over. If you need anything, the housekeeper's name is Clarisse. It's her day off today, so I'll introduce you to her tomorrow."

She looked at me like I had lost my goddamn mind. Maybe I had. Who the hell knew?

Paislie slowly stood and followed me down a hall. The guest bedroom was on the opposite side of the house from the master. It was probably bigger than her apartment.

"If you want your cat to roam around the whole house, that's fine. Janet wasn't sure so she just had everything set up for her in your bathroom."

We got to the end of the hall and I opened the door. Paislie's eyes widened as she took a step inside and mumbled something under her breath.

"My goodness. This is a bedroom?"

"It's the guest bedroom. My parents usually take this room when they're here. The bathroom is to your left. If you need anything from the store, just let me or Clarisse know. Janet and her husband will be leaving for Mexico for two weeks, but normally they stay in the smaller guest house down from the main house."

Paislie spun around and flashed me a huge smile. "You sent them to Mexico?"

I grinned and said, "Well, she's earned it for putting up with my grumpy ass for the last two months."

She let out a soft chuckle.

"I'll leave you alone to get settled."

"Wait! What am I supposed to do when we're not doing therapy?"

My dick jumped at the things I wanted to do with her, yet the guilt for feeling the way I was feeling was tearing me up inside. With a dull smile, I said, "Use your imagination. As long as you're here, everything is yours to use."

Paislie pinched her eyebrows together as she stared at me with a tense expression.

A part of me wished I hadn't even called to have her come out. Seeing her did insane things to me. After talking to Janet, I was even more confused about my feelings, especially my feelings for Casey and that pissed me off. The last thing I wanted to do was take it out on Paislie again.

Turning, I made my way out of her room and shut the door behind me as I let out the breath I hadn't even realized I was holding.

I may have just made the biggest mistake of my life by having her here.

Eighteen

PAISLIE

THE POUNDING OF THE GROUND under my feet felt good. It cleared my mind and that was what I needed. After my first therapy session with Malcolm this morning, I was more confused than ever. Yesterday, I'd spent almost two hours going over all of his medical information and coming up with a treatment plan.

I came to a stop and leaned over, placing my hands on my knees as I sucked in deep breaths. I could smell the spring flowers in the crisp cool air. Something about the air out here made me feel alive. Closing my eyes, all I could see was how scared Malcolm's eyes were this morning.

"Fuck!" I shouted.

The compound fracture had damaged some of Malcolm's nerves. He'd be able to fully walk again, I just wasn't sure he'd ever be able to get clearance to get behind the wheel and race. Not one single person had bothered to tell him how extensive the nerve damage was.

Then there was his knee. That was a whole other beast of its own.

Standing, I drew my arms up over my head and inhaled deeply. Right now I needed to get him walking and build up the strength in his leg. The whole time we were together this morning he didn't utter a single word to me. I cut the session short only because I couldn't take the silence anymore.

I knew my comment about finding another therapist pissed him off. I saw it in his eyes. I can do this. I can help him. I just need to pray and ask God to help me with these confusing thoughts I'm having. After looking over all the medical information, this job no longer was about the money. It was about helping Malcolm and I knew I could.

My cell phone went off as I pulled it out of my shorts.

Annie: Waco? What in the fuck are you doing in Waco?

I rolled my eyes as I let out a chuckle.

Me: It's paying me really well. Plus I'm staying at a damn mansion and my patient happens to be utterly handsome.

Annie: Have you fucked him yet?

My smiled dropped. *What in the hell? Does everyone think I'm a slut?*

Me: Just three times last night and twice this morning.

Not a minute later my phone rang.

"Hey."

"Are you kidding me? Tell me you're kidding because I know you and you wouldn't mix business with pleasure."

With a giggle, I replied, "Yes, I'm kidding. Gesh. Do you really think I'm that much of a slut?"

Starting to walk, I could see Malcolm's house. I swear his driveway was at least a mile long.

"Okay, well tell me why you're there. Is this guy like a germaphobe who won't leave his house?"

I nibbled on my lip nervously. "No. I kind of knew him before he had his accident."

"Oh . . . this just got very interesting. Who is he?"

I lifted my hand up and waved her off like she could see me. "No one you would know."

"Try me. You'd be surprised."

"Malcolm Wallace."

Silence.

Pulling my phone out, I checked to make sure the call hadn't dropped. "Annie?"

"Malcolm Fucking Wallace? You're staying at Malcolm Wallace the NASCAR driver's house? In Crawford? His ranch?"

I pulled my head back in surprise. "Since when did you become a NASCAR fan?"

She let out a roar of laughter. "Since I saw him at one of my father's benefit dinners. Holy fucking cow bells. Paislie, that guy is hot as hell. Where did you meet him and why didn't you tell me?"

"Um . . . well, I met him at a race in Vegas. Trey had VIP tickets and I literally ran right into Malcolm. We got to talking and I don't know, we hit it off. Then he sent me a ticket to the Texas race and I kind of had dinner with him one night and was there when he had his accident."

More silence.

"You there?" I asked.

"I. Hate. You."

Pressing my lips together, I shook my head as I tried not to start laughing. I knew she would be pissed I kept her in the dark about Malcolm.

"Do you know why I hate you, Paislie?"

"No, but I'm sure you're fixin' to tell me."

"First, you fuck Trey Rogers for months. Then while with Trey Rogers you met the best looking guy on the planet, then go out with said hot guy, and now you're probably massaging his upper thigh while you contemplate whether or not you're going to accidently graze his dick. I hate you."

And that was it. I lost it laughing. "When was the last time you had sex, Annie? I think you're overdue! You could always call Trey. I hear he likes to keep one on the side from his girlfriend of six years."

Annie made a disgusted sound. "Fuck him. He was an asshole. I feel sorry for that girl, but if she's stupid enough not to see, then that is her problem."

As I got closer to the house, I saw Sophie outside riding her bike. She still had the training wheels on it and I could hear her yelling out from way down the driveway. *Man, sound travels out here in the country.*

"Agreed. Anyway, Malcolm feels more comfortable here. So . . . here I am."

"Huh. So do you like him?"

Now it was time for me to be quiet.

"Paislie? Oh my . . . you do, don't you? Hold on. I need to shut my office door."

I slowed my walking down a bit. I could see Sophie jumping as high as she could to get my attention.

"Okay, tell me what's going on. In all the years I've known you, any time I ask if you like a guy you pop back with a for sure no. Even Trey, I knew you were only with him for the sex."

I loved my best friend, but sometimes I wanted to tape her mouth shut. "I'm not really sure what I'm feeling right now, Annie. I've never . . . well I mean . . . he makes me feel . . . I guess I . . ."

"Jesus! Spit it the hell out."

"That's just it. I don't know how I feel! I've never felt like this before."

She gasped. "Have you talked to Sister Elizabeth? What does she say?"

I rolled my neck a few times to get the tension out. "Hey, I've got to go. I have an almost six-year-old barreling at me on a bike with training wheels and she's out of control."

"What! He has a kid! Holy fu—"

Hitting end, I smiled as Sophie rode her bike up to me and hit the brakes hard and fast. *Must run in the family.*

"Paislie!" She turned to Clarisse and waved. "Paislie is gonna watch me now. She's my new best friend!"

Clarisse and I had met last night in the kitchen when I was sneaking around the house trying to find my way about. She gave me a tour of the house and then made us both a cup of tea. We talked for three hours about everything and anything. I instantly loved her. I knew it was because she reminded me of one of the nuns back at St Patrick's.

"Sophie, Virginia will be here any minute to get you."

Glancing up, I gave her a questioning look. "Her nanny. Malcolm insisted Sophie only go to after-school care three days a week. Monday's and Friday's Virginia comes. She's running late today."

With my hands on my hips, I flashed Sophie a huge smile. "Well, if it's okay with Clarisse, I'd love to hang out until Virginia gets here."

Sophie jumped off her bike and ran to the older woman where she dropped to her knees and begged.

Clarisse shook her head and said, "Fine. You be a good girl for Ms. Paislie, you hear?"

"Yes ma'am!" Promptly turning, she got back on her bike and started peddling while Clarisse got in the little golf cart she had been riding in while following Sophie, and headed back to the house.

"Do you like it here?" Sophie asked.

I shrugged. "Well, I haven't gotten a chance to really look around yet. I did hear there are horses here though!" I said with excitement in my voice.

"And ponies! Uncle Malcolm bought me one for my birthday last year and then said it was lonely so he bought another one. I didn't really get to visit them much when we lived with Daddy, but now that Mommy and me live here all the time I can see them anytime I want!"

Wow. Malcolm really likes spoiling Sophie. "That was nice of him to do that for your pony."

Sophie nodded her head. "Yeah. Mommy said Uncle Malcolm likes to spoil me because he has a broken heart."

That piqued my interest. "He does? Oh how sad! Why?"

"Casey."

That was unexpected.

Casey? Who's Casey?

"I don't think I've met her yet," I said, hoping that would pull more information out of her.

Oh, good lord. I'm pumping information from a five-year-old.

"Oh, she's dead!"

I stopped walking and stared at her. "She's . . . dead?"

Sophie did a circle around me. "Yep. I'm not allowed to talk about it 'cause it makes Uncle Malcolm really, really sad."

"Oh," I said, disappointed I wouldn't get any additional information.

"But I can talk to you 'cause you won't be sad 'cause you don't know her."

I fist pumped internally and I knew God was shaking his head at me. Glancing up toward the heavens I mouthed, *Sorry Lord. Forgive me.*

"Nope, I don't know her so you can tell me. Why does it make him so sad?" I asked.

"Promise not to tell?"

I crossed my heart. "Promise."

I'm totally going to Hell.

"Uncle Malcolm got hit when he was driving and she went to heaven while he held her and said goodbye."

My heart dropped to my stomach. I covered my mouth as I let the little bits of information Sophie fed me sink in. *Who was Casey and how long ago did this happen?* In all my research I hadn't found anything about a girlfriend named Casey.

"How sad," I mumbled.

"Yeah. Do you want to run while I ride my bike? I'm fast."

And like that, Sophie had moved on. "Ahh . . . sure! Let's go!"

She took off as I ran next to her. By the time we got up to the house and she rode around me a few more times, Virginia pulled up and off Sophie went to head to some jumping place.

I waved goodbye as I watched the car drive off. Turning, I went to head up the porch stairs only to find Malcolm standing at the top. My breath hitched as I took in the beautiful sight before my eyes. His scruff was trimmed to perfection and I quickly found myself imagining it rubbing against my skin. My nipples hardened at the thought.

Ugh. Stop it, Paislie!

"She really likes you," he said with a genuine smile.

I returned it with one of my own as I pushed all naughty thoughts away. "I really like her. She has more energy than the Energizer Bunny though, I swear!"

He threw his head back and laughed. The sound rippled through my body like my very own energy shot. "Tell me about it."

His eyes moved across my body and the butterflies went crazy in my stomach at his intense stare.

Shit.

"How does your leg feel?" I asked.

He looked down at it and said, "A bit sore, but nothing too bad."

"Did you take a pain pill?"

Malcolm shook his head. "Nah, I only take one when I really need it."

I licked my dry lips and couldn't help but notice the reaction from Malcolm as his eyes flickered down to my lips. "Well, I should go shower. I went for a run."

He simply nodded as I lifted my hand and said, "See ya,"

Before I got to the front door, he called out for me. "Paislie, do you think you could drive me into town? I need to get the hell out of here and I don't want to bother Clarisse."

The idea of spending time with him filled me with excitement and scared the hell out of me. "Sure, give me thirty minutes?"

Something moved across his face, but it was gone as fast as it came. "Perfect. I'll meet you right here in half an hour."

My body tingled with the promise he made and I quickly headed into the house before I did something I would regret. Like press my lips to his.

When the door shut, I leaned against it as I placed my hand over my racing heart. Looking up, I pressed my lips together and whispered a prayer.

"Father, please give me the strength and ability to resist my temptations."

I chanted the prayer all the way to my room, in the shower and while I was getting dressed.

MALCOLM

THE ENTIRE MORNING I HAD been fighting off a hard-on; first during my session with Paislie and then seeing her again with Sophie. For some reason, every time I saw them together I got that same damn feeling I had at Emmit and Adaline's house, but it was ten times stronger.

I didn't really need or want to go into town. I did however really want an excuse to be alone with Paislie. Her declaration of finding another physical therapist had pissed me off last night. I didn't want anyone else. I wanted her . . . in more than one way. She hadn't mentioned anything about it this morning, so I was hoping she had changed her mind.

I felt her walk into the kitchen before she even spoke. "Hey, you ready?"

Her voice filled the air and surrounded me in a warm fucking fuzzy feeling I wasn't used to.

Turning, I took her in while attempting to hold back my moan. She looked so damn adorable in jeans, pink Chucks, and a Houston Texans T-shirt.

"Oh, am I dressed okay? I can go change if you want."

My eyes snapped forward as I shook my head. "No. You look great. So great."

With a tilt of her head, she smiled and I saw something I hadn't seen since she got here. Happiness. "I look great? I'm just dressed in jeans and a T-shirt."

I wanted to tell her she'd look even better naked and bent over the table with my cock buried deep inside her. But I refrained.

Shit. I'll be hard all day if I keep thinking like this.

"Yeah, but you look great."

She drew in a breath and clapped her hands. "I got ready faster than I thought I would. Ready to go?"

"Sure."

It took a little effort for me to get down the stairs and to my truck. Paislie helped me get into the truck before taking the crutches and putting them in the back seat of the truck.

As she drove into Waco, I couldn't help but keep glancing her way. I was sure she felt my eyes on her. Each time I looked at her, she gripped the steering wheel a bit stronger. "Have you ever been to Waco?"

Paislie shook her head. "Nope."

With a jerk of my head, I looked at her. "Really?"

She shrugged. "Never had a reason to come here. Well, I take it back. I did visit Baylor, but decided it wasn't the school for me."

Now I was curious and wanted to know every single thing about her.

"Where did you go to school?"

"Texas Women's University in Denton."

I wasn't surprised she stayed in the Dallas area especially with how close she was with Sister Elizabeth.

"So did you ever go to college? I mean, I guess you probably didn't have time with as much as you travel."

"I actually started taking online classes in high school. I'd like to go back and get a degree. Just never enough time."

She nodded her head and stopped at a stoplight and turned to me. Her eyes moved over my shoulder and she threw on the blinker. "Are you in a hurry or need to be somewhere?"

"Nope, just wanted out of the house."

Paislie pulled into the parking lot of Woodway Park and parked. She turned off the truck, got and met me on the passenger side as I opened the door. I thought she was getting the crutches, but she got out a cane instead. "Let's get in some walking on your leg, shall we?"

My mouth dropped open as I looked at her. "What? I thought therapy was this morning."

With a raised eyebrow, she slowly shook her head. "If I'm going to be living with you twenty-four seven, and I see an opportunity to do something, we're doing it."

God, those last three words made my cock stir.

"Doing it, huh? Aren't you rushing?" I asked with a wink.

She rolled her eyes, but I couldn't miss the flush in her cheeks.

Placing her hands on her hips, she asked, "Are we in high school, Malcolm?"

"No ma'am, we most certainly are not."

She ignored me as she continued to talk. "Take your time walking, but the faster we build up the strength in your leg, the better." She pointed to a bench that faced the water. "Let's walk over there and then sit for a bit."

The distance to the bench looked easy, but by the time we got there, my leg felt like a ten-pound bag of cement was attached to it.

I sat down and moaned under my breath.

"How's it feel?"

"Like I just dragged a fuck ton of weight with my leg. It's still feels numb up the side here."

The way she was looking at me had me worried. "What? Why are you looking at me like I just lost my puppy or something?"

Her eyes lit up. "You have a puppy?"

With a frown, I replied, "No. I mean you're giving me a fucking pity look. I don't do those well, so if you could knock that shit off I'd appreciate it."

She folded her arms and narrowed her left eye at me. "Listen, if we're gonna make this work we need to get something straight right now. You're going to be in pain and it's not going to be fun, but if you're going to be a complete derk when we do this, I won't be sticking around. I don't like being treated like that."

"You mean jerk," I responded.

"No. I mean derk. You're being both a dick and jerk at the same time."

My head flinched back slightly as I frowned. "Isn't that the same thing?"

She shook her head. "No. It's like double the assholeness."

"That's another made up word, Paislie. You can't describe a made up word with another made up word."

Her lips twitched as she held back her smile. "Who says so?"

With a blank look, I said, "Everyone!"

She rolled her eyes and sat down next to me. "I read through all your medical notes. I need to ask you something."

My heart dropped as she stared at me with a concerned expression.

"Okay. What?"

"Has anyone talked to you about the excessive amount of nerve damage you sustained and the possible lasting effects?"

"That explains the weird tingling sensation."

"You'll also have random pain as they heal." She turned her body to face me. "I want to be one-hundred-percent honest with you, Malcolm. I don't think anyone has up to this point and I'm not sure if it's because they were trying to keep you positive or what the reasons are."

I swallowed hard as my heart felt like it was about to pound out of my chest. "Jesus Christ, tell me, Paislie."

"Don't use God's name in vain like that."

She was stalling. I closed my eyes and concentrated on my breathing. "Please, tell me."

"You're going to keep an open mind and not fly off the handle and say something mean?"

I sighed as I looked at her and was held captive by how beautiful her emerald eyes were. "Yes."

She looked down and fiddled with her hands before looking back at me. "With as much nerve damage as you have, coupled with the knee damage, you could have lasting effects. Such as pain that radiates in your leg, numbness on the side where a good portion of the nerve damage was, or you might not regain full strength of your leg and will need a cane to walk."

Bile moved into my throat as I stared at her. Not one fucking person had said anything to me like this. Not one damn word.

My hands shook and Paislie noticed right away. "Are you saying I might not ever be able to drive a racecar again?"

"I swear to you, Malcolm, I will do everything in my power to get you back to one hundred percent, but I need you to know we might not be able to get past ninety."

I locked my jaw down and clenched my teeth together as I balled my fists. The anger was moving through my body at warp speed and all I wanted to do was hit something.

Hard.

Paislie saw it immediately and her next response was not one I was expecting.

She stood and then sat down on me, straddling me as her warmth pressed against my dick.

"Malcolm," she whispered as she pressed her lips to mine and the surge I felt the first time we kissed flowed through my body again. This time it was ten times stronger. My hands gripped onto her hips as I dug my fingers into them, trying to release the anger somewhere.

"Kiss me back, Malcolm. Kiss me!" she demanded against my lips. My hand came up to her neck as I pulled her closer. Our kiss turned rough as I sucked her lip into my mouth and bit down on it while she gasped.

The moment she rocked her hips against me, everything vanished and all I could think about was her . . . sitting on me, pressing her pussy against me and both of us getting worked up.

My grip on her lessened as she ran her tongue along my lips before pulling back and leaning her forehead to mine. Her chest heaved along with mine.

"It was the only thing I could think of to take your mind away from the anger I saw building."

"It worked," I barely said as my voice cracked. Her eyes glanced down to where my rock-hard dick was throbbing in my jeans.

She placed her hands on my chest and pushed back as she stood up. "I'm sorry I did that. I don't think well when I'm under pressure and I acted unprofessionally."

My head was spinning with what she just told me and how my body wanted more of her. She's sorry she did that? She acted unprofessionally?

I took the cane in my hand and stood up. Paislie walked behind me in silence as we made our way back to the truck. When we got in, she started it and asked, "Where are we going?"

She acted as if nothing had happened between us, and it pissed me off that it bothered me so much.

"World Cup Café."

The only thing spoken between us was the driving directions I gave her to get to the café.

Once we ordered, Paislie tried to make small talk, but all I kept hearing in my head was what she said.

"So, what do people do for fun in this town? My friend, Annie, is coming this weekend and wants to hang out."

My head snapped up as I looked at her. "Bars. There's a lot of bars. Barnett's Pub or Crickets to name a few."

She smiled and looked away.

After paying for the check, we made our way out to the truck. "You can head back to the ranch."

The drive was pure fucking torture. I was still reeling over the way her body felt against mine, and on top of that, I kept replaying that damn kiss. I wanted to reach over and touch her. Anywhere, I just needed to feel her soft skin anyway I could get it. Her hands held the wheel like she had a death grip on it.

When we finally pulled up to the house, I tried like hell to get out of the truck before she came around to my side.

How could she crawl on top me like that and then act like nothing had happened? I was confused, in pain, and pissed off.

She placed her hand on my arm and I jerked it away as her eyes widened in surprise. "I'm fine."

Standing frozen in her spot, she watched me as I made my way up the stairs and into the house, slamming the front door behind me.

I'd give anything to have a mindless fucking right about now and was half tempted to call Ashley and see if she was still hanging with that douchebag.

By the time I reached my bedroom, the pain was so bad in my leg, I was sweating. My cock was still throbbing and all I wanted was some kind of relief.

Pulling my phone out, I pulled up her number and sent her a text. If I was lucky, she'd be here within the hour and I could forget the way my body was feeling, both from the pain in my leg and from Paislie's touch.

After hitting send, I closed my eyes and tried to forget everything.

Twenty

PAISLIE

I PACED BACK AND FORTH in my bedroom as I chewed on my thumbnail. "I can't believe I did that."

Sitting on the edge of the bed, I reached back for a pillow and buried my face and screamed into it. I knew he was getting angry and I should have just let him deal with his emotions, but I used it as an excuse to get closer to him. To feel his lips on mine.

Fucking hell. I practically begged him to kiss me while I rocked my body against his. Then I acted as if it never happened.

Stupid! Stupid! Stupid!

I reached for my Kindle and pulled up a book I was reading. It was far from the romance books I usually read. This book was recommended by Elizabeth. The Christian-based book was supposed to help me find my true inner self. The only thing I wanted to find was how not to be attracted to Malcolm.

Two and a half hours had passed since we got back from Waco. I couldn't take the silent treatment anymore. What we needed was to define the boundaries. Clearly, me jumping on top of the man paying me to help in his recovery was crossing a line.

I stood and dropped my Kindle onto the bed. "This is bullshit."

Racing into the bathroom, I checked myself in the mirror and pulled my long dark hair up into a ponytail and set out to talk to Malcolm.

We were two grown adults who clearly were attracted to one another. We needed to figure out a way to keep that under control while I was here . . . *working* . . . for him.

As I made my way through the house, I knew he wouldn't be upstairs.

I checked the back porch, the front, the kitchen, game room and both living rooms. Malcolm was nowhere to be found.

I stared down the hallway that led to the master suite. I knew which door was his bedroom because it was damn near straight across from the personal gym we were in this morning, which was ten times better than the gym I belonged to at home.

Pulling in a deep cleansing breath, I headed down the hall. Checking the gym, it was empty. Turning, I passed a long table that had a beautiful sculpture on it, which I had admired this morning. They were in a small niche that was on the wall opposite Malcolm's bedroom. Lifting my hand, I went to knock when I heard voices.

I held my breath as I leaned in closer. It was a female voice.

Did she just moan?

I slammed my hand over my mouth to keep from throwing up.

Oh. My. God.

He was fucking someone? It felt as if someone had kicked me right in the stomach as I quickly took a few steps back, bumping right into the table. Before I could stop it, the sculpture rocked and tipped right over, smashing against the travertine floor.

Fuck!

I dropped to my knees and started quickly picking up the pieces. Tears pooled in my eyes as I prayed for the strength to keep them at bay. *Please, God. Please don't let him come out here. Please don't let me see who he is with.* How stupid could I be to think this would work? How stupid was I to think I could work him up into a frenzy and then just walk away and he would be totally fine? He was a man. They only thought with their dicks.

The door opened and I trained my eyes onto the broken pieces of clay.

"Paislie, are you okay?"

I tried desperately to keep the sob from escaping, but failed. He reached down and placed his hand on my shoulder, causing me to pull away.

"Don't touch me!" I cried out a little too loudly. Not wanting to look at him, I reached for another piece and felt my finger slice open.

"Jesus Christ, Paislie, just leave it be and I'll get someone to clean it up."

Standing, I tried not to look at him. When I saw the towel wrapped around his waist, my mouth fell open. "I . . . I didn't . . ."

The overwhelming feeling of hurt fell over my body like a blanket. "Your finger is bleeding," Malcolm said as he reached for my hand. I shook my head and pulled it back.

"This was a mistake. I'm leaving."

His eyes widened in fear. "W-what do you mean you're leaving?"

A single tear fell from my eye as I brushed it away with my fingertips. "I can't do this. I'm so sorry."

A woman came walking around the corner and smacked right into me. She was holding a tray full of something that fell to the floor. She was dressed in all white.

"Oh crap! I'm so sorry," I mumbled as the woman cursed softly.

"Jessica is going to be pissed now. She likes to have the rocks heated up to the right temperature."

I reached for a rock and yelped as I fell back onto my ass. "What in the hell! Why is that rock hot?" I exclaimed.

"For Mr. Wallace's massage. Great. You go back there and tell her what you did, because she will be very upset."

"She already interrupted the zen we had, so don't worry about it, Natalie. Mr. Wallace has asked us to leave."

I sat there on the floor looking up at an older woman also dressed in white. She placed her fingers to her temple and let out a long, drawn out moan. Kind of like the one I heard in Malcolm's . . . bedroom.

Oh holy shit.

Fuck. My. Life.

"What are you doing?" I asked.

Her eyes shot down to mine and said, "Trying to find the inner peace. The quiet that makes everything okay. Mr. Wallace was in need of finding it and now you've just brought all this negative energy."

"Oh," was all I said. By the time I had my wits about me, Natalie had picked everything up that had fallen off the tray and both women were retreating away as they whispered, but loud enough for me to here.

"She ruined the whole environment. Next time I will insist he comes to the spa."

Staring at them as they walked around the corner, I continued to sit on the floor like an ass.

"Why are you on the floor?"

His voice no longer sounded angry. He seemed relaxed. *Yeah . . . I wonder why.*

I slowly stood and turned to him. I froze in place as I got a good look at him.

Jesus, Mary, and Joseph. Father in heaven, help me for I am about to sin.

My tongue instinctively ran along my lips as I took in the glorious site in front of me. Malcolm had an amazing body. His chest was broad and his abs looked like something out of magazine. The towel wrapped loosely around his hips, not leaving anything to the imagination.

My lower stomach clenched as my nipples hardened.

"I'm sorry I interrupted your little ménage à trois."

The smile that spread across his face pissed me off. "What were you doing at my bedroom door?"

The heaviness in my chest made it hard to breathe. No . . . the fact that he stood before me almost naked made it hard for me to breathe.

"I wanted to apologize for my . . . my um . . . um . . ." I couldn't even think straight with him looking at me the way he was.

"You're what?"

Finally shaking the thoughts running through my mind of Malcolm taking me up against the wall, I shook my head. "My actions earlier on the bench. It was insensitive of me to lead you on the way I did and my reaction was not at all professional."

He lifted a brow and stared at me. "You said you were leaving."

Trying not to focus on the V that dipped down into the towel, I mumbled, "What was that?"

"You said you were leaving."

The way his blue eyes were looking at me had me so confused . . . like I wasn't already confused enough, I needed his intense stare to add to it.

"You want me to leave?" I asked.

His face softened. "No. I don't want you to. But you said you were."

My lips were dry, but I was afraid to lick them.

My hands came up over my face as I let out a frustrated sigh. "I can't think straight with you standing in a damn towel!"

Spinning on my heels, I took off as fast as I could for my room. I needed space between Malcolm and myself.

A lot of space.

Twenty one

MALCOLM

I COULD HAVE EASILY TOLD Paislie that Jessica and Natalie were there strictly to give me a massage, but I kind of liked the idea that she got what she deserved.

Making my way into the kitchen, I gave Clarisse a wide grin as I slowly made my way over to her and kissed her on the forehead. "Smells really good. What's for dinner?"

"Fish tacos."

"Yum." I glanced around and when I didn't see her anywhere, I sighed. "Have you seen Paislie?"

Clarisse looked at me like I had grown an extra head. "She didn't tell you?"

"Tell me what?" My heart dropped.

"She said things weren't working out; she left a little bit ago, Mr. Wallace."

All the air from my body escaped in one breath. "S-she left?"

Clarisse nodded. "I thought you knew."

Shaking my head, I turned and headed out of the kitchen, "No, I didn't know."

Grabbing my truck keys, I moved as fast as I could.

"Malcolm! You can't drive!" she called out. I ignored her and made my way to the truck where I slowly pulled myself in. My truck wasn't a standard so I could drive fine.

Turning it on, I hit the gas and barreled down the driveway. Hitting the talk button on my wheel, I said, "Call Paislie."

"Calling Paislie."

My heartbeat was pounding in my ears as I drove faster.

I had to catch her.

I had to find her.

"You've reached the voice mailbox of Paislie Pruitt. Please leave—"

I hit the hang-up button as I yelled out, "Fuck!"

Once I got to the end of the driveway, I slammed on the brakes. Paislie's car was pulled over to the side. Throwing my truck in park, I carefully got out and made my way over to her as fast as I could. My leg was throbbing but I ignored it. My chest tightened with the knowledge that she only made it this far.

Her hands were on the steering wheel with her head rested on them. It was clear she was crying and that about killed me, knowing I was the reason she was so upset. The only thing I could focus on was her and making her understand how sorry I was.

I opened the door to her car and reached in for her. She didn't even look up as I pulled her to me, and she wrapped her arms around me while crying into my chest.

After a few moments, she pulled back and looked at me. All I saw was sadness in her eyes. I'd never felt my heart physically hurt like it did with the look on her face. I'd give anything to turn back time to just a few hours ago.

"What are you doing to me?" she whispered. "I don't know how to feel around you and that scares me to death."

My eyes closed as I said, "I feel the same way."

Her hands clutched onto my shirt as I looked back into her eyes.

"The only man I've ever loved left me." Her body shook again as tears fell freely once more. "He didn't want me and I couldn't understand what I did wrong. I just wanted him to love me. I begged him to love me."

Lifting my hand, I used my thumb to wipe away her tears. "Paislie," I spoke as my throat grew thick.

"I swore a long time ago I would never let another man into my heart to hurt me. Then I met you, and everything has been turned upside down. You do things to me . . . things that make me want to give you my very soul."

My breath caught as her words hit me.

She covered her mouth as she squeezed her eyes shut before dropping her hands and saying, "I would be completely destroyed if I let you in and you hurt me."

I cupped her face with my hands. "Nothing happened. Paislie, I've had Jessica come to the house so many times for a massage. I swear to God, nothing happened. I'd never do something like that to you. Never."

She bit down on her lip and placed her hands on my arms. "I tried so hard to leave. I couldn't make it past your driveway. I want to be here for you so badly. I know I can get you behind the wheel of a racecar again, but I'm fighting these other feelings and I'm so confused. I'm so scared."

My fingers lightly moved a piece of her brown hair that had been stuck to her face. "I feel the same way. You have my stomach in knots and half the time I don't know whether I'm coming or going, Paislie. This is all so new to me . . . these feelings. I've never done the exclusive girlfriend thing." I let out a frustrated sigh. "You drive me nuts, but the thought of you leaving kills me."

Our eyes held each other for the longest time before her gaze fell to my lips. Sliding my hand behind her neck, I pulled her to me and brushed my lips over hers.

"Your kiss is like a drug. I crave it constantly, Paislie."

She swallowed hard as her mouth parted, inviting me to take a hit of that drug. And take a hit I did. Pressing my lips to hers, our tongues explored each other like never before. The wind blew pieces of her hair slightly as I deepened the kiss, feeling the rush of energy between our bodies. I had never been so affected by a kiss before. I needed her to stay. We needed to see where these feelings would take us.

When we both needed air, I pulled back slightly and looked deep into her eyes. "Please don't leave. We'll figure it all out. All I know is I want you to stay, and not only to help with my leg. Please give us another try."

She nodded and pressed her lips together before smiling. I couldn't help but grin back as I asked her, "Why are you smiling?"

Her face blushed as she looked away and then back at me. "I just thought of a few new things we could try in your next therapy session."

A low rumble came from the back of my throat while her eyes burned with desire.

"UNCLE MALCOLM, DO YOU KNOW that Paislie has *never* had a pillow fight? Or a sleepover!"

It was Sophie's sixth birthday and she and I were out in the stables visiting Black Jack and Honey Dew. I smiled while Paislie's name seemed to float on the air.

After yesterday, with everything that happened and her trying to leave, Paislie and I spent the rest of the day doing nothing but sitting on the couch and talking. We finished the night out in each other's arms watching *Safe Haven*. It didn't take her long before she fell asleep. My arm was killing me by three in the morning and my leg throbbed, but I didn't care. It was the first time I'd ever slept with a girl in my arms. I never had the desire until Paislie. Her in my arms all night was amazing and something I could see wanting each night.

"You don't say?"

"I know!" Sophie gasped.

An idea hit me as I stopped brushing Black Jack and she followed my lead while Deuce snored away at my feet. "Sophie, what if we surprised Paislie with a slumber party on *your* birthday?"

Her precious blue eyes lit up like a Christmas tree. "Can we have a pillow fight?"

"Yes! We have to be sneaky about this though. Do you think you could be my little secret agent and find out what other things you love to do that Paislie hasn't done?"

She nodded her head enthusiastically. "I can do that! I'm six and a big girl."

My heart melted. I loved this little girl more than anything. In a way, I was glad her bastard father told Autumn to leave. I knew it was selfish of me to think that way. Deuce was lying at my feet as he looked up and barked. "I know you are, princess, and it appears Deuce does too."

Sophie ran and put the brush in the tack room and took off toward the house. "Hey, where are you going?"

"Oh, Uncle Malcolm! I have to get back to the house."

I pinched my eyebrows together and asked, "Why?"

"I have to make sure Paislie has an amazing slumber party! On my birthday! Paislie will need help picking out a dress to wear tonight now that she is part of the party."

"A dress for tonight, huh?"

Sophie gave me the sweetest look as she laughed. "Oh Uncle Malcolm, you're so funny. Did you forget about the ball?"

I chuckled. I had most certainly not forgotten about the ball. It's not every year a princess turns six. Autumn had been riding my ass for the last week because I promised Sophie a princess ball. How was I to know it would have taken so much effort? It's not every year a princess turns six.

"I have not forgotten the ball. I even have *my* outfit picked out."

Sophie beamed. "Mommy said you and granddaddy were wearing lexeo's."

Huh?

"What?"

"Lexeo's. I heard Mommy tell Clarisse that Paislie was going to shit her pants when she saw you in your lexeo." Sophie crinkled her nose and shook her head. "I hope not! She seems too old to go potty in her pants."

I pressed my lips together firmly to keep from laughing. I was going to have to let Autumn know her daughter was now in the stage where she repeated everything she heard.

"Oh! A *tuxedo*. It's called a tuxedo, Sophie."

Sophie looked at me like I had just said the stupidest thing in the world. "That's what I said!"

I rolled my eyes and silently moaned.

Women. They're all the same no matter what age.

Twenty two

PAISLIE

"**A** BALL?" I ASKED AUTUMN as I stood there stunned. "Like a real ball?"

She laughed and shook her head. "Scaled down for a bunch of five and six year olds."

"Um . . . I didn't bring any formal dresses."

Autumn's eyes lit up. "That's okay! I have plenty and we're the same size."

Sophie came running into the kitchen full throttle. *It must be in this families genes to want to do everything fast.* "Uncle Malcolm is coming too! He's super slow now that he hurt his leg. But I couldn't wait 'cause I'm so excited!"

Autumn and I both laughed. How could you not? Sophie's excitement rubbed off on you almost instantly.

"Why are you so excited, princess?" I asked.

She covered her mouth and giggled. "I can't tell you! It's a secret between me and Uncle Malcolm."

The air in the room changed and I placed my hand over my stomach when it dropped at the sight of him.

He was dressed in jeans, boots and a light-grey T-shirt that showed every single muscle he had. His messy, dark hair looked like he had just gotten out of the shower and ruffled it with his hand. Oh lord . . . then there was the scruff he had started wearing. Even with the added walking cane, he was hot as hell and made my panties wet.

God broke the hotter-than-hell mold when he made Malcolm. My eyes drifted over his body. The tattoos that stretched over his arm made me think of the Christina Aguilera song, 'Candy Man'. And man oh man would I love to taste that candy.

"I don't think you could eye fuck my brother any harder if you tried," Autumn whispered in my ear as I felt my cheeks heat. Tearing my eyes from him, I looked at her as she laughed and I gave her a light push.

"Shut up," I said while placing my hands over my cheeks to cool my face down. When I looked back at Malcolm, he was watching me. He slowly smiled and his damn dimple showed up just in time to push me damn near over the ledge.

I swear the sexual tension between us was going to blow and when it did, I didn't picture sweet and romantic. No . . . it was going to be more like fast, hard, and sweaty.

"Oh lord," I mumbled under my breath as I turned away from him.

Sophie took my hand in hers and pulled me. "We need to go buy you a pretty dress, Paislie, for the ball."

Peeking through my eyelashes at Malcolm, he shrugged and shook his head.

"Well ladies, if you'll excuse me, I'll go see what I can do to help with the . . . ball."

He shot Autumn a smirk as she gave him the finger without Sophie seeing. When Malcolm walked by, he stopped and looked at Autumn. "By the way, your child repeats everything you say."

A horrified look washed over Autumn's face as I giggled. "What did she say?"

"That Paislie was going to shit her pants when she saw me in my tux."

My breath stalled. "Tux?" *Holy shit. Malcolm in a tux. I can't even right now. I'm in hotness overload.*

Malcolm's blue eyes pinned me in place. "Yep," he said like it was nothing. Malcolm laughed as he headed to the living room and outside where they were setting everything up.

"Honestly, the party is more for the parents than the kids. That's sad to say, but there it is," Autumn said as she took me by the arm and led me to her room upstairs.

"Paislie is going to wear one of Mommy's gowns, Soph."

Sophie clapped and took off upstairs.

"Wow. I was happy if I just got a happy birthday!" I said as we headed upstairs.

Autumn sighed. "I know. It's terrible how spoiled she is, but damn it's fun!"

THREE HOURS LATER I WAS putting the last bobby pin in my brown hair. I decided to put it up in a French twist with a few curls hanging down to frame my face. Leaning in closer to the mirror, I took in my features. My green eyes were filled with something I'd never seen before.

Hope.

At almost twenty-six years old, I never paid attention to what my eyes said. Elizabeth always said your eyes were the window to your soul. For so many years I saw nothing in my eyes, so eventually I stopped looking.

The knock on my bedroom door caused me to jump before making my way over to it. When I opened it, I glanced down to see bright blue eyes staring up at me with a gaped open mouth.

"You're so pretty," Sophie whispered in awe.

I bent down and placed my hands on her shoulders. "Not as pretty as you, though." My finger curled around her black curl. Every time I looked at Sophie I imagined what Malcolm's little girl would look like. Would it be too much of a dream to imagine children together?

Tears threatened as I pushed the thought away.

"Thank you, Paislie. I'm in charge of bringing you your party dress for the ball!"

The thrill of tonight's adventures was heard in her sweet little voice. "Would you like to help me put it on?"

"Oh yes!" Sophie said skipping into my room and jumping up on the bed.

I hung up the red Versace gown and took a step back. The dress was gorgeous. I'd never worn anything so beautiful . . . or expensive. The dress hugged my figure with the tight bodice, but the flowing dress added a soft touch. The open back was just the right touch of sexy, but not too much. I thought it was too much, but Autumn reminded me the ball was more for the grownups so I went with it.

Opening my robe, I pushed it off my shoulders and heard Sophie gasp. Peeking over my shoulder, I winked. I totally forgot she was there.

Shit.

"Paislie! Where are your panties and what is that?"

Sophie pointed to the new garter belt I had bought the other day. Oh dear. It looked like I was about to give Sophie her first lesson in lingerie.

"Well, that is called a garter belt. It's used to hold up my stockings."

Her eyes roamed over my body and I felt slightly awkward. "Does your mommy not get dressed in front of you?"

The mesmerized face stared at me as she whispered a faint, "No, ma'am."

"How come your panties are not all there?"

Shit. How did I explain that one?

"They are. They are more of a big girl's panties."

"I'm a big girl. When I can wear them?"

Hmm . . . what would Autumn say?

Chewing on my cheek, I said, "When you turn twenty-one."

Sophie jumped. "Yay!!!"

Clearly she couldn't understand how far off that was.

"What's that called?"

She pointed to the black bra I was wearing. "It's called a bra. It's not a normal bra, it's made special for dresses and shirts with no backs on them."

Tilting her head in confusion, she let that one go. *Thank God.*

I reached for the dress and slipped it over my head carefully. The way it felt against my skin was heavenly. I'd always loved dressing up, I just never had a reason to. Sophie helped me zip up the small zipper on the side. I slipped on the heels I bought on the same shopping trip that I bought the garter and twirled around for my curious little friend.

Sophie stood there with a huge smile on her face. "Do you like it, Sophie?"

She nodded her head. "Oh yes! You really do look like a princess." I reached down and took her hand, spinning her and causing her dress to spin outward. "So, do you in your beautiful pink dress."

Sophie blushed and then started jumping around. "We're ready!"

She took my hand and started pulling me toward the door. "Oh wait!"

I called out. Walking over to the dresser, I picked up my favorite bottle of perfume and gave a quick spray.

"Me next!"

Bending down, I gave Sophie a quick spray. "Now we're ready!" I said with excitement. As Sophie pulled me down the hallway, she glanced over her shoulder and declared, "Uncle Malcolm is going to fall in love with you tonight!"

My smile dropped as my chest tightened. I struggled to get air in as she continued to pull me outside. The moment the fresh air hit me in the face, I took in a deep breath. Too bad it was hot and humid and offered no relief.

Ugh. Texas in June.

I sucked back a breath of air as I took in all the people. "Who are all these people?"

Sophie took off running over to a friend. So much for my party buddy.

"That is the million dollar question. I'd bet half of them don't even have a kid here."

I turned to my right and saw a handsome blond standing there with a smile on his face.

With a polite smile, I reached my hand out. "Paislie Pruitt."

"Jeremy Rice."

"Um . . . how do you know Autumn?"

He laughed and shook his head. "I know Malcolm. Anytime there's a party thrown by Malcolm, I'm there. We're old high school friends."

I nodded my head. "Oh, I see. So no little ones running around?"

His face fell in horror as he said, "Bite your tongue. I like sex too much to have kids right now."

Oh wow. Damn he's blunt.

A waitress walked by carrying a tray of wine. I quickly reached for a red and took a sip. I could feel Jeremy's eyes on me, instantly making me become uncomfortable. Five months ago I would have been flirting with this guy and probably would have ended up leaving with him.

"So what about you? Kids?"

With a chortle, I shook my head. "No. I'm married to my career."

He lifted his eyebrows as if I just gave him an invite back to my room. "You are for sure not from Waco; I'd remember such a beautiful woman."

Ugh. Cheesy line.

"Dallas. I'm a physical therapist."

"Oh. Are you helping Malcolm after his accident?"

I brought the wine glass up to my lips and nodded. I was ready for Jeremy to move on.

My eyes scanned around as I searched for Malcolm.

My breath caught in my throat when I found him. He was standing with a group of people as he listened very intently to an older man talking. I couldn't help but notice how the woman standing next to him kept touching his arm every time she laughed. She looked to be at least ten years older than me.

"Would you like to dance?" Jeremy asked.

I pulled my eyes off of Malcolm and focused back on him. "Oh, no thank you. Not right now, maybe in a bit."

He looked disappointed but perked up when I said maybe later. "Well, I'll hold you to it, Paislie."

My eyes drifted back over to Malcolm and anger seethed through my body. He had his hand on the woman's lower back as he threw his head back and laughed.

Jeremy was about to walk off when I reached for his arm. "I'm sorry I was distracted for a moment. So, tell me what you do."

The crooked smile did nothing for me, but I continued to stand there and talk to him. He was an accountant . . . boring . . . lived for hunting . . . yuck . . . could reel in a bass the size of Texas . . . whatever that meant . . . and was single. That one he told me at least four times over our conversation.

When I took a chance to look back over to where Malcolm was standing, he was gone. The older lady was still there and this time she had her arm around the older gentleman. When they kissed lovingly, I shook my head. I needed to get my insecurities in check.

"So, how about that dance now?"

Shit.

"Sorry, Jer. This one is with me."

The moment his arm wrapped around my waist, goose bumps spread over my body. The zip that raced through my veins caught me off guard. When Malcolm leaned over, his lips grazed my neck and my entire body shuttered. His mouth moved to my ear where he whispered, "Did he touch you at all?"

Wait. What?

Interesting. A possessive Malcolm . . . I could get used to this.

"No, all is good," I softly spoke.

When his lips moved lightly on the skin under my ear, I shivered. Slowly moving his lips back up he whispered, "You look beautiful. So fucking beautiful. You stole my breath when I saw you."

I turned and looked at him as he pulled back and looked at his friend. Did he have any idea how his words made my heart pound in my ears so loudly I could hardly hear around me? Or how he totally just swept me off my feet with his compliment. He doesn't do romance. *Pesh. I'm totally lost to him right now.*

He stood there totally calm as he spoke with his friend while I was an absolute mess.

Not being able to help myself, I wondered what type of lover Malcolm was. He came across as sweet, but I bet he was hot as hell in bed. Did he start off slow and romantic and then move on to something fast and hard? I could see him doing both, but the fast and hard was what was making my very thin panties even wetter.

Malcolm looked down at me and smirked. "Why are you breathing so shallow, baby?"

"Shallow? No . . . definitely not shallow," I numbly said.

His brow rose. "You're not breathing deep, baby."

Oh mother of God. Call me baby again, I silently pleaded.

"Deep?" I replied as I licked my lips. My eyes traveled over his body. He looked so damn good in that tux. What was the matter with me?

Malcolm's hand moved over my hip ever so slightly. Moving the dress against my skin in a way that was driving me mad. It felt like a silk sheet rubbing over my body. I'd always wanted to have sex on satin sheets. No. I'd always wanted to *fuck* on satin sheets.

I instantly pictured Malcolm over me as he moved in and out of my body.

Dear Lord, please ease this temptation.

"How long have you and Paislie known each other, Malcolm?"

Our eyes were locked and I knew he could tell I was turned on. I prayed to God he knew it was him who had me all hot and bothered, and not the jackass standing next to me.

"We met a few months back in Vegas at a race," Malcolm said, pulling his eyes from mine. I looked down and tried to concentrate on where I was. Sophie's birthday party. Or ball. Or the grownups ball. Whatever. There were children around and I was daydreaming of Malcolm in ways I shouldn't be.

I wonder if Malcolm wears boxers or briefs? Or does he go commando?

Oh, for Christ's sake Paislie. Get. It. Together.

Peeking back up at him, I looked at his handsome features. His strong jawline and soft plump lips that I wished like hell were exploring my body that very second.

Snapping my head away, I dragged in a deep breath as his grip on me tightened. His fingers dug into me and it felt like I was going to explode.

"Yes, Paislie is confident I'll be back in a racecar soon."

I flashed a grin to Jeremy and nodded my head. "Yep. Man . . . is it hot out here or what?"

Jeremy's eyes looked between Malcolm and me as he took a step back. "I'm going to go see who else is here." Turning to me, he reached his hand out for mine. When I lifted my hand, he brought it to his lips and kissed the back softly. It took everything I had not to pull it away before he touched me.

"It was a pleasure meeting you, Paislie."

My throat was dry as I fought like hell to form words. "Nice meeting you," I choked out.

When he walked away, I melted into Malcolm's side . . . which was not a good thing. The heat from his body was warming my already-overheated body.

Malcolm pulled me closer to him as he turned me. Our bodies were flush as I felt his dick twitch against my stomach.

A low moan escaped from my lips as I clutched onto his jacket.

God help me, for I wanted him more than I'd ever wanted anything, and it was taking everything in me not to drop to the floor and beg him.

Twenty three

MALCOLM

PAISLIE'S EYES WERE PRACTICALLY BEGGING me to touch her. Her breathing had changed the moment I walked up and it was clear she was horny.

I pulled her closer to me, my cock pressed against her stomach. The silk dress felt amazing as it moved over her skin. I brought my lips to her ear again as she grasped onto my jacket.

"Are you wet?"

Her body felt like her knees were going weak. "Y- yes."

"You have no idea how badly I want to fuck you right now."

Her head dropped against my chest as she whimpered. The fact that her body reacted to mine the way it had was the biggest fucking adrenaline rush I'd ever experienced. I wanted to see what else I could do to make her so turned on she would be begging me for relief.

"My lips want to taste you so badly, Paislie."

"Oh God," she whispered. "Malcolm. Please, I can't do this. Not here." She spoke into my chest as she continued to hold onto me for dear life.

"Do you have panties on?"

Her head jerked up. "Yes! Sophie was in the room with me when I got dressed. She was mesmerized by my garter belt and thong."

Fuck. Me.

Now my knees went weak. At least the good one did; the other one was numb with pain.

I glanced down to her lips and imagined my cock moving in and out of her mouth.

"The way you're looking at me, Malcolm."

Her eyes commanded mine. "How am I looking at you, baby?"

She clamped down on her lip before saying, "Like you're hungry for me."

My heart rate picked up as I slowly focused on where we were. "When can I have you, Paislie?"

"Jesus, if you keep this up I'll let you take me here."

With that, I took her hand and headed into the house. I hated that I needed the cane, but at this point, I would have sprinted on my bad leg to get her away from everyone.

"W-where are we going?" she asked as she glanced over her shoulder.

Opening the laundry room door, I pulled her in and pushed her against the wall.

"I need to feel you, Paislie . . . taste you."

Each breath was forced as the rush grew bigger. I'd been waiting for so long for this moment.

My hand slid up her dress and moved softly along her thigh where I brushed my knuckles across the thin lace material. *Son-of-a-bitch.* My cock was throbbing I wanted her so badly.

My fingers pushed the material to the side as Paislie lifted her leg, allowing me better access.

I slipped two fingers in and moaned as my dick hardened painfully more. "Fucking hell. You're soaking wet."

Her head dropped back as she whispered, "Please. Malcolm, I've waited so long for you."

My lips moved along her neck, placing soft kisses as I slowly moved my fingers in and out of her. Sliding another one in, I moved faster. "Yes," she hissed as she pumped her hips. I didn't want her coming yet. The first time she came, it was either going to be on my cock or my tongue.

Pulling my fingers from her, Paislie let out a whimper. I lifted her up and set her on the counter. It was going to kill my leg, but I needed to taste her.

"Lay back, Paislie. I want to taste you . . . now."

Her eyes widened with delight as she smiled and laid back. I lifted her beautiful gown and moaned when I saw the garter and panties.

"Jesus, you're perfect," I moaned as I pushed her panties out of the way and licked up her pussy. Paislie gasped and grabbed onto my hair.

"Oh . . . dear . . . God," she panted.

I've given plenty of women oral sex, but this was different. So very different. Paislie tasted sweet, addictive, like a drug. I instantly craved more as I licked and sucked her more. Her body quivered and I knew she was close. All I would need to do is concentrate on her clit and push my fingers in.

The knock on the door had us both freezing. Paislie lifted her head as we looked at one another. She shook her head and mouthed, *Are you fucking kidding me?*

"Uncle Malcolm? What are you and Paislie doing laundry for?"

My eyes widened in horror as Paislie pushed me away from her. She fixed her panties as I helped her smooth her dress down. I wanted her to taste her own desire for me before we opened the door. The idea that she might let me kiss her about had me coming in my pants. I pulled her to me and slowly made my way to her lips. When she ran her tongue across them, I took that as a yes and devoured her mouth with mine.

Her low rumbled moan zipped through my body as she tasted herself.

When I pulled back, I whispered, "That was fucking hot."

"Uncle Malcolm?" Sophie was now yelling. Paislie reached for the door and yanked it open.

"Hey, peanut!" she said, trying to sound normal, but her voice was jagged. Sophie took Paislie's hand in hers and pulled her through the house and back outside as I adjusted my dick.

Once we were back outside, my precious niece occupied all of Paislie's time while I sat there trying to understand what in the hell was going on with my emotions. Even watching Paislie with Sophie had my mind spinning with thoughts I never dreamed I would be having.

"She's certainly beautiful," my mother said as she sat down next to me.

Even though my attention was on Paislie, I nodded my head and said, "She has good genes."

My mother laughed and bumped my shoulder. "Malcolm Wallace, I was talking about Paislie."

With a smug smile, I turned to her. "Paislie is beautiful, there is no doubt about that."

"How long have you known each other?"

Not taking my eyes off of her, I replied, "Since the Vegas race."

Mom laughed. "Why is everything measured by which race it was?"

I looked at her with a stupefied look. "Isn't it?"

She rolled her eyes and let out a huff. "Are you dating?"

Were we dating? I just had my face all over her pussy in my damn laundry room. I wanted her and only her. Every waking moment she filled my thoughts, and even in my sleep she controlled my thoughts. I'd never in my life wanted anyone like I wanted Paislie.

"We're taking things slowly, but yes. I think we're dating."

"You think?" she asked as we both looked at each other. "You either are or you're not, Malcolm."

My eyes drifted back to Paislie. I hadn't dated anyone in a very long time. Did I want to open up my heart to the possibility of it being hurt again?

Pushing my fingers through my hair, I shook my head. "It's complicated, Ma."

"Really? The last time I checked it was pretty easy. Is it because of Casey?"

The mention of her name caused my heart to drop. "I don't want to talk about Casey."

"Why not? She was a huge part of your world before you started pretending like you never wanted to open your heart again."

My head snapped over toward my mother as she continued to look at Paislie. "I don't want to talk about her. She's gone and there is no use bringing her up."

My mother looked me straight in the eyes. "She's not Casey."

I pulled my head back and gave my mother a stunned expression. "No fucking kidding, Ma. I know that." Casey and Paislie had total opposite personalities. Casey was more quiet and much more reserved than Paislie was. Paislie wasn't afraid to laugh at herself, whereas Casey took everything seriously.

She narrowed her eye at me. "Don't use that language in front of me, Malcolm. I'm just saying you'll never be able to replace her." She looked back out at Paislie and said, "You don't find it a coincidence that Paislie resembles Casey?"

I practically broke my neck looking back at Paislie. She didn't look anything like Casey. "She looks nothing like her."

She stood and looked back down at me as she lifted her eyebrows. "Really? I find the resemblance very striking."

I swallowed hard as she turned and headed over to where Autumn was standing.

My chest tightened as I watched Paislie carefully. The brown curls framing her beautiful face caught my eye as I took her in. Casey had brown hair, green eyes and a personality that could make an entire room light up when she walked in.

Paislie had brown hair and green eyes, and was so much more independent and strong than Casey was. She knew who she was and what she wanted. The only things she had in common with Casey were the same hair and eye color and that was it. Their personalities were total opposites.

Her smile pulled me in like nothing I'd ever experienced before. There was something about her that made me long to be near her. The things I felt for Paislie were so much stronger than what I had felt for Casey.

She grabbed onto Sophie's hands as they played Ring Around the Rosie. My heart broke that she never got to experience a childhood like Sophie's. I wanted to make up for the shit her father did to her.

When her eyes lifted and met mine, I felt a jolt of electricity whip through my body. My mother's words played over and over in my head. I'd been with plenty of girls with brown hair and green eyes. I slowly shook my head. No . . . Paislie was her own person and she held me captive the moment she opened her mouth and spoke. I'd never felt that way about anyone before . . . or had I, and I just buried it deep down in my memory?

Twenty four

PAISLIE

A S MUCH AS I LOVED playing with Sophie, I was so worked up sex-
ually I was about to burst into flames. It didn't help having Malcolm
eye fuck the hell out of me since our little escapade in the laundry room.

As the night went on, I was introduced to more people, got to know
Shirley and Paul, Malcolm's parents, better and had the distinct feeling
Malcolm was wanted by more than just me attending this party. The
amount of women trying to give him their attention turned my stomach.

"Paislie! The next part of the party is about to start. You need to get
into your party pajamas."

I stared at Sophie like she had grown two heads. "Huh?" *Really, Paislie?
That was the best you could do?*

My body knew he was there before he uttered a word. "Paislie has her
pj's in her room and she'll be up soon, princess. You go with the rest of
the girls and get ready."

Sophie's big blue eyes darted between Malcolm and me. "Are you going to help Paislie get ready?"

Oh how I hope so.

"Oh no, Sophie! I'm a big girl and can get ready on my own," I practically spit out as I felt both Autumn and Shirley staring at me. When my
eyes lifted, Autumn was smiling, but Shirley was staring at Malcolm.

With a little jump, Sophie grabbed two of her friends and darted for
upstairs. Autumn laughed and said, "The party's in the game room. See
you soon, Paislie!"

She had an evil look in her eyes and I had a feeling something was up
between her and Malcolm. I knew she had played a hand in me being

a part of all of this tonight, and I was positive it was at the request of Malcolm.

Malcolm slid his arm around my waist and my body was engulfed in heat. Glancing up, I had to remind myself to breathe. I was so lost in his blue eyes.

I pulled in a breath of air and turned to Shirley who was now staring at me. "So, Paislie, what do your parents do for a living?"

My breath caught and I wasn't sure why. I was used to answering this question, but for some reason I felt like Shirley was putting me on a judging table and checking me out with a fine-tooth comb.

"I actually grew up in an orphanage. My mother passed away when I was young and my father . . . well my father basically didn't want to have to deal with me."

There it was. No use in sugar coating it. She asked and I gave her the answer. Malcolm held me tighter, as if I needed the extra strength. I appreciated the gesture, but I wasn't ashamed of my childhood. Do I wish it had been different? Of course I did. But Elizabeth was like my mother and I was the way I was because of her and God.

"Oh, I'm so sorry, I didn't know."

I gave her a polite smile and attempted to ease her guilt for asking. "Oh no worries, you wouldn't have known."

"Paislie actually thought for a little while she might want to be a nun."

My mouth fell open as I looked at Malcolm and then back to his mother, who now wore a smile from ear to ear.

Oh. Okay. I get it. The fact that I thought about becoming a nun made me appear a bit more innocent. Like maybe I wasn't trying to get my claws into her baby boy's money. She probably thought I was still a virgin too.

The memory of Malcolm's face between my legs popped into my head. It didn't take long for me to get hot and bothered. Malcolm moved his lips along my neck and to my ear.

"What are you thinking about?"

I grinned an evil grin as I simply said, "I need to do laundry."

His eyes lit up and I could see the desire building.

"Well, I guess I should go get ready for the next part of the party!" I exclaimed with a smile.

Shirley looked lovingly at Malcolm and something passed between the two of them. I wasn't able to put my finger on it, but something for sure was exchanged.

"I'll walk you to your room," Malcolm said as he placed his hand on my elbow and led me in that direction.

Oh. Shit.

Glancing back over my shoulder, I asked, "Will I see you upstairs, Mrs. Wallace?"

"Shirley, call me Shirley, sweetheart. And oh no," she said with a chuckle. "Those days are long over. I'm heading back out to the big people party."

Malcolm and I both chuckled as he said, "See you in a few minutes, Mom."

She nodded her head. "Hurry along, Malcolm. I want to introduce you to Katelyn McDermott. She's dying to meet you."

Turning away, I tried not to let that bother me, but it did. I got the feeling Malcolm's mother wouldn't approve of a relationship between us.

Malcolm placed his hand on my lower back and guided me to my room. When I got to the door, I turned and said, "Thanks, but I've got it from here."

His eyebrows pinched together. "The fuck you do."

Reaching behind me, he opened the door and guided me in. "Listen, I got the feeling your mother didn't care for me all that much or she's looking to set you up with Katelyn McDermott. Either way, you should probably get back to the party."

He stared at me like he was trying to let what I said soak in. Slowly shaking his head, he started moving toward me, causing me to back myself right up against a wall. "Do you really think I care about Katelyn McDermott?"

I shrugged. "I don't know. Do you?" I asked as my heart pounded in my chest.

His eyes searched my face. "No, I couldn't care less about her. What I care about is finishing what I started."

My face felt heated as I thought about Malcolm's lips on me.

"It's unfortunate that my knee is bothering me right now, because I would get down and fuck you with my tongue."

"Oh. My," I whispered.

"So my fingers are going to have to do, Paislie."

I will so take fingers, lips, dry humping, or anything else he wanted to do at this point.

"O-okay," I mumbled.

He reached up under the gown and quickly found his way as he pushed his fingers inside me. It didn't take long for me to start bucking my hips like a damn virgin girl about to get off for the first time.

Taking a hold of his jacket, I dropped my head back and pumped my hips against his hand. "That's it baby, fucking hell; you look so good about to fall apart at the mercy of my fingers."

My orgasm was quickly building and I prayed like hell no one knocked on my door.

When my legs trembled, I knew it was about to hit.

"I'm going to come!" I cried out as he pressed his lips to mine and finger fucked me to one hell of an orgasm. It felt naughty . . . knowing he had a whole party outside waiting for him and yet he took the time to finish pleasing me. It was almost as naughty as my first-ever orgasm. In the back hallway of the sanctuary with Peter . . . oh, what was his last name?

He was two years older and when he told me he wanted to put his fingers inside me and make me come, I had no idea what he was talking about. Ten minutes later I was begging him to do it again. We snuck around for four months, finding spots to kiss and make each other come until he finally took my virginity before he left for the Army.

"I need to feel your pussy come on my cock . . . tonight."

I was still trying to recover my breathing from the orgasm when his dirty talk practically had me falling over the edge again. I closed my eyes and took in a deep breath.

"Do you like when I talk dirty to you?"

I nodded my head, afraid to look at him.

"You better change into your pj's, baby. Sophie's waiting for you."

My eyes slowly opened and I wanted to argue so badly. "I . . . I don't really have appropriate pj's to wear to her um . . . her um . . ."

He lifted an eyebrow. "Slumber party?"

"Yes."

Malcolm's eyes drifted over to my bed as I followed his gaze. There sitting on the bed were two different sets of pajama's. One was flannel and was from the movie Frozen, very much for Sophie's party. The other was a white lace two-piece set of lingerie. My lower stomach clenched at the idea of parading around in front of Malcolm in it. Teasing his hard dick as I rubbed against him.

"Oh Lord in heaven," I softly spoke.

His lips were on my neck as he chuckled. "I take it you saw what I want you to wear for me tonight."

My mouth parted open as I stared at it and then glanced back to him. "Um . . . tonight?"

With a wink and flash of his panty-melting smile, he turned and headed out the door. Leaving me alone to wonder what tonight would bring.

I'D NEVER BEEN TO A slumber party. Granted I was twenty-five, having one of the best nights of my life, and feeling like a five-year-old, but I didn't care. It was so much fun watching Sophie and her friends playing and just doing what little girls their age did. The knock at the door had Sophie jumping up. "They're here! Mommy, come quick. Paislie help!"

I was surprised to see it was only Autumn and me along with six other little girls. The fact that I was included made my heart want to burst from the giant happiness bubble I was currently living in.

When the door opened, six guys came walking in, each carrying at least four pillows with them.

Narrowing my eyes, I looked over at Autumn and asked, "I thought the girls were sleeping in their sleeping bags. What are all the pillows for?"

Autumn's smile started off innocent and small. Then it grew bigger and had a bit of evil sprinkled in there.

I never saw it coming. From all sides of me little girls holding one to two pillows each were hitting me. Sophie screamed out, "Pillow fight!"

My hand came over my mouth as I was overcome with emotion. My first pillow fight! I spun around to say something to Autumn when she clocked me right on the side of my head . . . rendering me dazed for a good ten seconds. She covered her mouth and lost it laughing.

"Oh. Oh you just opened the gate of h.e.l.l!" I said as she screamed and took off running. It wasn't right, but I pulled a pillow out of Sophie's best friend Jordan's hands and took off after Autumn.

"Run! Mommy, run!" Sophie shouted as she laughed.

"Get her, Paislie!" Sophie exclaimed.

I stopped running and turned to Sophie. "You can't cheer both of us on, Sophie! It's one or the other."

Her face fell. "But I want you both to win."

I went to say something when Autumn came up from the rear and got me again. This time I was prepared and retaliated with a quick spin and landed a hit right on the side of her face . . . causing her to drop to the ground.

"Yes!" I screamed as Autumn jumped back up with stealth moves. "Oh . . . you think because this is my first pillow fight, I ain't got the moves?"

Autumn pressed her lips together in an attempt not to laugh.

"Ain't isn't a word, Ms. Paislie!" Jordan called out.

"It is tonight, Jordan!" I shouted and took off after Autumn.

This night would by far go down as one of the best nights of my life.

Twenty five

MALCOLM

THE DOOR TO THE WORKOUT room opened as I peered up and saw her. "Morning."

I wanted to be pissed off, but her beautiful smile and sparkling eyes wouldn't allow it. I could hear the girls up almost half the night laughing and having fun. My heart wanted to burst knowing Paislie was enjoying herself so much.

"I take it you had fun last night?"

She chewed on the corner of her lip as she took a few steps in and shut the door. I'd been looking forward to seeing her in the lingerie I'd bought for her, and at first I was upset she stood me up. That was before I saw her and Sophie skipping into the kitchen and making hot chocolate last night. I imagined Paislie didn't have any birthday parties like Sophie's and that broke my heart. With a tray full of hot chocolate, they headed back upstairs, but not before Paislie turned to see me watching them. With a smile and a wink, I told her to go have fun. My aching dick paid me back most of the night and had me jacking off at three am because I couldn't fucking sleep.

"I had a whole lot of fun. I'm slightly concerned that I had more fun hanging out with a bunch of five and six-year-old girls than I do with my own friends."

A small chuckle passed through my lips as I took her in. It was then I noticed she was wearing a long coat.

"Um . . . why are you wearing a coat?"

Her eyes glowed with eagerness as she leaned back against the door and reached behind to lock it.

She took a few steps closer to me and I could feel my cock coming to life.

"I thought since you weren't able to see me in the beautiful lingerie you bought for me, we might take a little detour today during your therapy."

My tongue moved over my lips as I swallowed hard. "You're off today," I mumbled in a wavering voice.

Her eyebrow rose. "Am I? Would you like me to leave and—"

"No!" I exclaimed.

The wicked smile that grew across her face made it hard to breathe.

I was sitting on the weight bench as she walked up and stood in front of me. "It's a little hot in here, don't you think?"

My mouth mumbled something I couldn't understand as I lifted my eyes up to hers. With one fluid movement, she opened the coat to reveal the most amazing fucking body I'd ever put my eyes on.

"My God," I whispered as I lifted my hands and placed them on her perfectly flat stomach. The sharp intake of air told me Paislie wanted me as much as I wanted her.

There wasn't an inch on her body I didn't want to taste with my lips or feel with my hands. Her body trembled as I moved my fingers lightly along her lace panties.

"You look so fucking hot, Paislie."

Her hands came up her body to her breasts while her head dropped back.

A low growl emitted from the back of my throat while my hands found their way to her ass. Taking it in my hands, I squeezed her and pulled her closer, touching my lips to her soft skin.

"Oh God," she gasped as her hands dropped to my hair.

Fighting the urge to rip her panties off, I took a deep breath and blew over her mound as her fingers wrapped tightly around my hair. I wanted the first time with Paislie to be different. Slow, romantic, everything I never had before.

"What do you want from me?" she asked in a husky voice.

My heart and mind were in a bitter battle. "I want so badly to make love to you, baby. But I'm gonna be honest, my cock is so hard for you it hurts. All I want is for you to put your pussy on it and ride the hell out of me until I spill every ounce of cum into your body."

"Jesus," she whispered as I stood. For one brief moment I forgot about the pain in my knee and leg as I removed my workout shorts.

Paislie's eyes lit up with a dark passion as she took a step back and slowly pushed her panties to the ground. She stepped out of them and kicked them off to the side.

"You're so naughty, Mr. Wallace."

With a wicked grin, I slowly shook my head as I pulled her closer to me, pressing my cock into her as she sucked in a breath. "You have no idea how naughty I can be, Ms. Pruitt."

I slowly sat back on the bench as she moved over me, each leg on either said of the bench. Her body trembled when I took myself in my hand and stroked. Paislie's eyes widened in delight as she zeroed in on my hand and licked her lips.

"Are you wet?" I asked as her teeth sunk down onto her lip and nodded her head.

Not removing my eyes from her face, I said, "Touch yourself and tell me how wet you are."

Her eyes snapped up and her face flushed. Her breathing increased as her chest rose and fell, each time turning me on more. "W-what?"

"Touch. Yourself."

For one brief moment she hesitated and then did as I said. I moaned when she pushed two fingers inside herself. "Very wet," she whispered.

"Are you ready for me, baby?"

With an eager nod, she moved over me as I placed both hands on her hips. Slowly sinking down, her breath stalled when my cock barely pushed inside of her.

My hands felt like they were shaking as I gripped onto her hips harder. Jesus H. Christ. I wasn't going to last a minute inside her.

"Wait!" she exclaimed. "Condom."

Fucking hell what would she feel like with no barrier? I couldn't wrap my head around it. "I . . . I don't have one!" I practically shouted.

Her mouth snapped shut as she gave me a blank expression. "Please don't say that. I've never in my life had sex with no condom, Malcolm. It's my number one rule and I've never broken it."

This is not happening right now.

"I haven't either, Paislie, and I get tested regularly as well."

The way we looked at each other had my cock getting even harder.

"Me too."

Jesus, please tell me I've died and gone to heaven if she answers this next question with a yes.

"Are you on birth control?"

Her lips pressed together, knowing where I was going. "Yes," she softly said.

I pulled her body down more onto my cock, filling her with a few more inches.

Her eyes closed as she said, "Malcolm, it's too risky."

My lips went to her neck as I softly dragged my tongue along her skin. "We can stop, baby. Just say the word."

She moaned as she let herself sink down a little more.

Son-of-a-bitch. I'd never been inside a girl with no rubber on. Paislie was no ordinary girl. She had my heart clearly thinking for my brain.

Another inch and we both moaned. "You're so big," she panted as she sunk all the way down letting out a gasp when I filled her completely.

Warmth radiated throughout my body as I wrapped my arms around her. I'd never be the same after this.

"Oh my God," she spoke as her fingers laced through my hair. My cock twitched inside her body, begging her to move, yet relishing in the absolute blissful moment.

"Fucking hell, you feel so good," I said as held her close to my body. "Fuck me, Paislie. I'm yours."

Her body trembled as she placed her hands on my shoulders and looked into my eyes. I loved her eyes. They said a million things at once, yet said nothing at all. She confused me, thrilled me, and had me longing for more.

Then she moved, slowly at first as my hand went to her hair and pulled it, forcing her to bend her head back.

"Fuuuck," I panted out. "I've never . . . felt anything . . . so fucking amazing."

"Malcolm," was all she said as she picked up speed. It was true, I'd never in my life experienced anything like this before. My head was spinning and my heart was racing. For the first time in a long time, I felt something.

I desired something more than sex. For the first time in a long time . . . the guilt about Casey was gone and I was allowing myself to feel.

Paislie brought it out. My sweet beautiful Paislie.

twenty six

PAISLIE

O H. DEAR. GOD.

It felt so wrong. Yet it felt so incredibly right. The feeling of Malcolm moving inside of me, with nothing between us was amazing. The fact that I didn't feel the need to have the barrier . . . even more amazing.

I'd finally let my heart open up and it felt fantastic. And it scared the hell out of me. I had just given my whole self to him in hopes he wouldn't ruin me.

"Fuck me! Fuck me faster, baby."

His dirty talk had me all kinds of worked up. I could practically feel the wetness running down my legs. "Mal . . . Malcolm!" I cried out as I moved faster, feeling my orgasm build. My body heated from head to toe. My skin was on fire everywhere he touched.

My stomach fluttered as he whispered against my lips, "You're so beautiful. I need to come inside you, baby."

That was it.

That was all I needed to unleash the most intense orgasm of my life. My legs shook and I wasn't sure if it was from fatigue or the orgasm. My body clenched down on Malcolm's dick as I rode it out. I was finally coming down from my high when I felt him grow bigger. The feeling was heavenly. I'd never experienced this feeling of having a man in me with no condom. It was as if I could feel everything ten times better.

"Oh God . . . not . . . again!" I cried out as Malcolm grunted and called out my name. His hips pumped hard while he held me in place, pulling more from me. The knowledge he was the only man to ever fill me with his cum and give me not only one but two orgasms while having sex, had my heart quickening.

Malcolm's arms wrapped around my body as we came to a stop. Our breathing rough as we attempted to get it under control.

"That was the hottest moment of my entire life," I spoke into his neck.

With a rumbled laugh, he pushed me back as he gazed into my eyes. My body was spent and if I hadn't known any better, I'd have thought I had just finished a marathon. When his hand came up and cupped the side of my face, I leaned into it.

"Please don't ever leave me. You've changed my entire world."

The sadness in his eyes brought tears to my own. I heard the hurt in his voice and I wanted to know why it was there.

"Why do you think I'd leave you?" I asked as I ran my finger down his tattooed arm.

He shook his head. "My leg hurts like a bitch."

I jumped up and looked down. My heart stopped as I watched his cum travel down my body.

Oh my God. I had sex with no condom. I just fucked a man on a workout bench in his workout room with his family in the house!

My emotions were so mixed. I loved that he came inside me, yet it felt like I had given him a sacred piece of me and that scared the hell out of me. The last man I gave my heart to broke it into a million pieces.

The small knock on the door had both of us freezing. "Mr. Wallace, it's Jane. Would you like me to clean in there?"

My eyes widened as my hands covered my mouth. Dropping my hands, I reached for my coat. Malcolm quickly put his shorts on, grabbed his cane and walked over to me with the sexiest smile I'd ever seen.

"What if she heard us?" I whispered.

When he pushed his fingers inside of me I gasped as he moaned before answering. "No, it's okay. It doesn't need to be cleaned in here, Jane."

My heartbeat was pounding in my ears so loudly I could hardly hear my own breathing.

Malcolm continued to use his fingers to make me complete mess. "Okay, have a good day, Mr. Wallace."

Malcolm grinned as I grabbed onto his arms and shook my head. What was wrong with me? My mind was all over the place. Someone was on the other side of the door and Malcolm was fingering me, clearly turned on again. "You too."

My hand grabbed his arm to stop him. "I . . . I can't think. Wait."

His lips moved slowly and softly over my neck while his other hand cupped my breast as his finger moved over the fabric teasing my nipple. "Malcolm," I panted out as he continued to drive me crazy everywhere he touched.

"You're so wet, baby."

The feeling in my body was unlike anything I could explain. I was on fire everywhere. "That would be your cum."

I'm going to Hell. Good lord, Elizabeth would be appalled at my behavior.

"Mmm . . . mixed with yours."

Dropping my head back, I gave in to the desire and pumped my hips, I needed more. I wanted more. God help me I wanted to come again.

Malcolm snickered as he finger fucked me faster. "You're greedy for orgasms, Paislie."

So close. God, I was so close.

"Uncle Malcolm!"

Her voice pulled me out of the spell I was under. I pushed Malcolm away as I took a step back. My chest heaving as I fought to drag in air.

"What are you doing to me?" I mumbled as I put my coat on.

His smile did crazy things to me. He started for the door as I quickly made my way to the bathroom on the other side of the gym. Barely making it in time, Malcolm threw the door open to a very happy Sophie.

"Uncle Malcolm! What were you doing in here? We heard funny noises."

"Yes, what *were* you doing in here? Jane had to come get me because the door was locked."

My lips pressed together tightly. Holy shit. Malcolm's mother.

"I was getting in a workout."

The silence that followed told me his mother was probably giving him a look only a mother can give.

Glancing up, I saw the window.

Autumn laughed and asked, "Is Paislie *working out* with you this morning?"

Damn her. I thought she was on my side. I was going to smack her the next time I saw her.

I quickly looked around for something to use to get me closer to the window.

"As a matter of fact, she did."

What is he doing? Oh God. I have to get out of here! Now!

"That would explain the locked door then, wouldn't it," Shirley said.

"Great," I whispered. I had the feeling Malcolm's mother didn't like me for some reason. This was not going to help the situation any.

"Paislie! Where is she, Uncle Malcolm?"

"Going potty. Paislie! What are you doing?"

I fell back against the door. I was going to take his balls and twist them until he begged for mercy.

Glancing down at my coat, I opened it. "I can't go out in this," I mumbled under my breath.

I quickly opened doors and practically screamed when I saw some of Malcolm's stuff. It was a pair of sweatpants and an old T-shirt. I kicked off my shoes, unclipped my garter belt and slipped the pants on. They were huge but oh well. The T-shirt practically swallowed me whole.

Shoes! Fuck! I don't have any shoes.

"Paislie?" Malcolm called out as I balled my hands up, took a deep breath, and opened the door.

Please don't make it look like I just had sex. Please.

With a smile, I walked out like I didn't know they were there. "Oh, hey there, y'all. Did you come to join the yoga workout I had planned for Malcolm?"

Malcolm nearly choked on his own spit, which made me smile bigger.

Autumn did her best attempt at hiding her smile as she tilted her head and looked at me. "Don't you look all cute dressed in . . . wait . . . are those Malcolm's clothes?"

I'm officially defriending her.

I looked down and shrugged. "Yep."

"Why are you dressed in Uncle Malcolm's clothes?"

I peered over to Malcolm, silently begging him to help me out. He stood there with a goofy-ass smile on his face. Meanwhile, Sophie jumped around with excitement, Autumn hid her laugh under her hand and

Shirley, well she stood there staring at me like I was the devil himself.

I never could lie. Ever. Even before I went to live at St. Patrick's.

At this point I had nothing to lose. It was clear Malcolm couldn't care less, Autumn thought it was a game and Malcolm's mother clearly hated me, so what did I have to lose?

With a shrug, I said, "I couldn't really work out in the lingerie Malcolm had bought for me, it would have been too cold."

Autumn lost it laughing as Malcolm coughed while he grabbed my arm and dragged me across the room. I risked looking at Shirley. That was a mistake. She glared at me like I was trash that needed to be taken out.

"What in the hell, Paislie?"

I stood there with my mouth hung open as my body trembled in anger. "Are you serious right now? What did you want me to do? Lie? You put me in that spot, Malcolm."

Glancing up, Autumn picked up Sophie and said something about getting ice cream from Clarisse. My eyes caught Shirley's as I held my breath for a few seconds before turning back to Malcolm. "And by the way, why does your mother hate me so much?"

Malcolm pulled his head back in shock. "She doesn't hate you," he said in a low voice.

I pushed past him and made my way out of the room.

"Yoga lesson cancelled," I said as I walked past Shirley. "Have a wonderful day today, Mrs. Wallace."

The entire way back to my room I fought like hell to keep my tears at bay.

I was not liking this overly-emotionally Paislie at all.

Not one bit.

Twenty seven

MALCOLM

P AISLIE STORMED OUT OF THE gym and past my mother while
she placed her hands on her hips and shot me a dirty look.

Lifting my hand, I shook my head. "Before you utter a word, Mom,
I'm a grown man and Paislie is a grown woman. What we do in private is
our business."

"Malcolm, I don't give a rats ass who you have sex with, from what I've
read it happens often, but to do it in your own home with an employee of
yours. And to top it off, you don't really know what this Paislie girl wants
from you. Let's not mention how she probably found out about Casey
and is using the fact she has similar looks to her advantage. She's taking
your money and having sex with you. That's not right."

I couldn't believe what I was hearing. "Stop it. Mom, just stop."

She rolled her eyes and shook her head. "I'm trying to protect you.
Clearly you have a thing for her and I'm just saying you're worth a lot of
money and honestly, for her to come down to your gym in slutty under-
wear? Good lord, Malcolm what am I supposed to think about her now?"

"Mom! I bought it for her to wear and I would appreciate it if you
didn't talk about Paislie that way. You know nothing about her."

"I know she's living in your house and you're paying her a ridiculous
amount of money to be here, on top of paying her rent on her place in
Dallas."

I felt my heart drop. "How do you know that?"

She shrugged and said, "I asked Janet a few questions and she assumed
I knew about your arrangement with Paislie. She might have told me a
little more than she should have under the impression I knew."

With a look of disappointment on my face, I turned away from my mother and stared out the window. It was then I saw Paislie walking to the barn. Her pace was fast, as if she needed to get as far away as possible. I longed to go after her.

With a deep breath in, I tried to make sense of what my mother was trying to do. "Mom, you don't know anything about my personal life, and I find it extremely rude that you would go poking around asking Janet things about it."

"I'm only looking out for you, Malcolm. Now, I think you should stop and think about this thing you have going on with Paislie. She's not Casey and she'll never be able to replace her."

Spinning around, I felt my heart pounding in my chest. "Jesus Christ, will you drop the whole fucking Casey thing!"

Her eyes widened in surprise. "Don't you use that language with me, Malcolm."

My hand pushed through my hair as I let out a frustrated moan. "Mom! I know she is not Casey. I'm not trying to find a replacement for her. I've spent the last I don't know how many years trying to bury the guilt of her dying. Trying to forget the words she said to me before her life ended. I've been dead inside, not allowing myself to feel anything for anyone. And yes, what you read was true. I fucked around . . . a lot. But Paislie is different and I don't know why you can't believe that. She wants *nothing* from me. She's had a hard life and made something of herself. Why can't you believe that I've actually fallen in love with someone and it doesn't have a damn thing to do with Casey? I never loved Casey the way I do Paislie."

With a gasp, she walked up to me. "You . . . you love this girl?"

I hadn't even realized I said I loved Paislie. And hell I said it twice. "I don't know what I'm feeling. All I know is I want to be with her every second of the day. Her smile makes me smile. Her laugh calms me down and her strength is inspiring. She believes in me, Mom. She brought me back to life and I need her."

Her eyes softened. "Oh, Malcolm. Sweetheart, I hadn't realized how strongly you felt about her. I didn't realize the two of you had grown so close. But do you know how she feels about you?"

"I hope the same."

She chewed nervously on her lip. "What if she's only after your money?"

"Mom, how could she be when I'm the one who pursued her?"

Her expression was one of surprise. "I see."

I shook my head and started for the door. "Mom, I love you, but you need to stay out of my business. I would also appreciate it if you apologized to Paislie. I'm not the only one who noticed the death stares you were giving her."

She simply nodded her head. Turning, I decided to make my way to the barn . . . after I took a pain pill for my damn leg.

WALKING INTO THE BARN, I took a quick look around and finally saw Paislie sitting on a bale of hay. Talking to a horse.

Okay. So she likes to talk to herself and horses. It was kind of cute.

She must have sensed me because she looked up. Her smile took my breath away. I couldn't believe I had finally made her mine. The limp in my leg was obvious as I headed her way. She quickly stood and watched me walk toward her.

"How bad does it hurt?" she asked as her eyes landed on my leg.

With a shrug, I replied, "It's fine. I'm more concerned about you."

Her face lit up as a flush swept over her. "Me? I'm fine. Totally fine."

I took another step as she took a step back, only to bump into the stall. "Really? You weren't fine when you stormed out of the gym a little bit ago."

She squared her shoulders and lifted her chin. I already knew this was her defense mode. One she probably learned early on when she pretended everything was okay. "Well, it's hard to stand there when your mother is shooting me daggers. If looks could kill I'd have fallen over."

I let out a dry laugh. "I talked to her about that. She knows how I feel about you and how much you mean to me. I'm pretty sure she won't be giving you that response again."

Paislie swallowed hard. "H-how do you feel about me, Malcolm? What's happening here, because I'm all kinds of confused. Earlier when we were together, I've never experienced those emotions before and I'm going to be honest with you, it scares the hell out of me. I don't think . . . I mean . . . I know I couldn't take it if you were to break my heart. Not you, Malcolm. You're the only person I've let in since my father left me and . . . I just . . ."

Her chin trembled and for the first time I saw vulnerability there I had never seen before. I dropped the cane and cupped her face within in my hands. Our eyes searched one another's face before her emerald eyes pierced my blue.

"Look into my eyes, Paislie. I've never felt like this about anyone."

"No one?" she asked, almost as if she expected a different answer from me.

"No one. Do you have any idea of how you've made me go almost out of mind since the first time you bumped into me. My life has been turned upside down. You're all I think about. You're the first thing on my mind when I wake up, and the last thing when I fall asleep."

A single tear rolled down her cheek as I used my thumb to wipe it away. "Paislie, please give me a chance to prove to you how much I've fallen for you."

Her lips pressed together as she attempted to hold back a sob. She slowly shook her head. "What are you saying, Malcolm?"

I never in a million years thought I would be uttering the words I was about to say. "I'm falling in love with you, Paislie."

Her breath expelled as she grabbed onto me to keep her balance. "Um . . . I um."

I wrinkled my brow and said, "Damn . . . I was kind of hoping you would say the same thing back to me."

More tears as she gave me the biggest grin I'd ever seen as she softly said, "I think I fell in love with you on my first date with Deuce. Something about the stars and that kiss."

I couldn't hold back my own smile as I pressed my lips to hers. The kiss started off slow and gentle. Our tongues dancing in a perfect rhythm as a low growl formed at the back of my throat.

Before things got out of hand, I took a step back. Both of us gasping for air as we stared at each other. "What are you doing to me?" I asked.

Her lips formed a wicked smile. "The same thing you're doing to me apparently."

My eyes glanced over to Black Jack. She had been talking to him when I walked in. "Black Jack here is an old friend of mine. First horse I ever bought."

Her eyes filled with excitement. "How about we go for a ride?"

Wiggling my eyes, I said, "Okay! I'll meet you in your room."

She lightly hit me on the chest. "Stop! You know what I meant. Want to take a few horses out?"

My right hand hit my chest as I let out an exaggerated gasp. "You ride? If you say yes, I'm marrying you this very second."

Paislie rolled her eyes and walked toward the tack room. "St. Patrick's had a camp every summer I went to. I quickly found out horses made me happy. I forgot everything the moment I got on one. I love horses."

Jesus . . . I just fell a little more for her.

"You can saddle 'em up?"

She glanced over her shoulder and shot me a dirty look. "Excuse me? You don't think I've got a little bit of country in me, Mr. Wallace?"

With a crooked smile, I shook my head. "No. I don't think you've got it in you, city girl."

Her left eye narrowed as she thought for a moment. "What will you give me if I prove you wrong?"

"I'll let you pick."

Her mouth slightly opened and I was pretty sure I heard something in the form of a growl come from the back of her throat. "Have a seat, baby, while I show you what this city girl can do."

A few minutes later Black Jack and Snowflake were both saddled and ready to go as Paislie stood before me with a look of satisfaction plastered across her face.

"Are you able to get up on him okay?" she asked with concern in her eyes.

I dropped the cane and used my good leg to mount Jack. He wasn't used to me mounting from the other side and tried to take a few steps back, only to have Paislie instantly calm him down. She talked softly to him and I couldn't believe how he seemed to be mesmerized by her voice.

"Even the damn horse likes you."

She snickered as she got on Snowflake.

"Where to?"

I motioned for her to follow me as we took off down one of the trails that went all over the ranch. This one happened to lead to a small lake on the property. As we rode along the trail, we fell into an easy conversation. Paislie mentioned some ideas for therapy and I could really hear it in her voice the passion she had for her job.

"Will you answer something honestly, Paislie?"

"Of course I will. You know I'm all about honesty."

My breathing picked up as I grew nervous about what her answer would be to my question. "Do you think I'll ever race again?"

Our eyes met and I saw it before she ever answered me. "I'd say there is a fifty-fifty chance either way. I'll push you as hard as I can, but you really need to mentally prepare yourself for not being cleared to race again."

I knew it deep in my heart. I had no doubt Paislie would get me walking fine again, but I wasn't sure about the pain that would occasionally shoot through my leg, or the numbness I felt. If my leg was bent very long, my knee went stiff and that was probably the most painful thing.

"What am I going to do if I can't race?" I asked, not really expecting her to answer.

"Why couldn't you do something other than drive? Like buy a car and be an owner, or do the thing where the guys talk on TV." She looked up and scrunched her nose in the most adorable way. "What are they called . . . commentary dudes?"

With a roar of laughter, I shook my head. "Jesus, there is no way I could do that shit. I'm getting behind a wheel again. I need to be behind the wheel. I need to feel the rush. It's the only thing I've ever known."

We rode for a few minutes in silence before my knee started aching. "I guess we should turn around and head back."

Paislie gave me a look. "Is your knee hurting?"

"Nope. Just not in the mood to ride I guess."

I had no idea why I just lied to her. Or maybe I did. I needed to get back in a car.

Twenty eight

PAISLIE

TWO MONTHS HAD PASSED SINCE I first came to stay with Malcolm. His progress was beyond amazing. Everything was beyond amazing. I was to the point where I now slept in his bedroom each night. We would spend half the night making love and talking before we would pass out wrapped up in one another. I'd sneak out in the morning and make my way to my room for my morning wake up from Sophie. Neither Malcolm nor I wanted her to know I was sleeping in his bedroom every night. Autumn said we were being stupid and old fashioned.

The last few days Malcolm had been holding back in our therapy sessions. His frustration was growing and I could see it in his face.

I walked into the local gym and headed to the pool. The girl at the front desk lifted her hand as I waved back.

"Hey, Paislie!"

"Hi, Carrie. How are you?"

She smiled big. "Good."

I wanted to like her, but the way she eye fucked Malcolm every time he walked by her drove me insane. He never looked twice at her, but I knew if given the chance, she'd be all over him.

Pushing the door open, the humidity hit me right in the face. "Ugh," I mumbled. Malcolm was standing in the pool talking to the same woman he had been talking to on Tuesday. I tried not to let the jealousy take over as I said a quick prayer and made my way over to them.

When she threw her head back and laughed, I rolled my eyes. Malcolm clearly was enjoying the attention she was giving him.

I cleared my throat to get their attention. She glanced up and smiled as Malcolm flashed me that crooked grin of his. "Hey, baby. Guess what I did today?"

Lifting my eyes, I replied, "No telling."

"Ran on the treadmill."

My eyes widened. "What? You were supposed to do the bike, Malcolm. Not run. That's too hard on your knee."

His smile faded but returned when his personal cheerleader defended him. "Well, he did a great job! I could hardly keep up with him." My eyes snapped over to her as I gave her a back-the-fuck-away-bitch look. Her smiled faded as she looked between Malcolm and me. "Listen, I'll see you next time, right?"

When she placed her hand on his arm, he didn't even flinch. "Okay, see ya later."

Malcolm climbed up the steps as he grabbed a towel and dried off as I kept my eyes trained on his new workout partner. "So, you seem to enjoy her company."

With a confused look, he turned from me to look at her and then back to me. "It's nothing. She's fun to talk to when I'm walking in the pool. It's a nice change."

Ouch. That hurt.

"And running on the treadmill?" He didn't bother to answer. "Why didn't you do the bike, Malcolm? You need to be careful about your knee."

He pushed past me, clearly in a bad mood. Maybe I interrupted something? Oh God. What if he liked her? No . . . Malcolm would never do that to me. I know he wouldn't.

"I was in the mood to run."

Suppressing my anger, I asked, "How did your knee feel after?"

After he slipped on a T-shirt, he made his way over to the exit. "Fine," he said as he pushed the door open.

Following him, I didn't say a word when Carrie jumped up. "Bye, Malcolm! See you tomorrow maybe?"

He flashed her his famous melt-your-panty smile. "Maybe, Carrie. Have a good day."

She practically melted at his words, causing me to roll my eyes.

Well, his leg was feeling better, considering he was walking full speed to his truck.

"Malcolm, do you want to tell me what's wrong? Why are you acting like an ass to me right now?"

He lifted his hand. "Not now, Paislie. I'm not in the mood to deal with you and your nagging."

I stopped dead in my tracks and stood there as I watched him walk to his truck. He threw his bag into the back seat and got in the driver's side and pulled out.

My heart raced in my chest and I wasn't sure if it was from his words or the look on his face when he drove off.

SOPHIE'S VOICE COULD BE HEARD coming from the kitchen as I walked in and laughed at the sight before me.

"Oh wow. What happened in here?" I asked as I looked at Clarisse.

She shook her head and said, "Sophie felt like making brownies. Needless to say, when she turned the mixer on high and dumped the flour in, I wasn't ready."

I covered my mouth in an attempt to hide my smile. "Did you need help cleaning up?" I asked.

She gave me a thankful look. "That would be amazing." She turned and dropped down to Sophie's level. "How about you go put on a movie, and I'll call you when it's time for more mixing and baking."

"Okay!"

Just like that, Sophie bolted from the kitchen and headed into the family room.

"Oh, Clarisse! I'm so sorry this happened," I said as I started to clean up the flour.

She shrugged. "I don't mind really. It's been nice having little Sophie in the house. Makes it feel alive."

I nodded. There had been plenty of times I dreamed what it would be like to have a child with Malcolm. The way he was with his niece made my heart melt every time.

After a few moments, I got up the nerve to ask Clarisse if she had seen Malcolm. The last I had saw him was almost six hours ago when he pulled out of the parking lot of the gym.

"Hey, have you seen Malcolm?"

"No, I haven't seen him all day. I figured he was with you."

I tried not to show my anger, but deep down I was pissed as hell that Malcolm dismissed me like he did and drove away leaving me standing in the parking lot.

I sucked in my lip as I bit down on it. "No. He was a bit upset earlier."

"Oh, really? Why?"

With a shrug, I answered honestly. "I'm not really sure."

"Well his parents will be here soon for dinner, so he better get his butt home."

My heart dropped. I still had a sneaking feeling Shirley didn't like me very much. She tried to be polite, but something was off. If Malcolm left me stranded here to deal with his parents, I was going to hurt him.

"Do you need help with dinner?" I asked with a hopeful eye. I desperately needed something to do to keep my mind from swimming with thoughts.

"Only if you want to occupy your mind."

With a chuckle, I put my hands on my hips and asked, "How do you do that? How'd you know I needed to keep my mind busy?"

She gave me a wink and said, "Experience my child. Experience. Now grab a mixing a bowl. I'm going to show you my secret recipe for one of Malcolm's favorites. Chicken and dumplings."

Clarisse was like a mother figure to me and I quickly found myself enjoying her company more and more. Her words of wisdom were always spot on.

Soon we were laughing and cooking up a storm. Two things I never really got to experience before. Elizabeth and I would sometimes bake cookies together, but it was nothing like what I had imagined a mother and daughter would do. I wanted so badly to talk about cute boys and what styles were hot, and she wanted me to practice prayers.

Time went by so fast that soon Shirley and Paul were standing in the kitchen, looking between Clarisse and myself. "Mr. and Mrs. Wallace, how are you?" I said with a smile. They both returned a warm smile in my direction.

"Paislie, sweetheart, please call us Shirley and Paul."

Progress. This was good. "Okay, Shirley and Paul. How are you both doing?"

Paul walked in and reached for a piece of celery. "Doing good, considering it's the middle of August in Texas and I'm too old for this hot weather."

I tried to hide my giggle but it slipped. Shirley hit him on the arm and shook her head. Janet came walking into the kitchen with a bright and cheerful smile on her face.

"Janet! I didn't know you were in town!" I exclaimed. Janet and I had hit it off extremely well. She was the only person who really knew Malcolm and there were so many times I would talk to her about things. I really needed to talk to her tonight to ask her if she noticed something off with him like I had.

She tilted her head and gave me a look that asked, *what did he do now?*

"Where's my son?" Paul asked. "There is bound to be a fight or something on we can watch."

I peeked over to Clarisse and then over to Janet who slowly shook her head. No one knew where he was.

Oh God. I was going to be stuck entertaining his parents. "Where's Autumn and Sophie?" I asked when I realized the house was too quiet.

"They were rushing out as we were walking in. Autumn said something about spending a few days in Dallas. Sophie's father wanted to spend some time with her. Imagine that," Shirley said with sarcasm dripping from her mouth.

I had to admit I was sad they rushed out without saying good-bye.

After Janet and I set the table, we all sat down to eat, including Clarisse. I had insisted she eat with us. "I can't imagine where Malcolm is," I said with a polite smile.

The conversation around the table was easy. I was surprised to see how much Shirley and I actually had in common. We both loved classic romance novels and Jane Austen was one of our favorite authors.

The table erupted in laughter after Paul had told a joke and then quickly fell silent. "Is that . . . a helicopter?" I asked, as the noise grew louder.

Clarisse and Janet exchanged worried looks as Shirley and Paul did the same.

"I guess we know where Malcolm was," Janet said as she stood up from the table.

I looked around confused. "Wait. Malcolm has a helicopter?"

Clarisse excused herself as she gathered up a few plates. "I'll go heat up some food for Malcolm."

Shirley smiled. "He used it a lot when he was racing. He liked to come back to Texas a lot and it was quick and easy for him."

Clarisse reached for my plate as she said, "Ashley used it a lot when she would come and . . . um . . . visit."

My head snapped up to look at her as her face blushed. She must have known she slipped.

Oh. My. God. It never occurred to me that Malcolm had actually had sex in his house with other women. All of a sudden I felt dirty. How many women had he screwed in his bed? Placing my hand over my stomach, I felt sick. Why did that bother me so much? Why was I under the allusion he never brought a girl here? Hell . . . if he flew Ashley here just to fuck her, I'm sure there were plenty of other women he did the same for.

I jumped up, sliding the chair back, scaring both of Malcolm's parents.

"Are you okay, Paislie?" Shirley asked, "You look white as a ghost."

I shook my head. "I'm sorry. If you'll excuse me."

Quickly turning, I bolted out of the dining room. I needed air quickly. This feeling of being jealous of women who were in Malcolm's past was foreign to me and I didn't like the way it made me feel. I hated it as a matter of fact. It was Malcolm's past.

Before I made it out of the room I ran smack into Malcolm, who reached his hands out to stop me from falling over.

"Where's the fire?"

My mouth parted open, but words wouldn't form. What if he flew to her today? What if he had been and I didn't know? I'd been here for two months and never even knew he had a helicopter.

"Where were you?" I asked.

"I flew into Dallas . . . business meeting."

Bile formed in my throat. "W-what kind of business meeting?"

"I talked with Mr. Elliot, my boss. Told him I met with one of the NASCAR doctors and they cleared me for racing."

It felt like a piece of lead was in my stomach. I stood there dumbfounded as I let his words soak in. "You've been cleared to race? Malcolm . . . you still have issues with your knee and I know you're hiding the pain. I can see it on your face."

Something moved across his face as his eyes turned dark and not in good way. "You don't know shit, Paislie. I need to be in that car. You don't understand."

I took a step back, my eyes filling with tears. "No. I don't understand. Please enlighten me, Malcolm. Why do you have such a need to be behind the wheel? Are you trying to kill yourself?"

A look passed over his face . . . as if a memory hit him.

"I need the rush."

"And you can't get that rush from something else? From someone else?"

He looked at me like he wanted to say something, but kept his mouth shut. I scrubbed my hands down my face. "Why do you even bother to have me here doing therapy if you're just going to do the things you want to do?"

"I don't need therapy anymore. I'm fine now."

It felt like I'd been slapped across my face as he gave me a blank stare. "So that's it? Does that mean we're through?"

His eyes softened. "Why would you say that?"

"Oh I don't know, Malcolm. Because you've tried at least three times today to say or do something to push me away or cause me to hurt."

"Hurt?" he asked with a puzzled look on his face.

"Call me crazy, but when the man you love tells you he liked the company of another woman today, tells you to shut up, then walks away from you and drives off with not so much as a goodbye. That fucking hurts. I stood there like a damn fool while you drove off without saying a word to me. Nothing! You don't do that to someone you care about." I didn't even care that his parents were standing in the room.

Horror filled his eyes as he glanced over my shoulder to his mother and back to me. "You don't love me, Casey, you just think you do."

My heart dropped and I couldn't breathe. That was the final blow. I never imagined I could actually feel my heart breaking like I did that very moment.

Shirley gasped as I heard her walk over to me. I used to think the woman hated me, but in that moment, her hand on my shoulder told me she understood what I was feeling.

I slowly shook my head as tears rolled down my cheeks. Standing up taller, I squared off my shoulders and attempted to talk without my voice cracking while I quickly wiped my tears away. My chest felt as if someone had placed a hundred pound weight on it as I fought for the words to speak.

"You're so wrong, Malcolm. I do love you and I'm sorry you don't feel the same. I let you in and I honestly thought you were the last person in the world who would ever hurt me." With the back of my fingers, I wiped more tears away as I turned my body but stopped. Slowly looking over my shoulder at him, I managed to say one last thing. "And my name is Paislie. Not Casey."

His eyes widened in shock while he stumbled back a few steps. "Shit. Baby, I didn't mean to call you that."

I turned to face him as I let a sob slip through my lips. "Don't call me that."

He took a few steps toward me. "Paislie, wait I'm so sorry and I'm not sure why I've been acting this way . . . but let me explain one thing."

My hand came up to stop him. "Stop. Just don't say anything else. I'm leaving."

He grabbed my arm. "Wait. Let me just talk to you."

Pushing his arm away, I shook my head. "You've had plenty of chances to talk to me. I can't do this. You promised me you wouldn't do this. I'm not your dead girlfriend and if that's all I was to you . . . a replacement . . . then you're more fucked up than I thought you were."

He shook his head. "No, it's nothing like that. I swear to you." His head jerked back. "Wait. How did you know about Casey?"

My phone beeped with a text message. Glancing down, I saw my father's name scroll across along with the beginning of his message. *Baby, I need to borrow some money. Can you ask your rich boyfriend?*

I didn't even have the energy to talk. It felt as if every ounce of strength I had vanished.

"I can't do this."

Not even bothering to go to my room to get anything, I grabbed my purse and keys and ran out to my car.

Malcolm called out after me as I opened the car door. "Paislie! Please just give me five minutes! Paislie!"

Tears streamed down my face as I drove off. Leaving everything behind, including my damn cat.

This was why I never opened up my heart up to anyone.

I wasn't meant to love or be loved.

Twenty nine

MALCOLM

" **M** ALCOLM?"

The sound of Janet's voice filled the empty room, causing me to open my eyes. "Did they leave?"

"Yes."

"Is all of her stuff gone?"

Janet paused. "Yes, are you sure you don't want to try and call her?"

"That's all, Janet. You can head back to North Carolina tomorrow. I've been cleared to race this weekend."

She paused for a moment and took in a deep breath. "Are you sure you're doing the right thing? I mean, with the race and with letting Paislie go."

Just the mention of her name caused my heart to ache. I tried so hard to hide the pain in my knee and leg from everyone that I started taking it out on Paislie. The one person who was doing her damnedest to help me and I fucked up. I promised her I wouldn't hurt her. She trusted me. I'd never be able to forget the look of hurt in her eyes.

"Have a safe flight back to North Carolina, Janet."

I had never dismissed her like that, but I needed to clear my head. It had been a month since Paislie had walked out of my life. After a few appointments with the NASCAR doctors, I had them convinced I was ready to drive again. I needed to get back behind the wheel. The need to be racing around a track at almost two hundred miles an hour was greater than ever before. The rush I had with Paislie was the only thing that compared to the rush I felt driving, and even racing wasn't nearly the same kind of feeling.

My phone buzzed as I glanced down at it.

Emmit: When are you coming in to town?

Me: Tomorrow.

Emmit: Dinner? My house? Addie would love to see you and so would Landon.

The thought of seeing them made my stomach drop. Emmit had everything I wanted.

Me: I'll try but I may be busy trying to get back into the swing of things.

Emmit: Totally get it. Let me know if you can.

I stared at the text messages. It was hard to believe I now considered Emmit to be one of my closest friends. It wasn't long ago we practically hated each other. Now I was having dinner at his house and playing with his son.

My hand dropped to my side as I stared out the window. Paislie was nothing like Casey. So why did I let it slip?

I brought the beer that was in my other hand up to my lips and drank the rest of it. I needed to feel numb. I needed to forget about Paislie Pruitt if I wanted to get back into the swing of things.

Forget Paislie.

I could never forget the only woman I'd ever loved.

My eyes closed as I dropped my head back and slowly let sleep take over. I barely heard the bottle hit the floor as I drifted off into a dream.

RICHMOND—ONE OF MY FAVORITE tracks and the best place for my comeback race.

"How are you feeling, Malcolm?"

"Emmit?" Hearing Emmit's voice over the radio made me smile bigger than I wanted. "What in the fuck are you doing?"

"Applying for your crew chief position."

I let out a roar of laughter as I waited for the green flag to drop.

"Hey, in all seriousness, be careful out there today. Listen to your body."

I gripped the steering wheel harder as my emotions had me damn near choked up. "It means a lot to me you're here for this."

"I know. I can't wait to rub it in your face when you lose."

With a smile, I shook my head. "Fuck off, asshole."

"One more to go," Russ said into my ears. Damn it was good hearing his voice. I missed this. Missed us chasing each other around in a circle.

As we came around turn four, I said a quick prayer my leg and knee would cooperate today. I was stunned when I got the pole in qualifying. Goes to show this shit was in my blood.

"Green . . . go go go," Russ shouted.

I hit the gas and gave it my all. "Let's do this," I said as I focused on nothing other than winning. Nothing else mattered. The only thing I had in my life was this racecar. As fucking pathetic as that sounded . . . it was true.

A hundred and ten laps in and I could feel my leg and that wasn't a good thing.

"Shit," I mumbled under my breath as I tried to ignore the throbbing around my knee.

Russ counted me down as I came in for a scheduled pit stop. "Five, four, three, two, one."

Dalton barked out orders as I waited for the signal.

"Go, go, go!" Dalton yelled in my ear as I took off in the race off pit road. I only had to get ahead of the number twenty. He was a rookie and I hadn't raced against him yet. Little bastard was trying to do his best to get around me. Either he would be going into the wall or I would be and I was going to make damn sure it wasn't me.

"Twenty to go . . . wreck in turn two. Stay on the apron."

Oh fuck.

I was going into the turn blind, with only Russ telling me where to go. It's not like I hadn't done it a million times, but this was the first time since my accident. The sweat was pouring down my face as my heart practically beat out of my chest.

"Go. You're clear."

I hadn't realized I had been holding my breath until I blew it out.

"How ya doing, Wallace?" Dalton asked.

My leg was feeling numb. The pain no longer there . . . it was replaced by numbness. "Fine," was my only response.

"Ten to go."

"Where's the twenty?" I asked.

"A car length back and falling. You're coming up to lap traffic. Stay on your run. Stay outside."

I did like Russ said. The adrenaline was pumping through my body and I loved every second of it. Fuck I missed this. The only thing that would make it better was if Paislie was waiting for me on the bus. I couldn't imagine what it would be like to fuck her on the high I was on right now.

A memory hit me hard as I sucked in a breath.

"You only want me after you've won a race, Malcolm. I want to know you want me all the time. Not just when you're pumped up from winning."

The memory of Casey flashing through my mind had me confused. I'd never thought of her when I was in a car. Never. This was my escape from all of that.

"Focus, Wallace! You're sliding all over the fucking place."

I shook my head to clear my thoughts.

"One to go. One. To. Go. Keep your line; you're clear all the way. Twenty is dropping back."

Is this fucking for real? My first race back and I'm going to win. Hell yes!

Coming out of turn four, I gripped the steering wheel like it was my lifeline. The checkered flag dropped and all I heard were cheers.

Dalton went crazy screaming in my ear. He finally settled down enough to say, "Welcome home, Malcolm. Welcome home."

The words hit me like a brick wall.

Home.

Was this what I wanted? Week after week, racing around a track chasing after what? What in the hell was I running from? The ghost of a dead girlfriend? The rush that used to be better than sex? The drive to win no matter what the cost?

I pulled up and took the checkered flag as everyone stood on their feet. The feeling was amazing and I proved I could do it. I proved I could come back and win a race. Bad leg or not, I fucking did it.

But at what cost?

THE INTERVIEWS WERE OVER. THE pictures done. I was exhausted and clearly limping on my leg. No one said a word. They didn't even bother to ask, except for Dalton and I brushed it off as being stiff.

Walking up to the bus, I saw her standing there.

"Malcolm, it's been a long time."

With a nod, I kissed her on both cheeks. "It's been a while, Kathleen."

She smiled and motioned for the bus. "Shall we head inside?"

I knew what I was about to do was wrong, but I didn't care. There wasn't much I cared about anymore.

thirty

PAISLIE

"PAISLIE? IS THAT YOU?"

Glancing up from my book, I saw Peter. "Peter Clarkson!" I finally remembered his last name. "Oh my gosh, is that you?"

With a nod of his head, I jumped up and walked into his arms. "It's so good seeing you."

He pulled back and laughed. "It's been a while." His eyes roamed over my body and lit up. "You haven't changed a bit, Paislie. Still beautiful and still rocking a sinful body that caused me plenty of Our Fathers during confession."

My cheeks warmed as his eyes grew darker. Peter had been my first, and boy did we have a past together.

"Stop it," I said as I motioned for him to sit down.

He pulled the chair out and took a seat. I couldn't help but notice his body. Holy hell . . . he must work out six hours a day to have a body like that.

"I can't believe I ran into you. What a crazy small world," he said with a smile that pulled something out from the past and hit me right smack in the face.

Lust.

Want.

Desire.

How I had a crush on him at one point. Then he went off and left me to join the Army and get as far away from St. Patrick's as he could. I didn't blame him because I knew how he felt. Both of us wanted out. I had always felt so comfortable with him. He was just another man who left me.

Clearing my throat, I nodded. "Totally. What have you been up to?"

"Came to visit some friends."

His eyes were hungry as he looked at me. Swallowing hard, I tried to keep myself in check. For weeks I had buried myself in my apartment with Princess as I mourned the loss of Malcolm. My mind drifted back to my conversation with Elizabeth.

My head was buried as I knelt silently in the nave of my beloved St. Patrick's. My safe haven and the only place I'd ever truly felt loved.

"Paislie, you look troubled."

I lifted my head to see Elizabeth, my dearest friend, standing alongside Father Tim. With a smile, I stood and made my way to them both. Elizabeth wrapped me in her arms and I finally let go of the tears I had been trying to hold back.

"I'll leave you be," Father Tim said as I pulled back and quickly wiped away the evidence of my weakness. He smiled and my heart felt light. I had always had suspicions that Father Tim and Elizabeth carried a torch for one another. They were both young and attractive. "Paislie, I'd love to see you sitting in the pews this Sunday."

My face flushed as I looked down in guilt. "Yes, father, I'll be there." And I would. If I made a promise to either one of them, I always kept it.

"Good. It will do your heart good to sit in the Lord's house more often." He flashed me a bigger smile and gave Elizabeth a slight nod before turning and walking away.

Reaching for my hand, Elizabeth guided me to the front pew. "Talk to me, Paislie. I'm filled with worry."

Her eyes looked me over as she pulled me down into a seated position. "You've lost weight."

With a shrug, I barely said, "I haven't been hungry."

"What happened?"

With a dry laugh, I shook my head and looked up at the crucifix. "I let him into my heart. Gave him a piece of myself that I swore I'd never give away."

Elizabeth took my hand in hers. "Do you love him?"

A single tear rolled down my cheek. "I thought I did. Maybe I longed for some-one to love me so much, I deceived my own heart into thinking I was in love."

"Did he do something to hurt you?"

I jerked my head to look at her. "No." His blue eyes invaded my thoughts as I closed my eyes and whispered, "He treated me like a princess."

"Did you get scared?"

I shook my head. "I didn't run because things were getting serious." With a chuckle, I looked back at her. "There were moments I fantasized about having a family with him."

Elizabeth smiled. "Paislie, that's wonderful."

My smile faded. "It was until he started pulling back. Flirting with other women. He might have been sleeping with someone else, I have no clue. He lied to me about his knee; he went behind my back."

Concern washed over her face. "What did he do?"

I stood up and shook my hands, trying to shake away the feeling of dread looming in my heart. "Elizabeth, I just want to forget him. Forget men all together. I want a simple life like yours."

She pulled her head back and laughed. "You think my life is simple, Paislie? That I don't struggle with the feelings you struggle with?"

My eyes widened. "Well . . . I . . . I'm not sure."

She shook her head. "Paislie, I've been fighting a demon of my own for some time. The heart is one that is hard to deny when it falls in love."

I sucked in a breath of air. "Father Tim?"

She swallowed hard. "All I'm trying to say is that even though your head is telling you walking away was the answer, it might be time to listen to your heart."

My head dropped as I slowly shook it.

"Listening to my heart has only ever lead to hurt." Lifting my eyes to hers, I pressed my lips together. "I'm tired of being hurt."

She wrapped me in her arms as I let myself cry one more time. After that I would never shed another tear for Malcolm Wallace again.

"Paislie? Earth to Paislie?"

I laughed and shook my head as I looked Peter in the eyes. "I guess I got lost in a memory."

With a lift of his eyebrow, he tilted his head and gave me the sexiest smile ever. "Oh yeah? I hope you picked a good one."

Was I really going to do this? Go right back to my old habits of getting lost in sex?

I took every inch of him in. Damn, I bet he's good in bed. I quickly imagined his rock hard body over mine.

My phone buzzed, pulling me out of my naughty thoughts. When I glanced down it was a reminder telling me the NASCAR race was on.

Reaching down, I dismissed it.

"NASCAR? I never imagined you would follow that."

Attempting to swallow the frog in my throat, I casually asked, "Do you?"

His face lit up. "I was going to meet a few buddies to watch the race. One of the drivers is making his comeback race."

"Malcolm Wallace," I whispered.

Peter pointed to me. "Yes! How did you know?"

With a fake smile, I replied, "I was his physical therapist during his recovery."

His tongue moved over his bottom lip. "Why is that so fucking hot sounding?"

Heat surged to my lower stomach as I focused in on his lips. "Peter, how would you feel about skipping that race and heading back to my place to catch up a little better?"

"What race?" he replied as he stood and reached for my hand.

I packed up my things. "I walked here."

His breathing picked up a bit as he said, "My rental is right around the corner."

Pulling in a deep breath, I slowly let it out as I tilted my head and gave him another once over. Making sure I eye fucked the hell out of him.

"Lead the way."

Twenty minutes later and we were all over each other in his car that was parked in front of my apartment building.

"Fucking hell, I don't want to screw you in my car, Paislie."

I crawled over him and began grinding myself against his hard dick. God he felt big. It had been too long since I had an orgasm and my body was screaming for relief.

"You haven't changed at all, baby. So responsive."

I ignored his comment and focused on giving myself the much-needed orgasm. The thin layer of my panties was soaked as my relief built.

"Peter . . . oh God!"

He grabbed onto my ass and pulled me closer to him and kissed me. It was nothing like Malcolm's kisses. My body didn't tremble, my stomach didn't flutter, and I felt absolutely nothing.

Just like before, mindless sex to hide the pain.

His fingers pushed my panties out of the way as he slipped them inside of me. Before Malcolm, I would have been pumping my hips against Peter's hand. Guiding him on how to fuck me with his fingers.

"Fuck waiting," Peter mumbled as he pushed me off some and unzipped his pants.

"Condom?" I gasped.

Peter magically made one appear in his hand as he placed it in his mouth and rubbed the tip of his dick against me.

Instead of it turning me on more, it made my stomach turn.

Everything felt wrong. Me on him, his hands on me, his dick pressed against my body.

No.

This isn't what I want.

"Wait," I panted as I placed my hands on his chest.

Stopping him now would be a total bitch move and I knew it. I slid off of him and wrapped my hand around his dick, moving it up and down slowly as he dropped his head back.

"Jesus . . . you've gotten better at hand jobs."

I smiled as I fought to keep the bile down.

"Suck on me, Paislie. Show me what you've learned."

I swallowed hard. I hated what I was doing and I sure as hell didn't want to put his dick in my mouth. It dawned on me it was the middle of the morning and anyone could walk by and see us.

Looking around quickly, I sped my hand up as he pumped his hips. "Oh fuck."

Twisting and pulling, I quickly had him calling out my name as he covered his dick and came in his hand.

"Fucking hell, that was nice."

Nice? What a dick.

When he opened his eyes he looked at me. "Your turn."

I shook my head and chewed on the corner of my lip. "Peter, I'm sorry I led you on. I . . . well I recently broke up with my boyfriend and I thought I was ready to do this, but I can't. Hell, I mean . . . I want to . . . but I'm not ready."

His eyes softened. "Is that why you finished me off with your hand?"

I slowly nodded. He grabbed a shirt that had been in the back seat and cleaned himself up. When he was finished, he placed his hand on the back of my neck and pulled me closer to him. His lips softly kissed mine. I wanted to feel something so desperately, but I felt nothing.

Peter sat back and searched my face. "He really hurt you?"

With a shrug, I winked and said, "Should be used to it, right?"

He slowly shook his head. "No. And I'm glad you stopped us, Paislie. I would never want you to do something you didn't want to do."

With a weak grin, I shook my head. "I wonder what would have happened if you hadn't left."

His face grew into a huge smile as his cheeks flushed. "I would have gone to college, struggled to pay my way, asked you to marry me and you probably would have said yes because we are the only thing we ever knew. Maybe had a kid or two and probably would have ended up divorcing by the time we hit thirty."

I couldn't help it as I busted out laughing. "You've thought about this?"

He shook his head as he chuckled. "Nah, but I have thought about you a lot."

"Be careful out there fighting for our country," I whispered as I leaned over and kissed him lightly on the lips. "Enjoy the race."

On that note, I quickly got out of the car. "Wait. At least let me walk you up to your apartment."

I narrowed my eyes as he held up his hands. "I honestly only want to use your bathroom super quick and I swear I'll behave."

Before motioning for him to head in, I caught a glimpse of a man standing across the street.

Ugh. He probably just got off by watching us in the car.

Turning quickly, I shut the door and silently made a vow that I'd never try public sex in the daytime ever again.

MALCOLM

KATHLEEN WALKED ONTO THE BUS and placed a manila envelope on the counter before turning and looking back at me. "It's been
a while since you've sought me out for work."

Reaching into the refrigerator, I grabbed a beer for each of us. She
reached her hand out and happily took it. I popped the top off and took a
long drink.

"Congrats on the win by the way."

With a fake smile, I replied, "Thanks."

She gave me that look only a mother could give as she waited patiently
for me to explain why I had asked her to have Paislie followed for the last
few weeks.

"I just wanted to make sure she's okay."

"Did you hurt her? Break up with her or something?"

"Something like that."

Kathleen dragged in a deep breath and quickly expelled it as she
opened the envelope.

"I didn't do the work. I had one of my guys who works the Dallas area
for me on it. From the reports it seems like your girl has had herself buried inside her apartment and barely ever leaves."

My head pulled back. "Work?"

"She's going to work, but that's about all. She does go to St. Patrick's a
lot and recently started going on Sundays."

I couldn't help the small smile that played across my face. I knew how
much that church and Sister Elizabeth meant to Paislie.

"Looks like she has a friend by the name of Annie McCarthy. She stops by often but they never go out. She usually brings take out and stays for a few hours before leaving."

My heart sank, but at the same time I was relieved to know Paislie hadn't been going out or seeing anyone.

"But then today I got a call from my guy. Said he was sending me some pictures. Looks like your girl met someone at a small café earlier this morning. Couldn't get info on the guy; he was driving a rental car."

I swallowed hard. "She met a guy? You said she had breakfast with him?"

She smirked and shook her head as she pulled out some pictures. "They had more than breakfast."

Placing the pictures on the counter, my heart leapt to my throat and I instantly felt sick to my stomach. The pictures showed Paislie on top of the guy in a car.

"Did they . . . were they having sex?" I asked clearing my throat.

Kathleen shook her head. "He said it looked more like foreplay, but at one point the guy had a condom in his mouth and your girl crawled off of him. Finished the job with her hand."

Turning away before Kathleen could see the rage on my face, I closed my eyes and counted to ten.

I drew in a deep breath and slowly blew it out. "What about after that?"

"He went up to her apartment. My guy had to leave because Paislie looked directly at him so he took off."

Both hands went up to my head as I pushed my fingers through my hair and cursed under my breath.

"I'm going to safely guess you still have feelings for the girl since you're paying me to keep tabs on her."

My arms dropped to my sides. Paislie had moved on. "I don't need you to watch her anymore, Kath. Let me know what I owe you and I'll have Janet get it over to you as soon as possible."

"Okay. You're the boss." I could hear her gathering up the pictures and sliding them back into the envelope. "Do you want the pictures?"

As much as I wanted to tell her to find out whatever she could on the asshole Paislie was fucking, I didn't. With a slow shake of my head, I turned back to her. "Burn them."

With a quick nod, she walked over to the small stove. She turned it on, lit the corner of the envelope and dropped it into the sink.

"Malcolm, I know you're not asking, but may I offer you a bit of advice?"

Kathleen had been a family friend for as long I could remember. I had her investigate the guy who hit me, resulting in Casey dying. She also did a background check on Janet before she came to work for me.

With a weak smile, I said, "I'm all ears."

"Instead of having her followed around to make sure she's okay, why don't you find out yourself? She obviously is hurting from what ever happened between the two of you and you care enough about her to see what she's doing."

Letting out a gruff laugh, I said, "She must not be that upset if she's fucking some guy in a car for a little afternoon delight."

She shot me a dirty look. "I don't think she had sex with the guy. My thoughts are she was going to, decided not to and finished him off to lessen the blow."

I stared at her like she was insane. "He went up to her apartment with her. Maybe they decided they weren't into the public sex thing after all."

She shrugged. "You'll never know unless you go to her."

"I can't."

"Why?"

My heart was pounding in my chest as I clenched my fists together. I was so angry for what I did to Paislie I wanted to punch myself. "I promised her I wouldn't hurt her and I did. She'll never trust me again."

Kathleen looked at me before turning and heading to the door. She opened it and was about to step out when she said, "That's the crazy thing about love."

I waited for her to finish her sentence but she didn't, causing me to ask, "What's the crazy thing about love?"

"If she truly loves you, she'll risk it all for you."

With that, she was out the door and gone as I glanced at the burning pictures in my sink. I brought my beer up to my lips and finished it off as I turned the water on and put out the small fire.

With a frustrated moan, I glanced up and saw Deuce lying on the sofa. "You still mad at me?"

He lifted his brows but never moved. "I know, boy. I miss her too."

The rest of the week flew by with meetings, strategizing about the race, practice runs and interviews. My mind wasn't focused and I knew Dalton and everyone else could see it. When the knock on my bus came, I knew exactly who it was going to be from.

Opening the door, I grinned and motioned for him to come in.

Emmit walked in and took a look around before heading over and sitting down next to my damn dog. "Hey boy, how's it going?"

The traitor gave him a few licks before looking at me and barking.

"Little fucker. He's two seconds from being taken to the pound."

Emmit laughed and gave Deuce a rub down before looking back at me. "So, how did the first race feel after being gone so long?"

With a cocky smile, I shrugged. "It's like riding a bike."

"How's your leg?"

"Hurts like a son-of-a-bitch." There was no sense in lying to him. I knew he would see right through it.

"Taking anything?"

I shook my head.

Emmit nodded and took a look around. "Do you miss it?"

With a smile, he glanced back my way. "Ya know, I thought for sure I would. That thrill you get from racing around the track. God how I've loved that feeling for so damn long."

I chuckled. "Tell me about it."

His eyes turned serious. "Addie's pregnant. We're expecting another baby to arrive on Valentine's Day."

I stood up and reached my hand out. "Holy shit, dude. Congratulations. Planned?"

He shook my hand and smiled bigger. "Yep. Not the due date though. That was all Mother Nature on that one."

"You hoping for a boy or a girl?"

With a shrug, he replied, "Don't care, as long as the baby is healthy and Addie has a smooth pregnancy. I'll take whatever he gives us."

I sat across from him and laughed. "Damn. It's crazy to think you're gonna have another one."

"Yeah, tell me about it. To answer your question though, I do miss racing, especially the adrenaline rush I got out of it. But I don't really know how to explain it, the rush I get from being with Addie and Landon is ten times better. It's different . . . but so much better. I think the decision I made was the best decision of my life."

"Really?" I asked as I thought about how happy Emmit looked. There was something so different about him. He seemed at ease.

With a slap of his hands on his legs, he pointed to me and said, "So, let's talk about you."

I held out my left arm and said, "Got another tattoo. That's about all that's new in my world."

His eyebrow lifted. "Yeah, I'm pretty sure I didn't get a phone call asking me to fly here because you got a new tattoo."

I leaned back and stared into his eyes. "Who called? Dalton?"

"Yep."

"Asshole."

Emmit let out a small laugh. "He cares about you, Malcolm. Your whole team cares about you and he said you're not focused at all."

"Well fuck, what does he expect! I've been gone for a few months. I came back and won my first fucking race. Give me a damn break."

He remained silent as I sat there and let the events of the last week replay in my mind. I knew what I wanted and I was miserable because I didn't have it.

I stood up and cursed.

"Fucking hell. I can't do it, Emmit. I thought I wanted this. It was the only thing I ever knew. The only thing I ever thought I was good at. Then she came into my life and turned it fucking upside down. I can't eat, sleep, or think straight. She's got me hiring a damn private detective to follow her."

"What?" Emmit asked as he stood up. "You didn't."

My hands scrubbed over my face as I let out a frustrated moan. "I don't know whether I'm coming or going anymore."

"Have you tried to talk to her?"

"No. I called her Casey."

Emmit's eyes widened as he scrunched his damn face up. "Tell me she didn't know who Casey was."

"No . . . she knew. I'm not sure how, but she knew."

Emmit walked into the kitchen and grabbed a beer from the refrigerator. Opening it, he handed it to me. "Why did you call her Casey?"

My hand pushed through my dark hair. "Fuck if I know. I honestly have no idea. Maybe it was because she had started to lecture me about driving and Casey used to do that. The only difference is Paislie wasn't trying to keep me from racing . . . she was trying to keep me from hurting myself more. Or worse yet, someone else."

Emmit leaned back against the counter and folded his arms across his chest. "So?"

The way he was looking at me, as if I had the answer to everything, pissed me off. "So? So what?"

"Do you love her?"

It felt as if time stood still after Emmit asked me that one simple question. It was simple because it should have been easy to answer, yet I was struggling with my answer.

"No."

He lifted his brows and looked me right in the eyes. "No. You don't love her?"

"I'm not what she needs, Emmit. I'm not what she deserves."

"And that is?" he asked with a smug look.

I felt nauseous as I struggled to keep talking. "Someone who will devote his entire world to her. Not someone who is going to lie and go behind her back. Treat her like dirt instead of confide in her when I'm pissed off at the world. She needs a guy who will make a promise to her and keep it. I didn't do any of that."

"You fucked up, Malcolm. Don't you think she's worth trying to find out if she'll give you another chance?"

The pictures Kathleen showed me popped into my head. "She's moved on, so it's really a moot point."

Emmit laughed as he shook his head. "You really are a thick headed son-of-a-bitch, aren't you?"

"Fuck you, Lewis. You can stand there and judge me with your perfect little world. You got what you wanted."

"I did," he replied with a smirk.

"Well good for you, because I don't want that life."

"I never said you did."

Anger was beginning to build as I balled my fists. "Yeah, well good. The last thing I want to be is tied down with some clingy-ass woman and a bunch of kids running around screaming and yelling."

Deuce took that moment to jump down and run to the door and bark.

"Fuck!" I shouted.

"You want to get rid of the dog too?"

I flashed him a dirty look.

"I get the feeling you want exactly what I have, Malcolm, and you want it with Paislie."

Walking up to Emmit, I grabbed him by the shirt and pushed him against the wall. "Shut the fuck up, Emmit or I swear I'll punch you."

He never once made a move to stop me. "Why don't you tell me the real reason you're pissed off, Wallace?"

I pushed him as hard as I could before turning and grabbing the dog's leash. "Please be gone by the time I get back."

Emmit grabbed my arm and pulled me to a stop. "Don't let her go. I've made the mistake of letting the woman I loved go and lost out on so much time. Trust me, Malcolm, you've got to let the guilt of Casey and the past go and look at what you have waiting for you now."

Yanking my arm free, I turned away from him and pushed the door open. I needed air to breathe. Emmit was right behind me as I dragged in a deep breath of air.

I stared off toward the lights of the track as I slowly shook my head. "I'm no good for her. I'll end up hurting her again and I'd rather die than see that look in her eyes like I saw before she left." Looking over my shoulder at Emmit, I whispered, "If I stay away from her . . . I can't hurt her."

Emmit called out my name as I quickly started walking away with Deuce.

PAISLIE

"SO, DO YOU WANT TO tell me what's on your mind, Paislie?"

I looked at Elizabeth with a questioning look. "Nothing. Why?"

She shrugged and replied, "Let's see, where should I start? You've been coming to mass for the last few Sundays. I've found you sitting in that same pew at least once a week with your head bowed down in prayer for the last month, you look like you've lost about ten pounds, you have dark circles, and your eyes hold a look of sadness."

I snarled my lip at her as she talked.

"Shall I keep going?"

Shaking my head, I said, "No. Please stop before you really depress me more than I already am."

She bit out a laugh then took a drink of her tea.

I pushed my food around on my plate before peeking back at her. "My eyes look sad?"

With a nod, she took a bite of her chicken potpie. "Yep."

"How do you know it's sad? Maybe I'm just tired from working this week."

Her head snapped up as she peered at me. "I know sadness when I see it. It's a look I've seen many times in my own eyes."

My breath stalled as I chewed the corner of my lip. "Elizabeth, do you regret—"

"No."

My mouth dropped open. "You don't even know what I was going to ask you!" I exclaimed.

"I do. You were going to ask if I regretted becoming a nun. You always ask me that when you think I've been locked away for years crying my eyes out from a long lost love."

Dropping back in my seat, I stared at her. "Father Tim."

Her gaze fell.

I knew it!

I knew she had feelings for him.

"Does he feel the same way about you?" I asked as I reached across the table for her hand.

Her silence was my answer.

"Elizabeth, you can't go through life denying how your heart feels."

She laughed and shook her head. "I'm not sure I should be taking advice from someone who clearly is hiding from her own feelings."

"Ouch!" I said as I shot her a dirty look. "If you weren't a nun I might tell you to fuck off."

"Paislie Pruitt, ask for forgiveness this instant!"

With an evil grin, I shook my head. "Maybe we should just get an apartment together and buy a few more cats. I'll pine over Malcolm and you'll dream of what sex might be like with Tim. I obviously can't call him Father Tim, because that would be weird."

"Dear Lord above." With her hands, she made the cross symbol over her chest. "Paislie, you cannot talk about a man of the cloth like that! Especially *that* man!"

With a frown, I tossed a piece of bread in my mouth and asked, "Why not? He's a man even if he is a priest."

Elizabeth rolled her eyes and took another bite of food.

With a pop of my head, I gave her a smirk. "Look me in the eyes and tell me you haven't thought about him like that, even in your dreams?"

She swallowed hard and said in a quiet voice, "Paislie, I'm certainly not going to tell you what my dreams are."

With a huge grin, I leaned back in the chair and folded my arms over my chest. "So you have had naughty dreams about him."

"Stop!" she shouted as I clamped my mouth shut.

Giving her an oh shit look, I asked, "Too much?"

Reaching for her water, she dipped her fingers in and flicked water on herself. I couldn't help it . . . I busted out laughing.

When I glanced over her shoulder and saw Father, er, Tim walking up, my laughter stopped on a dime and I mumbled, "Oh no."

I sat up and quickly ate as I looked directly at my food.

"Why hello there, Paislie, Elizabeth. How are you both doing today?"

When I peeked up, Elizabeth was giving me a look of horror. Oh hell. Wait until she turned around and saw him. It was his day off and he was dressed in jogging pants and a tight blue T-shirt. I had to admit I was impressed that his body was as nice as it was. Of course, he was only in his mid-thirties and I knew he worked out often.

I slowly shook my head in an attempt to warn Elizabeth.

Don't. Do. It. Don't look at him, Elizabeth.

Elizabeth took a deep breath and turned slightly as she looked up. Her eyes widened and the only thing I saw was a look of pure desire move across her face. Clearly he saw it too, because Tim's breathing picked up.

Elizabeth seductively bit down on her lip. "Oh my Lord," she mumbled as I kicked her under the table, causing her to get her wits about her. The table nearly fell over when she stood quickly.

"Tim . . . um . . . Father . . . oh, ah um I mean . . . Father Tim . . . Tim."

Holy crap. I'd never seen Elizabeth stumble over her words before.

"Elizabeth, are you okay?" he asked as he reached out for her. When she jerked away from him, she tripped over the chair and almost fell.

"Elizabeth!" I cried out as I jumped up. Tim quickly grabbed her before she fell.

When she pushed out of his arms, she turned to look at me for help. Of course I picked that time to wiggle my eyebrows and glanced down to his pants in the exact location of what she longed for. She gasped and said, "I've got to go. I'm late!"

Tim and I stood there and watched as she practically knocked people over in her attempt to get away as fast as she could.

"Is she feeling okay today?" Tim asked.

Pressing my lips together, I shrugged. "I think she hasn't been getting much sleep."

"Really? I wonder why?"

"Dreams, forbidden dreams about something she can't have," was all I said as I saw his head snap over in my direction.

I'm totally going to Hell for this.

WITH THE BOWL OF POPCORN, a bag of black licorice, and three Diet Cokes, I sat down on the sofa and turned on the race. I wasn't sure if I should watch it or not. Last week Malcolm nearly wrecked three times and I swore I wasn't going to watch another race. The problem was I was letting my heart call the shots and not my head, therefore I was sitting down and getting ready to settle in as they were doing a few warm up laps before the race went green.

My phone buzzed as I picked it up to see a text from Annie.

Annie: Let's go out tonight? I need dick.

Rolling my eyes, I let out a chuckle.

Me: I can't. Princess and I are watching movies.

Annie: Pussy. Don't' you mean you're stalking your man on TV? Jesus Christ will you snap the hell out of it. You need to get fucked and as soon as possible.

I knew she was probably right. On both accounts. I was somewhat stalking Malcolm on a daily basis. I did a Google search of him every night before I went to bed. Not really sure what I was looking for . . . or hoping not to find . . . but each night I held my breath and typed in his name.

The moment I saw a picture of him, a warm feeling rushed through my body. Maybe I did need to go out. Even some mindless touching and kissing might be kind of nice. What harm would come of a little innocent fun?

I was about to text Annie back that I would go out with her when the announcer mentioned Malcolm's name and my breathing stopped.

"Looks like Malcolm Wallace is having a bit of trouble again this week."

I swore I could feel my heart beating in my ears. I needed something of Malcolm and if it had to be just the mention of his name, then so be it.

Me: Enjoy your night and get enough dick for both of us.

Annie: Pussy.

Me: You called me that already. Be careful! Love ya!

Annie: Tomorrow I'm dragging your ass somewhere. Love you too!

I dropped my phone next to me on the sofa and turned up the television.

"I've started wondering if his leg really is giving him trouble and that's what has him so distracted."

My lower lip tingled when I realized I was chewing the living hell out of it. Closing my eyes, I said a prayer that Malcolm would be okay. I didn't know why I was torturing myself by watching him race. I hadn't heard anything from him since the day I walked away. Even when they delivered my stuff along with Princess, there wasn't even so much as a note. I wasn't sure what broke my heart more. The fact that I was hoping he would reach out to me, or the fact that he hadn't reached out to me.

Pushing a handful of popcorn into my mouth, I picked up my phone and checked my email. There was one more lap before the race started. The name Emmit Lewis stood out like a sore thumb on my phone and I knew instantly that was the Emmit who used to race with Malcolm.

I clicked the email and opened it as I started to read it. My eyes drifted up to the television as I watched the race. What happened next had me jumping up and knocking the popcorn to the ground.

My hands covered my mouth as I whispered, "Oh God, Malcolm."

Thirty three

MALCOLM

STOOD AND STARED DOWN at the gravestone as I took in a deep breath. It was the first time I had been here since the day Casey was buried.

My hands were in my pockets as I fought to say the words I had been fighting to say since the day she died.

With a slight smile, I shook my head and said, "I quit racing. I was half a lap away from starting a race and I pulled down onto pit road and just drove back to the garage. You'd be happy; I know how much you really hated me racing. I loved it though and for the longest time, it helped me deal with the guilt of you dying. I guess not so much of you dying, but the fact that I've never been able to promise you what you asked for right before you died.

"I need you to know that I loved you, Casey, but I think even then I knew deep in my heart what we had wasn't going to be forever. I sometimes wonder if God took you because he knew I couldn't make that promise to only love you.

"For so many years I avoided the idea of falling in love with anyone. I wasn't sure if it was because if I did, then it would make it all too real and I knew I wouldn't be able to give you what you asked."

Kicking at a stick, I closed my eyes and drew in a deep breath before slowly letting it out. "I met someone, Casey. She's changed the way I look at everything in my life. That rush I longed for that I got by racing or doing crazy shit like jumping out of planes, I didn't need it any longer. The only thing I need is to see her smile. Feel her touch. She's the rush I've been searching for this whole time."

Tears built in my eyes as I stared at her name etched into the stone.

"I can't promise myself to you forever because I promised my heart to Paislie. I think before I even met her my heart was hers. I kept it guarded, waiting for her to bump into me and give me that smile that I would see every time I closed my eyes. I tried to move on with other women and none of them ever made my heart feel so alive like she does."

The warmth from a single tear felt like it burned a path on my face as it slowly continued on before I reached up and wiped it away. I placed the single yellow rose, Casey's favorite, on the ground and took a few steps back.

"I never knew I was holding onto my past until I saw the hurt in Paislie's eyes and I never want to see that again. I love her, Casey, and for the longest time it hurt knowing that I loved her more than I loved you. The guilt was confusing at first, but I realized had you not died that night, I would have come to my senses before I promised you something I wouldn't have been able to give to you. You see, Casey, my heart has been waiting for Paislie and it's time I let go of the past and look to my future. I'll never forget you, Casey, but it's time for me to say goodbye."

The feeling of a huge weight was instantly lifted off my shoulders as I took a few steps back and turned around. I was frozen in place by her emerald eyes.

"Paislie?"

She quickly wiped her tears away as she gave me the smile I had been longing to see for the last few months.

We both walked toward one another and stopped as we got within a few inches of each other.

My eyes searched her face as I whispered, "I can't breathe without you. I need you to know that. You're everything I need."

A small sob escaped her mouth as she brought her hands up to her lips. "I'll do whatever I have to do to beg for your forgiveness. I swear to you, Paislie, I will never hurt you again. I don't need you to save me . . . I need you to love me as much as I love you."

Her hands dropped to her sides as her eyes peered into mine. The ache in the back of my throat was almost unbearable as I waited for her to speak.

"Why did you drive off the track the other day?"

My hands reached for hers as I watched her breath catch. "Because in that very moment it hit me."

"What hit you?"

I pulled her body closer to mine. "That what I wanted wasn't on the racetrack or in that car. It wasn't the rush I got from living my life on the edge."

My thumbs wiped her tears away as I leaned down and softly kissed her lips. "It was seeing your beautiful smile every day. Hearing your voice first thing in the morning, feeling you in my arms as I drift off to sleep. Paislie, I love you and I want to spend the rest of my life showing you how much I love you. I have no idea why I called you Casey that day but I swear to you, I've never thought of you as a replacement. I love you, Paislie. God I love you, and only you, more than anything in this life of mine. You're the reason I wake up each day."

Her hands came up and grabbed onto my arms. "Please tell me I'm not dreaming."

A wicked smile crept over my face. "How about if I show you?"

We were soon lost in a kiss. I never wanted to let her out of my sight again. When we finally pulled back for air, I searched her face. "Wait. How did you know I was here?"

She smiled and said, "Your friend, Emmit."

My head pulled back in confusion. "Emmit?"

"He sent me an email, we talked on the phone, and I meet him and his beautiful wife and son this morning."

I looked over her shoulder to see Emmit leaning against a car, giving me a fucking grin from ear to ear.

I shook my head and snickered. "I told him I was letting go of my past today . . . I guess he's smarter than I gave him credit for."

Paislie giggled and lightly hit my chest. Taking her hand in mine, we headed over to Emmit. He pushed off the car and reached his hand out for mine.

"Glad to see you took my advice."

With a chuckle, I gave him a light push. "Glad to see you didn't give up on me."

"Nah. I was even thinking, now that you followed in my footsteps and seeing how much Addie and I miss Texas, maybe we should talk about a future together."

"Now, Emmit, I know we've moved into a comfortable area with our friendship, but I don't think I'm ready to take it any further."

His smile faded as he pinched his brows together. "That's not what I meant, asshole. I'm talking about going into business together."

I was certainly intrigued. "What did you have in mind?"

Emmit stole a glance over to Paislie and then back to me. "Why don't you two get . . . caught up on things first. Addie and I are staying at a bed and breakfast in Waco. How about we meet for breakfast tomorrow."

Warmth radiated through my body at the idea of being with Paislie. "Let's make it lunch."

Both Emmit and Paislie laughed as he shook my hand and said, "Deal. I'll wait for your call tomorrow."

Paislie dropped my hand and walked up to Emmit. She reached up and kissed him on the cheek. "Thank you for everything."

Emmit's eyes softened as he nodded and said, "You're welcome. I'll talk to y'all tomorrow."

Paislie and I stood and watched Emmit drive off before I turned her to me. "If I take you home, Sophie is going to freak and want you to play pretty pretty princess or some shit like that."

She frowned. "Emmit just drove off with my bag that had all my stuff in it."

Reaching into my pocket for my phone, I hit Janet's number.

"Hey, boss."

"Janet, I need you to see if the Russell place is available. The cottage."

"Oh my goodness! Please tell me she's with you."

I couldn't help but smile like a fool. "Yes ma'am, she is standing right here."

Paislie blushed and looked down. "Okay, I'm on the other line, give me two seconds."

My hand slipped behind her hair as I pulled her to me. Our lips crashed together and quickly grew hungry as Paislie's hands moved to my chest. Her low moan vibrated through my entire body.

"You're a go! They're all in California."

Pulling my lips from Paislie's, I panted, "Thanks."

Not giving her time to answer, I hit End, shoved my phone back in my pocket and picked Paislie up as she squealed in delight.

"I missed you, baby," I said as I let her slowly slide down my body and pushed her against my truck, pinning her with my body.

Tears were threatening to build in her eyes as her chin trembled. "I missed you too. So very much."

"God give me strength to get you to the Russell's place. I want nothing more than to rip your panties off and take you right here." Paislie looked around as I said, "Well, maybe not a cemetery, but you know what I mean."

She smiled but then it faded and was replaced by a look of worry. The images of her on that fucker flooded my memory.

"Malcolm, I need to tell you something."

Closing my eyes, I fought to keep the jealousy away. "It doesn't matter what happened when we were apart, Paislie."

When I opened my eyes, she looked so conflicted. "It does to me. I'm not sure if you were with anyone, but I . . . I um . . . well I ran into an old friend who I grew up with in the orphanage. I was feeling really lonely and confused and we went back to my apartment."

I wanted so desperately to tell her to stop talking. The last thing I wanted to hear about was her and this old friend rolling around in bed together. The only reason I held back was it was clear she wanted to get this off her chest.

"Things got a little intense in the car and for a moment I thought I was going to just let him take me there in broad daylight. Before I had a chance to even have an orgasm, I came to my senses and stopped it."

I slowly let out the breath I wasn't even aware I was holding. "Paislie, baby you don't owe me any—"

She put her finger up to my lips. "Please let me finish." I nodded and waited for her to keep talking.

"I felt terrible for getting the poor guy so turned on, so I gave him a hand job. He wanted to take things further but I told him about you and that I wasn't ready."

My heart was pounding against my chest wall as I waited for her to keep telling me what happened. "He asked to come up to my apartment to clean up. I let him and that's all that happened. I didn't even kiss him goodbye."

Thank God.

This whole time I had let myself believe she had sex with him.

I placed my hand on the side of her face and looked deeply into her eyes. "I haven't been with anyone, Paislie."

"Not even . . ."

Her gaze fell as I lifted her chin with my finger and made her look at me. "Not even Ashley. She is madly in love with some computer programmer dude from Dallas. We were only ever meant to be friends."

Paislie chuckled as I opened the door and held her hand while she got in. Before shutting the door, I kissed her gently on the lips. "I really hope we make it and don't stop on the side of the road."

She cocked her head to the side and said, "Patience, Mr. Wallace. I promise it will be worth the wait."

My dick jumped in my pants as I adjusted it and moaned. "Let's get the hell out of here."

Thirty four

PAISLIE

M ALCOLM TALKED MY EAR OFF while he drove to whatever the Russell's was. I prayed like hell it wasn't a bed and breakfast like Emmit and Adaline were staying in. The last thing I wanted was for people to be around us when I screamed out Malcolm's name in pleasure.

My body was in overdrive as I pressed my legs together to keep from sticking my hand down my pants. Each bump Malcolm hit had me moaning internally.

Jesus why am I so horny? Oh wait, maybe it had something to do with the fact I needed to feel the hands of the man I loved on me, bringing me to a state of euphoria like never before.

Trying to focus on what Malcolm was saying, I sucked in a breath when his hand moved further up my leg. He must have noticed because he smiled.

With a snicker, he turned and pulled up to a large iron gate. "We're almost there."

"What is this place?" I asked as he typed in a code.

"The Russell's place."

Horror swept over my body. "Someone's house? Malcolm we can't just go to someone's house and have sex."

He grabbed my hand and kissed the back of it. "Take a deep breath, Paislie. I promise it will be worth it."

I looked back out the front window as Malcolm drove down the long drive. Soon, vineyards appeared on either side of the truck.

"A vineyard?" I asked with excitement.

"A lot of people think the vineyards are all in the hill country, but we have a few hidden jewels up this way."

I couldn't help the silly grin on my face as I looked at the endless grapes hanging from the vines. "It's so beautiful."

"You haven't seen anything yet." Excitement bubbled up in my stomach as I tried to search ahead of us. "You ready?" Malcolm asked as I started laughing.

"For what? You're killing me here! What am I ready for?"

It was then I saw it. I let out a gasp as the French Normandy-style house came into sight. The gothic spires and archways were breathtaking. The closer Malcolm drove, the more I was in awe.

"What is this place?"

With a grin, he replied, "Heaven."

The truck came to a stop as I agreed. "I'll say."

Pushing the truck door open, I jumped out and took in as much as I could. The landscaping was out of this world with fountains sprinkled throughout. It truly was heaven on earth.

"The Russell's bought this place back in nineteen twenty. It has stayed in their family ever since."

He took my hand and led me up to the front door. "Wait. This is someone's actual house. Malcolm, no! We can't just go in there and desecrate their home!"

He threw his head back and laughed. "Trust me, I have their permission to be here. I've been trying to talk them into selling me this place."

My eyes grew wide. "What? As in like buy the house and the vineyard?"

He winked and said, "Yep."

Less than a minute later, I was standing in a grand foyer with my mouth gaped. I wasn't sure where to look first. The wood floors were beautiful, but what really had my attention was the amazing wooden staircase that stood in front of me. It branched off to both the right and left.

"You should see it at Christmas time. They line poinsettias along the stairs leading all the way up. Garland and lights are wrapped around the railing as well. I remember coming here as a young boy and thinking someday I would own this house."

I let out a dry laugh. "You'd have to be a millionaire to afford this place!"

Malcolm lifted his brows as I quickly changed the subject. "How big is it?"

"Over sixteen thousand square feet and four floors."

"Four floors!" I exclaimed.

Taking my hand in his, he walked around. "Two families live here. Each has two floors."

"Wow. I can't even imagine."

Malcolm showed me the lower two floors. The kitchen alone had me drooling. With the off-white cabinets and gourmet cooking appliances, I almost wished I was a good cook. We toured the master bedroom that was at least three times the size of my apartment in Dallas. The giant Jacuzzi-style tub had my thoughts wandering and in a very naughty place.

The other four bedrooms each had their own bathrooms. One had a fireplace in it like the master bedroom.

"So do the other two floors look the same as this?"

"Pretty much. Except on the main floor there is a wine tasting room. Bob Russell, who was the grandson to the original owner, had a tasting room put in years ago when they had the vineyards opened up to the public. But now they simply sell the grapes and no longer make wine on the property."

"Wow. I can't get over how beautiful it is. I would love to see it at Christmas time if they let us."

Malcolm squeezed my hand and pulled me closer to him. "They'll let us. Jonathon, Bob's son is a huge NASCAR fan. I've given him plenty of VIP passes."

With a smirk, I asked, "Is that why they let you just walk around their house?"

He laughed and guided me out the back and down a precious stone path. "Something like that." The feel of his hand on my lower back guiding me was the best feeling in the world.

When we came upon a small cottage, I looked at him. "Please tell me this is our last stop. I'd give anything to feel you inside of me."

Malcolm's eyes turned dark and he practically pulled my arm out of the socket.

Throwing the door open, he pulled me inside and slammed the door shut. My dress was up and over my head before I even had a chance to adjust my eyes to the lower light in the cottage.

His lips crashed against mine while my fingers laced through his hair and grabbed a handful. We were acting like sex-starved teenagers, and I wouldn't have it any other way.

"Malcolm," I moaned into his mouth as he lifted me and I wrapped my legs around him. Pressing me against the door he reached down and released himself.

"I missed you so much, baby," he whispered in my ear.

My head dropped back as I felt his dick tease my entrance. "More," I panted as he pushed in slightly.

Digging my fingers into his shoulders and squeezing my legs tighter, I begged him to give me more.

"I want you so much, Paislie. I'm going to come the moment I slip inside of you."

"Yes!" I cried out. "Please . . . I want you too."

My body was trembling as I anticipated what was going to happen next. Malcolm was going too slow, teasing me to the point where I wanted to scream.

"Damn it, Malcolm. Fuck me!"

That did it. He pushed his dick into me in one movement, causing me to whimper at being filled with him.

"Shit. Baby, did I hurt you?"

I shook my head and wrapped my arms around him. "Don't move," I whispered.

What started out as a desperate need changed the moment he pushed inside of me.

"Jesus, Paislie. No one makes me feel the way you do. I don't need anything in life but this."

Burying my face into his neck, I let my tears fall.

Being careful to not pull out of me, Malcolm brought me over to the sofa and gently laid me down.

His blue eyes locked with mine, while he ran the back of his hand down the side of my cheek. "When you're not with me I can't breathe. It's as if you are the oxygen I need to survive."

A small sob filled the air as I tried to form the words to speak. "No one has ever loved me like you have . . . I've never felt so alive."

He closed his eyes and slowly pulled out and pushed back in. The feeling was beyond any words I could ever use. My heart felt whole for the first time in my life. This was what love felt like.

"Paislie . . . I love you."

"I love you," I whispered as his lips brushed over mine.

My back arched as he continued to make sweet love to me. I didn't want this moment to ever end. Staying in this little cottage with Malcolm buried inside of me was my perfect heaven.

We were in perfect harmony as my hips moved in rhythm with his. The familiar feeling built as Malcolm kissed me gently. The feeling was deliciously slow as I wrapped my legs around him and called out his name. It wasn't long before he pushed in as deep as he could while my name flowed from his lips.

Collapsing on top of me, Malcolm's hot breath hit my neck. We both fought to regain our breathing as he pushed up and gazed into my eyes. "Tell me what you feel this very moment."

The feel of him still inside of me had me smiling. "Blissfully happy. Complete. Loved beyond belief."

His wide grin caused my chest to flutter. "You're a part of me, Paislie. I'm sorry it took me so long to get out of my own head."

I lightly ran my finger along his jawline and over his lips as I softly said, "You were worth the wait." We both let out a chuckle as I lifted my brow. "But, we do have a lot to catch up on."

"Like what?" he asked as he kissed the tip of my nose.

I lifted my eyes as if in thought. "Kissing. We have a lot of missed kisses we need to catch up on."

The crooked smile had my heartbeat quickening. "Kisses got it. What else?"

"Lots and lots of orgasms. At least a hundred."

The feel of his lips sliding across my neck caused me to let out a contented breath. "I bet I can think of ways to make up for those orgasms."

He pulled out of me and slowly moved his hand down and then stopped abruptly.

Closing his eyes, he cursed. "Damn it, let me grab something to clean you up before this gets on their sofa."

My stomach dropped. I had stopped taking my birth control pills over a month ago.

I was frozen still as Malcolm walked back over and cleaned me up. Sitting up, Malcolm gave me a concerned look. "You look white as a ghost."

Oh God. Why did I stop taking them? Why!

"I . . . I got the stomach flu and stopped taking them."

"What are you talking about?"

My stomach started to roll as I felt like I was going to throw up. "My birth control pills. I haven't taken them in over a month."

A look of horror quickly moved over Malcolm's face and I'm sure it matched my own look.

My hand flew over my mouth as I jumped up. "Bathroom!" I called out as Malcolm grabbed my hand and led me to the bathroom down the hall. The moment I stepped up to the toilet, I leaned over and threw up.

"Fuck! Does it happen that fast? W-why are you throwing up? Oh God. Oh God. Fuck, I'm such an idiot! Why didn't I think to ask?"

Malcolm was clearly in panic mode, as was I. Only I was throwing my guts up and chanting the same thing he was currently yelling.

When I had nothing left to throw up and the dry heaves stopped, I took off my bra and took in a few deep breaths. Turning the shower on, I stepped inside and softly sighed in relief. The feel of the hot water hitting my body felt amazing.

When I felt Malcolm's hands wrap around my body, I was instantly calmed. "Whatever happens it'll be okay."

I nodded my head as my tears mixed with the hot water. It's not that I didn't want to have a child, I did. Very much so. I just didn't want one now. Malcolm and I were just back together and there were so many things I wanted to learn and do with him.

"I know," I finally said.

He turned me around and cupped my face in his hands. "I don't want you to think I don't want to have kids because I do."

With a deep breath in, I smiled. "I do too, but not now. I think it's important we spend time together first, but . . . if . . . I mean . . . if I—"

Pulling me into his arms, Malcolm held me tight. "We aren't going to sit here and do the what if's. Let's just wait and see."

"Wait and see? How can you be so calm? Your sperm could currently be making its way to one of my poor innocent eggs."

"Why are your eggs innocent but my sperm isn't? They're just doing their job."

I rolled my eyes. "Oh lord. They're probably just like everything else in your world . . . fast! I bet they've reached the finish line already!"

Malcolm's chest puffed out and he flashed me a proud smile. The way the water ran down his body had my lower stomach pulling. I bit down on my lip and let my eyes travel over his body.

"No! I don't have a condom so stop looking at me like that."

His dick was already hard as I moved my hand over his shaft. His eyes lit up and soon he was pushing three fingers in me. My body was so receptive to his touch, and I wondered if it would always be this way.

God I hope so!

"Paislie, oh fuck I'm going to come!"

Glancing down, I saw his cum squirting out and that pushed my own orgasm to hit me as my legs shook and I saw stars as I closed my eyes and called out his name.

Malcolm was holding me up as he peppered my face with kisses. "That's two orgasms down."

With a laugh, I wrapped my arms around him as we stood under the hot water.

Deep in my heart I knew everything was going to be okay.

Peering into his eyes, I winked and said, "Ninety-eight more to go!"

THINGS FINALLY HAD CALMED DOWN and I felt like I could breathe again. I had done a few interviews about why I decided to walk away from racing. Job offers for commentating came in and I declined each of them. Now I know what Emmit went through. My knee was at about ninety percent and the pain had receded to a dull ache.

Paislie had given her notice at work and had accepted a position at Baylor University in the Physical Therapy department. She also got her period, which caused us both to celebrate with a trip to the doctor and a new prescription for birth control pills. Then a stop at Walgreens to buy a mega-size box of condoms, a bottle of cheap wine, and hot sex in the back of my truck on the ranch under the stars rounded out the evening.

The door opened and I glanced up to see Emmit standing there. "It's about damn time. You're late, asshole."

Shutting the door behind him, he laughed and reached for my hand, giving me a quick shake. "The only person here is you so I'm not late. You try moving your pregnant wife and a son who can't sit still for five minutes from North Carolina to Texas."

"Stop being a pussy."

Emmit dropped into a seat and shook his head. "I fucking can't wait until you have a baby." A grin appeared on his face as he let out a dry laugh. "Is it wrong if I start going to bed at night and pray you have triplets and all girls?"

My heart dropped as I pointed to him. "Fucker. Don't be praying for shit like that!"

The door to the conference room opened and Mr. and Mrs. Russell walked in along with two lawyers. Emmit and I both stood and shook hands all around. As we took a seat, Mrs. Russell gave me a sweet smile.

"So, the two of you want to take over our family vineyard?"

With a nod of our heads, I replied, "Yes, ma'am."

Mr. Russell leaned back in his chair and looked between the two of us. "Now, Malcolm, you've been coming to our place since you were a little boy. I remember you following me around in the barn talking my ear off about how you were going to take over my job and have a much better go at it."

My face was suddenly hot. "I . . . I forgot about that."

Mr. Russell smiled. "I haven't. I also haven't forgotten the countless times you walked through the vineyard because you said it helped settle your thoughts. You're comfortable in the environment and I have no doubt you won't take what my great granddaddy started and continue to make it thrive."

He turned his attention to Emmit, who promptly squirmed in his seat. "Now you, son, I don't understand. You enjoy wine?"

Emmit replied, "Yes, sir, very much."

"I heard you took a trip to Europe to tour some vineyards and spent some time in the hill country touring some newer vineyards."

"Yes, I did. I enjoyed the trips immensely. It was very educational."

Mr. Russell nodded his head and looked at his wife before turning his attention back to us. "What are your plans, boys? Are you going to turn it into a tourist trap and have people traipsing all through our family's beloved home?

Emmit and I both sat up straighter as I spoke first. "No, sir. Not at all. Our intentions are to keep the vineyard as it is, selling to the local wineries. We have no desire to get into the winemaking business, but we would like to expand beyond the vineyard and try new things."

His eyebrows rose. "Expand?"

Clearing his throat, Emmit said, "The ranch that backs up to the vineyard is rumored to be getting ready to go on the market. Malcolm and I would like to make them an offer and look into staring an olive orchard. My wife loves to cook and is obsessed with olive oil. It would be more of her baby to get that up and running."

Mrs. Russell smiled. "I love that idea and think it is amazing to see your wife taking such an interest as she is."

Emmit beamed with pride.

Mr. Russell lifted his hand and his lawyer slid a file over toward our lawyer.

"Everything is as exactly as we agreed upon. The suits here have both looked it over and if you're both ready, we are ready to sign on the dotted line."

Emmit and I looked at each other. Who would have imagined that two years ago we were trying to run each other off the racetrack and exchanging insults, and today we're purchasing a vineyard and another ranch if all works out.

Glancing over to Emmit, he nodded his head as I smiled and looked back at my old friend. "Where do we sign?"

WALKING INTO THE KITCHEN, I smiled at the sight in front of me. Paislie was holding Landon as Clarisse and Adaline were both gathered around the stove cooking something.

I couldn't pull my eyes away from Paislie as she danced and sang while Landon laughed. I'd never experienced such an overwhelming love before as I looked adoringly at my future.

"If I didn't know any better, I'd say that was a look of man who sees his future right in front of him."

Warmth radiated throughout my body as Paislie's eyes caught mine. When she smiled, I swear the earth shook. "I do believe you're right on this one, Lewis."

With a chuckle, he slapped my back and said, "Welcome to my world, buddy."

Emmit headed over to the stove and wrapped Adaline up in his arms as I glanced back over to Paislie. I made my way over to her and leaned down to look into Landon's eyes.

"Hey, Landon. That's my girl whose heart you're trying to steal."

He laughed and looked back at Paislie. My heart was pounding so loudly I could hear it in my ears. "How was your meeting?" Paislie asked, pulling me out of my daydream of her holding our own child.

"It went perfectly," I replied as I took a few steps back and looked over to Emmit. Adaline knew that we were buying the vineyard, but Paislie had no idea. My biggest fear was of her and Adaline not getting along. "How was your day with Adaline and Landon?"

Paislie's face lit up. "Adaline taught me how to make the perfect hard-boiled egg."

My mouth fell as my gaze bounced between Adaline and Paislie. "Okay, I hadn't realized you couldn't boil an egg."

Emmit let out a roar of laughter. "Damn dude, that's one of the first things you find out . . . can they cook?"

Adaline lightly punched Emmit in the stomach as Landon struggled to get down from Paislie's arms.

"That's not all we did. We actually had a wonderful time hitting all the little stores in Waco." Paislie spoke as she put Landon down.

Adaline turned and placed her hands on her stomach that was showing the signs of her pregnancy. "I can't believe how much we have in common."

Paislie nodded her head. "We really do!"

With a quick peek at Adaline, she gave me a wink. She knew I was worried and this was her way of letting me know all would be okay.

"Hey, Paislie, you up for running an errand with me?"

I could practically feel Adaline about to go crazy as she attempted to hold her excitement in.

Paislie smiled and gave me a shrug. "Sure. Adaline, did you need me to help with anything?"

"Nope. Emmit's here, so he can entertain the little monster while Clarisse and I cook up a feast for dinner. I think we'll even break out some bubbly!"

Pinching her eyebrows together, Paislie was about to say something when I took her hand in mine and pulled her out of the kitchen.

I concentrated on my breathing as we walked out to my truck. The last thing I wanted was for Paislie to figure out what was going on. Even with her leaving Dallas, changing jobs, and living with me, I wasn't sure if she might think I was moving too fast.

"Is everything okay?" she asked as I opened the truck door for her.

"Did you and Emmit get into a tiff?"

With a dry laugh, I kissed the tip of her nose and winked. "Far from it."

As I walked around the truck, I rehearsed what I wanted to say one more time.

Blowing out a breath, I whispered, "God, please let me get this right for her."

Thirty six

PAISLIE

MALCOLM WASN'T ACTING RIGHT, AND I couldn't put my finger on what was wrong. He seemed nervous. His left leg had been bouncing since he got in the truck. I wanted desperately to ask him if his leg was bothering him or was something else wrong.

I hadn't asked what his meeting with Emmit was about. Just because we were living together, I still didn't feel it was my right to be sticking my nose in his business. When Adaline told me they were moving to Texas, I about started jumping like a little girl. I loved spending time with her and Landon. The first time we met was a whirlwind of a weekend.

"What do you mean we're flying to North Carolina?"

Malcolm handed me a bag and said, "Just pack for a couple of days. I need to meet with the realtor up there so I can put my house on the market. Emmit and Adaline also invited us for dinner tonight."

My eyes widened in surprise. "So, we're just flying up there like that's it?"

He looked back at me like I had two heads. "Yeah. We'll get there around noon, meet with the realtor and then head on over to Emmit's place. I think you and Adaline will really hit it off."

The room felt like it was spinning. Even though Malcolm had left NASCAR, he still lived his life in the fast lane . . . all the time. The fact that he begged me to go rock climbing and I gave in only to find myself half way up a rock clinging for my life, should have been my first warning sign life was going to be very different with this man.

"But I have work on Monday. I can't miss work, Malcolm, I just started!"

Again, he gave me a dazed looked. "Baby, we'll be back Sunday night."

With a gruff laugh, I threw my hands up and said, "Oh, well why didn't you say!" With a roll of my eyes, I grabbed his arm to get him to stop. "Malcolm, I'm not used to just jetting off across the country to meet someone for dinner. I'm really not that hard to impress. I'd be perfectly fine with a burger from Sonic and a movie."

Pulling me into his arms, Malcolm kissed me. Not just any kiss. A toe-curling kiss that quickly had me pulling his shirt from his pants and pleading with him to make love to me.

His hand stopped mine as he pulled his lips away. "Nope. No time. The pilot's here and ready to go."

Wait. What?

"P-pilot? What's he gonna fly?"

Malcolm threw his bag over his shoulder and called out, "The helicopter."

Swallowing hard, I closed my eyes and said a prayer I'd make it through the next twenty-four hours.

I was so lost in thought, I hadn't even noticed Malcolm pull into the Russell's place.

"I need to check on something for Mr. Russell. It shouldn't take too long."

With a smile, I replied, "No problem. I love this place."

Malcolm's smile widened as he pushed the code for the gate and headed down the long drive. "So, how come the two families don't really live here anymore?"

"Mr. and Mrs. Russell bought a place in Sonoma, California, and spend most of their time there. Their son and his wife decided that grapes weren't their thing. They moved to Maine and run a bed and breakfast up there. They were traveling back and forth until recently when they decided they wanted to make Maine their home."

"Oh, how fun! My best friend, Annie, and I used to dream of having our own bed and breakfast."

Malcolm's head snapped over to look at me. "Really? No shit."

"Really! We talked about moving to Selado and opening one after we went to a bachelorette party there one weekend. The bride's sister rented out the entire bed and breakfast for us. It was amazing." I smiled at the memory.

"That's insane. Adaline wants to open a B and B."

That piqued my interest. "She does? Here in Texas?"

Malcolm nodded and I couldn't hide the jealousy that raced through my body. Closing my eyes, I quickly asked for forgiveness in thinking that way. I really liked Adaline and would never want to think ill of her.

When the truck stopped at the stone cottage, my body tingled as the memory of Malcolm and I making love there swept over me.

"Come on, I need to check on something in the cottage."

Pushing the door open, I jumped out of the truck as Malcolm quickly made his way to my side with his hand in mine.

Are his hands shaking?

"Are you sure you're okay? Everything is all right?"

He kept his eyes forward as we walked up to the door. "I sure as hell hope it is."

Frowning, I went to ask him what he meant by that when he opened the door and led me in.

My breath hitched as my eyes bounced around the cottage. Pink peonies filled the room. Everywhere I looked there were bouquets of my favorite flower. The smell in the room was amazing as I took a few steps in. In the middle of the room was the same quilt we sat on during our first date. Next to it, lying down, was Deuce. My hands came up to my mouth to keep from laughing. I was so overcome with happiness I could barely think straight.

"Malcolm, this is amazing! What is all this for?"

Spinning around, I gasped when I saw him down on one knee holding a ring box in his hand.

"Oh, Malcolm," I whispered.

"Paislie, from that very first moment I met you, I knew you were different. It may have taken us a few tries to get it right, but I knew in my heart you were always the one I was meant to spend the rest of my life with. Will you marry me?"

My body trembled as I looked at the love of my life as he opened up the box and a beautiful princess-cut diamond sparkled against the fire burning in the fireplace.

Tears fell freely as I reached up to pinch myself. *Is this really happening?* I'd finally found what I had been searching for since my mother died.

Love.

A beautiful timeless love.

Nodding my head, I tried to force the words to come between my sobs of happiness. "Y-yes! Yes! A million times yes!"

Malcolm laughed as he took the ring out and slipped it on my finger. Standing, he pulled me into his arms and kissed me passionately. I was completely lost in the kiss. Nothing else in the world mattered more to me than this moment. Everything about it was perfect.

Deuce barked, causing us both to laugh. "I'm glad to see you included my boy."

The crooked smile that spread over Malcolm's face had my lower stomach tightening. "I promised him your first date." He turned and looked at the boxer as he sat there patiently waiting. "As you can see, he's ready to start your date."

Placing my finger on his chin, I brought his eyes back to me. "First things first, Mr. Wallace."

Malcolm raised his eyes in question. "And what would that be?"

"I believe you still have a few orgasms to catch up on."

His eyes turned dark as he quickly picked me up and carried me to the sofa. "I'm on it, baby." Setting me down, I watched as my future husband stripped out of his clothes.

"And, Malcolm," I said as I pulled my dress over my head, "please go slow."

His hands cupped my breasts as I dropped my head and let out a moan. "Oh, baby, I can do slow."

And boy did he ever do slow. His hands and mouth explored every inch of my body before he slowly made love to me.

The smell of the flowers, the light from the fire, and the smell of chicken salad filled my senses as we whispered one another's names. Never in my wildest dreams would I ever imagine I could be so happy.

Nothing would ever be the same again. I'd finally found love and nothing or no one would ever take it away from me.

Ever.

Thirty seven

MALCOLM

LAY ON THE COUCH with Paislie wrapped in my arms as Deuce snored on the quilt in front of the fire.

With a giggle, she turned in my arms and looked up at me. "I should probably get over there to my date. It appears he fell asleep waiting on me."

I frowned and said, "Poor bastard."

Paislie gently kissed my chest before getting up and slipping her clothes back on. She made her way over to Deuce and plopped down next to him as I got dressed.

"I knew I smelled chicken salad!" she exclaimed as Deuce wagged his tail in anticipation.

"Oh look, boy! Janet made you a sandwich too and it's shaped like a bone."

She set the sandwich down onto a plastic plate and put it in front of the dog. He quickly ate it as Paislie took a bite of her sandwich.

Sitting across from her, I let out a chuckle. "You couldn't wait for me?"

With a shrug, she winked. "What can I say, multiple orgasms make me hungry. Then add an engagement on top of that and I could eat a dog!"

Deuce whimpered as Paislie laughed and said, "Not you, baby boy. You're too special to me."

Feeling satisfied with her answer, Deuce laid his head on Paislie's lap.

I slowly drew in a deep breath before letting it out. "So, I have some more news for you."

She took a drink of water from the water bottles that Janet had packed. "Is it bigger than this?" she asked as she held up her diamond.

I was suddenly overcome with nerves and scared as hell I might have jumped the gun. *Shit. I thought this was going to be easier than asking her to marry me.*

"I'm selling my house. I want to start our new life in a new home that we make together."

Paislie's sandwich stopped short of her mouth as she stared at me. "You're selling your house? What about Autumn and Sophie?"

"I've actually got a place lined up for her. Although I'm not sure how she would feel if she knew we had made love on the couch twice now."

Her eyebrows pinched together in confusion. "What are you . . . oh my gosh! Autumn and Sophie will be living here in the cottage?"

With a smile, I said, "If she wants. For all I know, she might want to move into an apartment in Waco. She really loves her job at the university."

"Oh wow. Does she know, I mean have you told her about wanting to sell your house?"

I felt guilty that I had kept Paislie in the dark, but I really wanted to surprise her with this new adventure we were about to take.

"I have. I was just waiting to make sure the sale of the new house went through."

Her hands came up to her face as she said, "Okay wait. Malcolm you have my head spinning. You've already purchased a house? Don't you think I might have wanted to have some sort of say in that? I mean, if we're getting married, I'd kind of like to be a part of the big decisions."

My heart was pounding in my chest as I nodded my head. "You're right and I normally wouldn't have kept you in the dark like this. But I knew you'd love the house. Everyone knew you would."

"Wait. How many people know about you selling your house?"

Oh. Shit.

"Um . . . just a few people."

I jumped up and reached for Paislie's hands, pulling her to me. Deuce stretched and went to the door and waited for someone to open it. "Come on. I'll show you the new house."

"What?" Paislie said as she glanced around the room at everything. "What about all of this? The fire?"

Walking up to the fire, I hit a switch and it went out.

"Holy crap! That was gas? I'd have never have guessed," she mindlessly said.

"Come on!" I was sure she could hear the excitement in my voice as I dragged her to the front door while Deuce barked.

"The food!" she called out as I laughed.

"That's what I pay Janet for."

Paislie rolled her eyes and pulled me to a stop. "Malcolm Wallace. We can clean up our own mess. Let's go back in there and take care of it so Janet doesn't have to deal with it."

My smile faded. "You're serious?"

Folding her arms over her chest, she nodded. "I most certainly am."

"But, Paislie—"

Holding up her hand to quiet me, she replied, "Malcolm, just because you're used to being waited on, I'm not. I don't want Janet to think I'm going to take advantage of her, especially now that we're engaged. Now come on, let's go back in and pack up the food."

I could see the spit and fire in her coming out and I loved it. It would be hard for me not relying on Janet to take care of almost everything in my life, but I knew Paislie was right. It was time I stopped relying on everyone else.

Fifteen minutes later, I placed the basket and quilt in the back of the truck. "What about the flowers?" she asked.

"I've already made arrangements to have them delivered to a local nursing home."

I could see something move over her face as she gave me that goofy smile. Biting her lip, she asked, "Are you sure we have to go see the house? I'm thinking maybe we should keep celebrating our engagement."

With a laugh, I took her hand in mine as we walked down the path and toward the large castle looking house. "Oh, I've been wanting to get a better peek at the house! I hope the next time the Russell's are in town maybe they'll invite us over for a dinner party!"

"Oh, I think you might be getting a better look sooner than you think," I said as I tried not to smile from ear to ear.

I continued to walk to the house as Paislie said, "Malcolm, I thought you were taking me to the house you bought?"

We stopped at the front door and stood there.

"So, are you going to tell me why we're just standing here?"

My heart was racing. "We're waiting."

Her eyes darted back and forth from the front door to me. "O-okay. Waiting for what?"

The door flew open and Sophie ran out. "Uncle Malcolm! Paislie!"

Sophie ran right into my arms as I hugged her and kissed her. "Can I tell her?"

We both looked at Paislie as she stood there stunned and confused as hell. "Sure you can, princess," I replied as I kissed her cheek.

"Paislie! This is your new house!"

The color drained from Paislie's face. "Come again?" she asked as Sophie looked at me with a confused face.

"What does that mean?" she asked as I threw my head back and laughed my ass off.

When I finally stopped laughing, I looked at the love of my life and said, "Welcome home, Paislie. The first two floors belong to us and the top two belong to Emmit, Adaline, and Landon."

"And the new baby!" Sophie cried out.

I kissed Sophie on the cheek and put her down. "Yes, and the new baby."

Paislie closed her eyes and shook her head as if clearing her thoughts. "Wait. Hold on, you bought this house?" She pointed back to the house and asked again, "This house? As in . . . the house that belongs to the Russell's?"

"Yes, but the house belongs to us. Emmit and I bought it, along with the vineyards."

She sucked in a surprised breath. "The vineyards?"

"Yep," I said with a nod of my head. "Emmit and I formed a corporation together." Wiggling my eyebrows, I said, "We're in the business of wine grapes now. And hopefully, olive oil."

Paislie looked more than stunned. "What about . . . I mean. Neither one of y'all want to do anything with racing?"

"Oh, hell yeah. We're going to build a team most likely and be co-owners. I'm thinking that will be a few years down the road; once we get the hang of all of this, we can concentrate on that." Flashing her a smile, I said, "You can take the boys out of racing, but you'll never take the racing out of the boys."

She stumbled back a few steps.

"Uncle Malcolm, Paislie looks sick."

Reaching out for her, I asked, "Paislie. Are you okay?"

"I . . . I . . . I need to sit down."

Thirty eight

PAISLIE

*D*ID HE SAY OLIVE OIL? *No. Did he? Holy shit, what is happening right now?*

"Sophie, run and let your momma know we need some water for Paislie."

My hand flew up as I called out, "Harder! I need something harder than water."

Malcolm laughed as Sophie gave me a puzzled look before turning and running into the house.

Glancing back to Malcolm, he flashed me a smile that made my stomach flutter. Damn him.

"Information overload?" he casually asked.

My mouth opened as I tried to speak. *Is he for real? Any other woman would be running for her life right now.*

Inhaling a calming breath, I slowly blew it out as I tried to clear my head. I'd give anything to talk to Elizabeth right now.

"So . . . let me get this all straight."

He took my hand and kissed the back of it as I continued to talk. "You bought this house with Emmit, along with the land."

"Yep."

"Autumn and Sophie most likely will live in the stone cottage."

He chuckled and then gave me a wink as he replied, "Unless Autumn finds out what we did in there, but most likely yes, at least for a little bit."

I let out a frustrated breath as I covered my face before dropping my hands to my sides. "Wait. You said Emmit and Adaline are going to live in this house too?"

His smile faded. "Um . . . well yeah. They were going to live on the top two floors and we'll take the first two floors. Keep it all just like the original owners had it. The only thing that was part of the contract is that we didn't turn the original house into a tasting room or anything. There are two private entrances and both houses each have three-car garages."

So I'm getting married and moving into a four-story house that we're sharing with another couple. Am I okay with this? He sure seems to be.

"Did you mention olive oil? Are there olive trees here also?"

With a smile, he shook his head. "No, that's where buying the ranch that backs up to this place comes into play. Since Adaline loves to cook and the idea of making the bed and breakfast on that land was hers, she mentioned growing olive trees and making our own olive oil."

My eyes widened as I stared at him. "So, you all have your futures planned out and what am I supposed to do?"

Malcolm looked at me with a stunned expression. "I . . . well I thought . . . um . . . I thought you would love the idea of living here. You've mentioned how much you loved the house. And the bed and breakfast. You mentioned it just a little bit ago. It's perfect."

I stood up and let out a dry laugh. "Malcolm, that's Adaline's idea. I can't just walk in and make myself a part of it."

"No, Adaline will be thrilled you're interested as well. She knew there was an old historical home on it. She simply mentioned the B & B idea. Her goal is to get the olive orchard going."

I turned away from him as I tried to calm my racing heart. Slowly turning back around, I looked directly in his eyes. "I have a job. I have a career I actually like, and you want me to just walk away from it and help Adaline start her own business?"

Swallowing hard, Malcolm pushed his hand through his hair and cursed. "Shit. Paislie I'm not asking you to walk away from anything. I thought this might be something that you would be excited about and want to be a part of."

I didn't know how I should be feeling. The excitement from the engagement had worn off and now I was being faced with a future I wasn't the least bit prepared for.

"I'd like to go home, please." I quickly turned and headed back toward the cottage and Malcolm's truck. He grabbed my arm and pulled me to a stop.

"Are you mad?"

Giving him a blank stare, I tried to figure out what to say. "I'm not mad . . . well hell I don't know, maybe I am. How did you know I would be okay with this?" Glancing back to the house, I looked at it. It was huge and we would probably go for days without even seeing Emmit and Adaline.

"The house is big, but did you even stop to consider that maybe Adaline and I wouldn't care for each other? That maybe I didn't want to go into a business with her? I originally wanted to do this with my best friend and to have something else forced down my throat doesn't sit well with me. You didn't even talk to me about any of this, Malcolm!"

"I'm not forcing anything down your throat."

My hands went to my hips. "Really? Oh hey, Paislie, I bought a house with someone else and we're going to all own it even though you're just now getting to know the couple. By the way, they will live upstairs from us and we'll share everything, the pool, the hot tub, the tennis courts. Oh yeah and we are now going to be in the wine grape business." I rolled my eyes. "Do you even know anything about wine grapes, Malcolm?"

He went to talk, but I kept going.

"Let's not forget to mention that you're also going to own racecars with the same man you couldn't even stand a few years ago. What if you disagree on something and none of this works out? You bought a damn house with him! You'll be traveling to races, and what about North Carolina? You sold your house there, but now you're talking about owning a team. Call me stupid, but aren't all the teams located there?"

Again he opened his mouth to talk, but I stopped him. "I think it's wonderful Adaline found something she's passionate about, but to expect me to just jump right on into someone else's dreams seems rather selfish on your part."

"I guess I didn't think about it like that."

"No, you didn't. I need to be alone for a bit to get my thoughts together. Please, will you take me home?"

Sophie came running out, calling my name. When I turned to look over my shoulder, Emmit, Adaline, and Autumn were all standing on the porch.

Shit. How much of that did they all just hear?

"Here's your water," Sophie said as she forced it into my hand. Lifting it up to my lips, I took a drink and handed it back to her. Adaline was looking at me like she wanted to say something but wasn't sure what she should say.

"Congratulations on the engagement!" Autumn called out as she bolted down the stairs and pulled me into her arms.

"I've never seen Malcolm as happy as he has been with you," she whispered into my ear. When Adaline and Emmit stood before me, Adaline gave me a sympathetic smile. "It took a little while for me to get used to the idea as well. Would you like to tour the whole house so you can see how the two separate living areas are laid out?"

Oh. My. God. I'm the last person to even see the whole house.

I shook my head and barely said, "Not right now. I really need to get back to the house. I'm not feeling well."

With that I turned away from everyone and forced myself not to run but to walk.

By the time I got to the truck, I jumped in and tried to get my breathing under control. It felt as if I was having a panic attack.

Malcolm got in the truck and silently we drove back to his house. Not saying a word, I made my way to the guest bedroom I had stayed in a few months back. Malcolm didn't even follow me.

Shutting the door, I leaned against it and slid to the ground as I dropped my forehead onto my knees and cried.

The different emotions running through my mind were confusing. The idea of being married to Malcolm thrilled me, yet at the same time I knew my life would be so different. Mansions, vineyards, assistants, cooks, and whatever else Malcolm decided to throw into the mix. The one thing I would not allow him to do to me is let me lose my independence or my voice. I wasn't sure how long I sat there on the floor before I finally got up and hit Elizabeth's number.

After she answered, I launched into a full on explanation of everything that just happened.

"So, what exactly are you confused about, Paislie?"

My eyes widened in shock. "Elizabeth, he planned all of this without talking to me!"

"Okay, so I get that the idea of the bed and breakfast thing makes you angry because it wasn't originally your idea, but have you not talked for years about doing something like that?"

I chewed the corner of my lips. "Well, yeah but that's beside the point."

"Why? Do you like Adaline?"

My heart jumped to my throat. "Yes. Very much."

"Do you not think Malcolm saw that and took that into consideration before he made this move?"

I shrugged even though she couldn't see me. "I guess so."

"Paislie, I get you're feeling like Malcolm made some serious decisions without consulting you, but stop for a few moments and ask yourself this. If he had asked you to marry him, then asked you about buying the house and vineyards with Emmit and his family, then mentioned the possibility of the bed and breakfast, what would you have said?"

I thought for a moment. "I would have said yes to all of it. I love that he and Emmit are reaching outside the box and trying something totally different, but it's also a little scary for me to think he's doing this with someone else. What if they have a fight? I mean they bought a damn house together!"

Elizabeth chuckled. "I see your point, but I also don't think of Malcolm as someone who would make such a decision without really thinking it through."

I nodded as I sat down on the bed. "I honestly think I'm more upset by the fact that I was the last to know any of this. Did he not tell me because he was worried I would say no to his proposal?"

"Maybe, or maybe he really thought he was surprising you."

My lip tingled as I realized I was biting it. Letting out a frustrated sigh, I asked, "Do you think I overreacted?"

"Yes and no. I would probably have a talk with him about future decisions and that you want to be a part of them."

"Totally," I barely said as I stood back up and paced the floor. "It all just seems so fast, Elizabeth."

"And there we are to the root of the issue."

My head dropped back. I knew she was right. One second I was engaged and the next, I discovered I had a house bigger than the one I was currently in, another family living there with us, a vineyard, olive trees, and possibly going into business with a person I hardly knew. Plus add in a wedding, my own career and the idea that as each day went on, I longed for a child more and more.

"Ugh! I want to scream!"

Elizabeth chuckled. "Then scream."

I followed her advice as I grabbed a pillow and screamed into it.

"Feel better?"

"Some," I said with a giggle. "I'm scared I'm going to wake up and this is going to be a dream and I'll be standing on the steps again looking up at St. Patrick's."

"Oh, Paislie, it's not a dream and if anyone deserves to find happiness it's you."

"It feels like a dream," I whispered.

The soft knock at the door had me spinning around and rushing over to open it. Malcolm stood on the other side holding a Diet Coke and a small tub of Ben and Jerry's. With a smile, I motioned for him to come in.

"Elizabeth, thank you for listening to me. I'm going to run now."

"He showed up, didn't he?"

Grinning, I replied, "Yes."

"I'll talk to you soon, Paislie. Remember, fall to your knees and seek guidance. He'll always be there for you."

"Thank you, I'll talk to you soon."

"Soon! Tell Malcolm I said hello."

"Will do."

I hit End and stared into his beautiful blue eyes.

"You brought me soda and ice cream?"

He gave me a small shrug and said, "Emmit's suggestion."

I took the spoon and the ice cream and sat on the end of the bed as Malcolm sat next to me. One bite and I felt like I was in heaven.

"I'm sorry I got so upset. It's just everything hit me all at once and I got a bit scared."

"Scared of what?"

"Malcolm, imagine dreaming of a life someday that you never thought possible. Then you meet your prince charming, he offers you the world, but he offers it to you all in one sitting. You'd be a little scared."

He closed his eyes and shook his head. "I know I should have talked to you about it, even Adaline told me I needed to tell you, but I honestly was just trying to surprise you. If this is something you're not interested in doing, we'll figure it out."

I took his hands in mine. "Malcolm, I really am excited for this new adventure you're going on, but I'm not going to lie and tell you it doesn't make me nervous. It does, especially with you not talking to me about any of it. One thing you have to do is talk to me about something before you go off and do it. We're a team now, Malcolm, and we need to decide on our future together."

He lifted my hand and kissed the back of it. I knew deep in my heart everything would work out, and a part of me was excited but I wouldn't let myself jump ahead.

"I agree with everything you said. I'm not used to sharing my decisions with someone else, and I've always kind of left everything up to everyone around me. I know that all needs to change and it will, I promise you. It may take me time adjusting to it, but I swear to you I'll never put you in a situation like I did today." With a smile that had my knees wobbling, he whispered, "It's you and me now."

The smile on my face grew as his words settled into my mind. "You and me always."

When he slowly lowered me to the bed, I let every worry slip away. "I'm going to make love to you, Paislie."

I couldn't help the smile that spread across my face. There was nothing better than being lost in Malcolm.

MALCOLM

"**A**RE YOU NERVOUS?"

Glancing over to Paislie, I smiled. "No. Should I be?"

She gave me a sweet grin in return. "I don't think so. Even though Elizabeth is like my mother, and father, and sister, and best friend all rolled into one."

My heart sank. "Okay, now I'm nervous. Do I earn any extra points for being raised Catholic?"

She chuckled and squeezed my hand. "Nope, but I'm sure she is pleased about that."

"She's not going to ask me to recite anything, is she? Paislie, I haven't stepped foot in a catholic church in a number of years. Even then I always had headphones on."

Shaking her head, she looked forward. "There, pull over and park in front of that store. The restaurant isn't too far from here."

I did as she said and parked her car. We got out and walked hand in hand down the busy street. I'd already been by St. Patrick's and talked to the bishop. The wedding date was set for six months out and he had insisted Paislie have a wedding with a mass. Memories of my cousin Jenn's wedding flashed through my mind. I'd never tell Paislie, but I got up thirty minutes into the ceremony and left.

When she stopped walking and took both my hands in hers, I knew she was nervous. "Are you sure you want a catholic wedding?"

It was as if she had been reading my mind. "What would you like, babe?"

Her eyes fell to the ground as she kicked at a pretend rock. "I've always wanted a traditional wedding, but if you want something simple, we can do that too."

Pulling her to me, I gently kissed her on the lips. "I want what you want, baby. I'm in this for the long haul."

Her eyes lit up and I knew there wasn't anything I wouldn't do for her.

"Paislie, there isn't anything I wouldn't do for you to make you happy."

"I love you so much," she whispered. "You ready?"

Taking in a deep breath, I nodded. "Ready."

The moment we walked into the restaurant, I searched for a nun. When Paislie said, "There she is!" I looked in the direction she was facing.

"Where?" I asked as I followed her. A slightly older woman stood and smiled warmly at us. "Is that her?"

"Yep!" she said as she wrapped the woman in her arms. "Elizabeth, I've missed you so."

I couldn't believe my eyes. The woman standing before me was beautiful. She was dressed in a simple black dress with a belt that wrapped around her waist, showing her figure. Her blue eyes took in Paislie with so much happiness, I could practically feel the love she had pouring out of her. Her hair was in a sleek ponytail and she wore very little if any makeup.

"Elizabeth, I'd like for you to meet Malcolm. Malcolm, this is Sister Elizabeth, but you can call her Elizabeth."

"Sister, I mean, Elizabeth. I um . . . well you're not what I expected."

Her brows rose as she tilted her head. "Pray tell what were you expecting?"

I motioned with my hands to look at her. "Not this. A habit, an older woman who was grumpy looking."

Paislie playfully hit my chest as she motioned for us to all sit down.

"Mr. Wallace, how long has it been since you have been to the church or spoken with a nun?"

My face burned as I sat. "Please, call me Malcolm. To be honest I couldn't tell you the last time I actually talked to a nun. Probably while taking my catechism classes. Sister Margret was old and grumpy. Had I had a teacher such as you, I might have kept going to church."

"Malcolm!" Paislie said with a look of horror on her face. Elizabeth laughed and told Paislie to loosen up some.

"It's okay, I'm rather flattered, Mr . . . I mean . . . Malcolm."

"So, when did you become a nun?"

"I was about sixteen when I felt the calling."

I about choked on my own spit. "Wow."

"I get that response a lot."

Paislie cleared her throat and said, "We just met with Bishop Mark. I requested Father Tim for the wedding.

Elizabeth forced a smile and moved about in her seat. "I'm sure he would be honored to perform the sacrament."

Paislie grinned from ear to ear. "He is very happy to do so; he said so himself when we asked him."

"He was there? I thought he was on his trip."

Something moved across Elizabeth's face, and if I didn't know any better, I'd say Elizabeth had feelings for Father Tim.

No way.

"He must have come back early because he was in the bishop's office," Paislie said. I could tell by the look on her face, she had the same thoughts I had.

Clearing her throat, Elizabeth picked up the menu and looked over it. "This is my favorite place to eat, Malcolm. They have the best lasagna in all of Dallas."

That was a fast change of subject if I'd ever seen one.

Peeking over to Paislie, our eyes met and I made a mental note to ask more about the relationship between the sister and the father.

Wait. That sounded weird.

I shook my head to clear my thoughts. It didn't take long for both women to fall into an easy conversation. I even got to hear about when Paislie was younger.

Sitting back, I watched the two of them as they talked about everything from the wedding to a movie they both wanted to see together. It was clear Paislie loved this woman very much.

"THANK YOU FOR DINNER, MALCOLM. I really enjoyed meeting

you. Everything Paislie has told me about you is so very true."

With a smile, I nodded. "All good I hope."

She let out a girlish giggle and said, "Yes! Of course it was."

As both of them locked arms and walked, I heard someone call out Paislie's name. Turning, I saw an older man come walking up quickly. He gave me a once over and stopped to look at me before turning to Paislie.

Both women had a look of horror on their faces as Elizabeth seemed to stand a little in front of Paislie, almost as if sheltering her.

"Paislie, my little girl. Look at you still hanging with sisters, huh?"

Elizabeth smiled but I knew it wasn't genuine.

"What do you want, Dad?"

Dad?

My head snapped back to look at the guy. Paislie hardly ever mentioned her father. On occasion he would contact her to ask for something, usually money. Seeing him standing there made him all too real.

"Now, why do you think I want something? I saw my daughter walking down the street and I wanted to say hello to her." He turned his attention on me. "And who are you?"

I went to answer when Paislie jumped between us. "None of your business."

He let out a whistle and reached down for her hand. "Holy shit, look at that fucking rock on your hand."

"Dad!" Paislie exclaimed as he looked over to Elizabeth.

"Forgive me, sister, I'll go to confession on Saturday."

I was stunned to see the look Elizabeth gave him. When Paislie pulled her hand from his, I wrapped my arm around her. "You're getting married. I think I have the right to know who the man is who is marrying ya."

With a forced laugh, Paislie shook her head as she said, "You gave up that right when you left me on the steps of the orphanage."

"Malcolm, I'd like to leave now."

Gripping my hand tighter on her waist, I led her away when my name was called out.

"Malcolm Wallace. I thought that was you." Looking at Paislie, he smirked. "Looks like you done good for yourself, Paislie."

"Let's go, please, Malcolm."

Doing as she asked, we walked away from her father. Taking one last look over my shoulder, I saw him watching us. I had the feeling that now he knew Paislie was getting married, and to someone with money, he wasn't going to just let her walk away so easy.

Next time he came sniffing around, I'd be ready.

"Elizabeth, where are you parked?" Paislie asked in a shaky voice. I hated the affect that asshole had on her.

"Around the corner. You're more than welcome to walk me to the car if you'd like."

"Please. I don't want him seeing my license plates. He'll know where I'm living."

My heart was pounding in my chest and when we rounded the corner, I pulled her to a stop. "Would he do something to you if he knew where you lived?"

Her expression was blank. "No. He'd just start sending me letters asking for money. I doubt he would show up if he knew you would be there. He's a coward, so most of the time he sends me a letter or text message."

Asshole.

We walked Elizabeth to her car and chatted with her a bit more before we headed back to the car. I could feel Paislie's body relax the moment we rounded the corner and she didn't see her father anywhere.

"I'll never let him bother you again, baby. I swear."

Giving me a weak smile, she looked straight ahead, lost in her own thoughts.

Once we got to her car, I opened the door while she got in. Pressing a number on my phone, I waited for Kathleen to answer.

"Hello?"

"I've got some work for you in the Dallas area if you get your guy on it."

She rustled some papers and finally said, "Send it over to me by tomorrow and I'll let you know."

"Thanks," I said as I hit End.

"Who was that?" Paislie asked.

Tossing my phone on the console, I replied, "An old friend who is doing some work for me."

I reached for her hand and held it gently. "Did you want to talk about it?"

"No, not really. I'd just rather focus on planning the wedding and him not finding out about it."

I let her words sink in as we drove almost the entire way back to Waco in silence while I tried to think of a way to keep the lowlife asshole who called himself Paislie's father, away from her.

Forty

PAISLIE

S TANDING ON THE PLATFORM, I stared at myself in my wedding gown while the seamstress made her marks.

I'm getting married.

Holy shit.

"I've seen that look of horror before on my own face."

Smiling, I looked at Adaline in the mirror. We'd become the best of friends and I thought of her as a sister. She looked amazing even though she was about to push out a baby.

"I find it hard to believe you were nervous to marry Emmit."

"Ha!" she said with a wave of her hand as if I had just said the most ridiculous thing ever. "Trust me, I was scared to death. Plus, all the craziness that surrounded our wedding."

"What kind of craziness?" I asked.

"It's a long story that I'll tell you all about when we're alone with a big bottle of wine."

Giggling, I shook my head. "My life has changed so much since meeting Malcolm."

"I bet," she said as she got up and made her way over to me. She was all stomach as she climbed the two steps and adjusted the dress. "You're going to make a beautiful bride, though."

My heart felt as if it would explode I was so happy. "You know, when I was younger I used to lay in bed and dream of having a family." Turning to her, I took her hands in mine. "I'm so blessed to have you, Emmit, and Landon in my life. I hope you know that."

Her lips pressed together as tears formed. Oh Lord. She was going to cry. I'd never seen anyone cry at the drop of a bucket like Adaline. Emmit said it was the pregnancy. Yesterday when I showed her one of the guest rooms I had decorated at the B & B she lost it in a crying fit and said I should have done all the rooms because she hated all the other ones. Never mind the fact that I had decorated nearly all the rooms. I let it slide due to her current condition.

"Don't cry, Adaline. Please don't cry 'cause then you'll make me cry and we'll both be standing up here crying looking like crazy women."

She instantly stopped crying. Damn if I knew that was all I ever had to say I would have been using that this whole time.

"Oh no."

Her face drained of all color. "Okay, well if you want to cry, sweetie, you can."

She shook her head and then grabbed my hands. I about fell to the ground when she started squeezing them.

"Ohmygawd!" I shouted as I was practically brought to my knees.

"Paislie, you have to stay still if you want me to get this measurement right."

I couldn't even form words. Adaline had a death grip on my hands. I was never going to tell her to stop crying ever again.

"Can't. Feel. My. Hands." I panted out as Adaline closed her eyes and breathed heavier.

"Lucy! Help me! She's trying to rip my hands off!"

Lucy jumped up and looked at Adaline. "She's having a contraction."

I sighed a breath of relief that she wasn't mad at me for talking about her crazy crying. "Thank God," I said with a chuckle as Adaline let up her grip.

"Wait. What? Contraction!" I exclaimed as Lucy helped Adaline down and to a chair.

I started spinning around in a circle as I tried to figure out what I was supposed to do next.

"Baby. The baby is coming?" I gathered up my dress and quickly made my way over to Adaline.

"The baby is coming!"

"You don't have to shout, Paislie. I'm in labor—not deaf."

My head snapped to Lucy. "What do I do?"

"Take her to the hospital."

"Right!" I shouted as I grabbed both of our purses and yelled over my shoulder, "I'll get the car!"

"Your dress," Lucy exclaimed as I slid to a stop.

"Shit!"

Heading back into the dressing room, Adaline called out, "No time! Paislie, I'm having another contraction."

A total look of fear covered my face as I stared at her. "What? No, you just had your first contraction. You can't go that fast!"

Adaline raised her eyebrows and gave me a shy smile. "Well, I've been having them the last hour or so, but I thought I'd be okay until after your alteration appointment."

My hand flew to my chest as I looked at Lucy. "Is she serious?"

A sudden flash of adrenaline raced through my body as Adaline said, "I texted Emmit and he and Malcolm are on the way to the hospital."

Panic hit me square in the face. "I can't let Malcolm see me in my wedding dress."

"I'll drive, you change!" Lucy called as she flew by me with my jeans, T-shirt and sneakers in her arms.

This was insane . . . but it would work.

Reaching to help Adaline up, I helped her walk out to Lucy's car.

"Another one is coming," she said as I opened the front passenger door and helped her in. "I need your hand."

With a gruff laugh, I shut her door and said, "The hell with that!"

I was barely in the car with the door shut when Lucy floored it.

"It's two minutes to the hospital, change fast," Lucy called from over her shoulder.

"I can't get it unbuttoned!" I called out.

Lucy threw up her hands. "Well, I can't get it; I'm driving."

Slipping on my jeans, I frantically tried to reach the buttons. Before I knew it, she was pulling up to the front entrance of the hospital and I was jumping out.

"You! Hey, Mr! Please, can you unbutton my dress?"

An older gentleman walked up as Lucy ran into the hospital to get a wheelchair.

"Do I want to know?" he asked as he unbuttoned the dress.

With a shake of my head, I said, "Nope. You don't."

He laughed and said, "You're done."

Turning, I kissed him on the cheek and then jumped back into the car where I slid out of my dress and put my T-shirt on.

"Oh God. Here comes another one!" Adaline cried out as she lifted her hand up as if I was crazy enough to give her mine.

With a roll of my eyes, I slipped my sneakers on and jumped out right as Lucy and a hospital volunteer showed up with the wheelchair.

Just as Adaline sat down in it, Emmit came running up, with Malcolm behind him carrying Landon on his shoulders. My lower stomach pulled as I looked at him. Nothing was hotter than him with a child in his arms . . . on his shoulders . . . playing hide and seek.

His eyes caught mine as I smiled.

"You look flush, baby. Is everything okay?"

With a nod, I peeked over to Lucy who gave me a thumb's up before I turned back to Malcolm. "I've never been better."

As I made my way over to my handsome fiancé, I said a quick prayer that I hadn't ruined my dress in my frantic state to get it off. Lucy gave me a hug and whispered she'd take care of the dress.

I was getting married in two months and I hoped like hell she got all the measurements she needed.

"Thank you," I whispered in her ear.

"Thanks, Lucy! I owe you!" Adaline called out as she was pushed into the hospital.

Malcolm's eyes bounced from Lucy, to her car, back to me. "Who was that and where is your car?"

Smiling up at Landon, I reached up and tickled his tummy as he laughed. "That was the seamstress who was doing alterations on my dress."

"Okay. Why did she bring y'all to the hospital?"

Now that I thought about everything, I had to laugh. "I was getting alterations done on my dress and Adaline decided to hide the fact that she was having contractions until it was too late. She said I didn't have time to change and there was no way I was going to let you see me in my dress." With a shrug, I said, "So, Lucy drove and I changed, of course after I jumped out and asked a total stranger to unbutton my wedding dress."

A look of pure shock flashed across Malcolm's face.

"Never a dull moment with you, is there?"

Shaking my head, I said, "Nope. Are you okay with that?"

Leaning down, Landon put his hands on Malcolm's head while he kissed me softly on the lips. "Perfectly okay with that. Now let's go watch Adaline pop out a kid."

Laughing, I hit him in the stomach as Landon started singing about being a big brother.

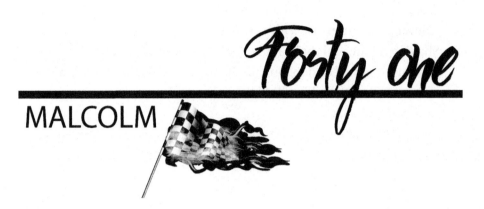

Forty one

MALCOLM

M Y CHEST WAS TIGHT AS I watched Emmit hold his daughter, Hailey. The look of love on his face was amazing. I'd never seen him with tears in his eyes before, except for when that wine bottle fell on his toe. Pressing my lips together, I tried to push the memory and the laughter away.

"Emmit, she is beyond beautiful," Paislie said as she looked adoringly at Hailey.

Beaming with pride, Emmit nodded his head, "She looks like her mother."

Adaline grinned as Landon snuggled up next to her in the bed, fast asleep from all the excitement.

"Would you like to hold her?" Emmit asked Paislie.

Her face lit up as she nodded frantically. The moment he placed Hailey in her arms, I felt my entire body go stiff.

Holy shit.

I cannot deny it any longer.

Paislie's eyes filled with tears as she rocked the baby softly in her arms. When she peeked up to look at me, she gave me the biggest most beautiful smile I'd ever seen.

Yep, there was no getting around this one. I wanted a baby. I wanted to see Paislie holding our baby.

The door opened and Ashley walked in demanding to see her niece. Paislie was still not too sure about Ashley and I couldn't blame her for being bothered by how open Ashley was about the two of us. I'd been honest with her about my time with Ashley. It was clear from the smile on

Ashley's face that Paislie had nothing to worry about, she was very happy with her fiancé, Jon.

We stayed until it was clear Adaline was ready to pass out. Paislie wrapped her arm around my waist as we made our way to the elevator.

"So, two more months and we're going to be hitched."

Laughing, I pulled her closer to me. "Two more months."

Paislie stopped and looked at me. "You know, I believe you still owe me a few—" Looking around to make sure no one heard her, she turned back to me and gave me a seductive look. Everything in that moment disappeared and I saw nothing but Paislie. "Orgasms," she whispered. My eyes quickly scanned the area as I grabbed her and pulled her around the corner.

Giggling, she asked, "Where are we going?"

I found the door I was looking for and pushed it open. I nudged Paislie into the cleaning closet and shut the door.

"Are we going to do some cleaning?" she asked with a naughty smile. "I have fond memories of doing laundry with you."

I had my pants unbuttoned and my zipper down as she took my cock in her hand and stroked it.

"How many more orgasms do we need?"

She swallowed hard and said, "Three."

Lifting my brow, I asked, "Three? Are you sure?"

"Um . . . yep . . . I'm sure." I loved seeing her chest heave up and down at the mere excitement of what I was about to do to her.

With a quick look around, I grinned when I saw the room was big enough for my next plan. "Take off your jeans," I commanded as I put a sheet on the floor and dropped to the floor onto my back.

Without hesitating, she did what I asked. Slipping off her sneakers, she pushed her jeans along with her panties down and off her right leg, keeping them on her left still.

"Sit on my face."

Her eyes widened in shock as she asked, "W-what?"

"I want to taste you, baby."

Her mouth parted slightly open as she gazed down at me while biting her lip.

Doing as I asked, she lowered herself to me as I ran my tongue along her lips and to her clit.

"Oh, God," she whispered as she started to move her pussy against my face.

Fucking heaven.

Grabbing onto her hips, I held her still while I worked on her first orgasm.

"Malcolm," she whispered as she slammed her hands over her mouth while her body trembled. I loved feeling her fall apart. It was one of my favorite things.

When she finally came down, I lifted her hips and said, "Turn around, I want to feel my cock in your mouth."

She gasped as she quickly moved. I knew she loved it when I talked dirty to her. When she put that sweet pussy back in my face, I slapped her ass, causing her to let out a yelp before taking me into her mouth. Letting out a moan, I let her work me for a bit before I pulled her back onto my face. When she moaned, it vibrated through my entire body, causing me to suck and lick her faster. My finger moved up and coated it with her wetness before I pushed it into her ass, causing her entire body to go rigid and her orgasm to hit her. Each whimper and moan against my cock had me fighting not to let go and spill into her mouth.

I tapped on her hip, signaling her to stop before I came. "Oh God . . . Malcolm . . . I feel myself throbbing."

Not sure how much longer we could stay in here, I told her to stand. She held onto the wall as she steadied herself.

I picked her up as she wrapped her legs around me while I slowly lowered her onto my cock. "Damn, baby you feel so good."

It didn't take me long before I was pouring every ounce of my cum into her body. When I sank down to the ground, I held her so she wouldn't be on the floor. We both dragged in air while trying to steady our breathing. The door handle moved and we both froze.

"Aw shit. Who locked it?" someone said from the other side of the door. Paislie jumped up and quickly put her panties and jeans back on while I tucked my guy back in and zipped up my pants.

Putting my ear to the door, I lifted my eyebrows and slowly unlocked the door. Barely opening it, I peeked out to see no one was around. We both quickly ran out of the closet and to the elevator like we were fleeing for our lives.

The second the elevator doors shut, we both lost it laughing.

Life with Paislie was amazing and I couldn't wait to see where she wanted her last orgasm since I only managed to give her two.

THE FEEL OF EMMIT SMACKING my back, had me about spitting out my beer.

"You ready?"

With a grin, I replied, "I sure am."

"You do know how long your wedding ceremony is, right?"

I rolled my eyes and nodded. "I'm well aware of how long it will be."

"I'm thinking Addie and I will have enough time to sneak out and get in a quickie before anyone misses us."

My mouth fell. "You're my best man; you don't think people will notice you gone?"

With a wave of his hand, he chuckled. "They'll all be asleep."

"Fuck you, Lewis. I don't even know why I asked you to be the best man, you bastard."

The front door opened and Paislie came running out. "Look what was printed in *The Dallas Morning News* today."

She held up the paper and smiled. The picture was of me, Paislie, Emmit, Adaline, Landon, and Hailey all in front of the house with another picture of the vineyards.

The caption read:

Two former NASCAR teammates find life in the slow lane peacefully blissful.

I took in a deep breath and let the cool April air fill my senses. Paislie had thrown bluebonnets out last fall and they were springing up everywhere with all the rain we had gotten this past winter. The smell was amazing.

I took a glance around and smiled. This place really was our home. Everything had been falling into place and I couldn't have been happier. When we landed a huge deal with a local winery in the hill country, The Dallas Morning News asked to do an interview. Once she got past all the

NASCAR questions, we really got to talk about our plans for the future, plus it was a great plug for the bed and breakfast.

"The phone for the bed and breakfast has been blowing up all day and at first I couldn't figure out why until I realized it was the article in the paper. We are booked up for the next year."

Emmit and I both looked at her with stunned looks. "What?" Emmit asked as I shook my head.

"Yep. One year out; I finally told Janet to start putting people on a waiting list until I could talk to Addie about how she wanted to do reservations that far out."

The smile on my future wife's face caused my body to heat up. Damn, I'd give anything to take her right here.

Elizabeth walked out and it felt like someone poured cold water over me. My semi hard-on was gone in an instant.

"Paislie, the caterer is on the phone."

A look of horror moved across Paislie's face as she dashed back into the house, followed by Elizabeth.

"So, what's it like having one of your wife's best friend's be a nun?"

Glaring at Emmit, I shot him the finger as he laughed. "Don't you have anything else to do besides sit here and harass me? Like go help your wife with your daughter, or anything other than being in my face."

Emmit stood and flashed me a smile that told me he was about to be up to no good. "Bachelor party tonight."

"No. Dude, it's the night before my wedding. There is no way in hell I'm going out with you."

Emmit shrugged his shoulders. "We're not going out. We'll be at the B&B having a grand ole time celebrating the last hours of your freedom."

A bad feeling swept over me as I stood. "Emmit, I don't think this is a good idea."

"It'll be fine. What happened to the old Malcolm I knew? The guy who looked for any excuse to be a dick and have a good time."

"I'm going to ignore the dick comment. I fell in love, grew up, and I really don't want to go to my wedding with a hangover."

Emmit grinned from ear to ear. "Then don't drink. We need to be there by eight."

Before I had a chance to even argue with him, he was gone.

"Shit," I mumbled as I glanced down to Deuce. "What do you think, boy? Hanging out with the guys one more time isn't going to hurt, right?"

Deuce barked and then put his head back down as if he was disappointed in me.

"What do you know? You're a dog."

Forty two

PAISLIE

"OH MY GOODNESS. PAISLIE, YOU look beautiful," Annie said as she straightened out my train.

I took a peek at myself in the mirror and gasped at the reflection. "Wow."

It was all I could say as I stared at the woman I hardly recognized. My brown hair had been pulled up and curled with baby's breath flowers tucked all through out. I wore a simple pearl necklace that Janet had given to me one afternoon while we were walking alone in the vineyard. It meant more to me than she would ever know. She had become more than just Malcolm's assistant; she was like my surrogate mother.

Adaline handed me a pair of pearl drop earrings that we had bought together that she had insisted would be perfect and she was right. I put each one on and smiled when our eyes caught. "They're totally perfect."

She smirked and replied, "Told you they were."

Turning back to the mirror, I took in the beautiful strapless ball gown dress. "I love the sweetheart neckline so much on you," Adaline said as she gave me a loving look in the mirror.

"I do too," I softly spoke.

The moment Annie and I saw the dress, I knew it was perfect. The lace bodice flowed beautiful into English net that covered the satin dress. Lace appliqué lined the bottom of the dress and added the perfect amount of elegance.

Pulling my wedding dress up, I looked at the Jimmy Choo shoes Malcolm had bought me for today. I almost fell out of my chair when I opened them. I wasn't used to getting such expensive gifts, and I wasn't sure I would ever get used to it.

"Please, Lord, don't let me break my neck walking in these," I whispered as Annie giggled. She was the first person I called after Malcolm gave them to me. Only she would understand that moment since she had practically begged me to use my savings to buy shoes like this.

Elizabeth walked up to me and placed her hands on my shoulders. I instantly felt calm with her touch. "Okay, it's time. Take a deep breath and slowly blow it out."

Doing as she said, I closed my eyes and inhaled through my nose and out my mouth. When I opened my eyes, I couldn't help but smile as Annie held my bouquet of pink peonies. I was instantly transported back to when Malcolm asked me to marry him.

With my eyes closed, I could practically feel his lips on my body.

Annie cleared her throat and said, "Um, Paislie I'm pretty sure I know what you're thinking about, but in all seriousness here, we have a nun in the room."

Everyone started laughing as I felt my cheeks heat as I glared at my best friend.

Three knocks on the door signaled it was time.

"Ready?" Adaline asked as I nodded my head. "Let's hope Emmit doesn't try to escape during the ceremony."

Chuckling, I shook my head as I thought about his comment during rehearsal.

"Mass? We're doing a mass? The title on the program should be 'Get ready for the longest celebration of the sacrament of holy matrimony in history.'"

As we made our way down the hall, I could hear each girls' shoes hitting against the marble floor. My eyes glanced around as I remembered running down these halls as a little girl. St. Patrick's was more than a church; it had been my home as well. I sought refuge here so many times.

Janet was making sure everyone was in position and knew what to do. She had been a huge help in planning the wedding. I nearly gave Malcolm a heart attack when I told him she should get into the wedding planning business.

Janet cleared her throat and said, "Okay, Landon and Sophie will be going first, then Adaline, followed by Annie."

Glancing back to me, she flashed a huge smile. "Don't trip!"

I moaned and said, "Oh, why did you say that!"

Elizabeth wrapped her arm around me tighter as I felt the tears threatening as I thought about when I asked her to walk me down the aisle. I'd never seen her cry before that day.

Janet gave me a wink and said, "I'll motion when it's time for you and Elizabeth to start walking."

"Got it," Elizabeth said in a chipper voice.

The music started and I watched Sophie guide Landon through the doors. My heart was pounding so loudly I was sure everyone could hear it. The sound of the guitar playing "Jesu, Joy of Man's Desiring" warmed my heart. As a little girl I used to dream that song would be played during my wedding.

As I stood off to the side, I watched as Adaline began walking. Annie turned and smiled before she started walking. The violins played as I looked at Elizabeth.

"I'm scared."

She smiled warmly and said, "You're not scared. You're nervous."

"It's the same thing."

With a light chuckle she said, "There is a very big difference."

Janet nodded and Elizabeth and I moved into position. Swallowing hard, I watched everyone stand and look directly at me.

"Okay, now I'm scared and nervous!" I said as Elizabeth grinned bigger.

"Paislie."

My heart dropped at the sound of my father's voice. Turning, I couldn't believe my eyes.

"What are you doing here?"

"Shut the doors, Janet," Elizabeth said. "Let everyone know everything is okay; we just need a few moments."

The tightening in my chest was causing me to have a hard time breathing. *What in the hell is my father doing at my wedding?*

"You're not welcome here, Mr. Pruitt, and I kindly ask that you leave please."

I was stunned at how calm Elizabeth sounded.

An evil smile spread over his face. "Oh, I have no intention of missing my little girl's wedding. How much did that dress cost, pumpkin?"

With a quick glance at my dress, my head snapped back to him. "I think if you want this day to go off without a hitch, you'll spread the wealth."

"You unbelievable evil man. You're actually standing here bribing your daughter before her own wedding!"

"Sister, why don't you for once keep your habit out of my families business?"

Elizabeth walked up to my father and stood directly in front of him. "The day you dropped Paislie off at St. Patrick's, you gave up any right to call her your family. She is my family. Our family here at the church, so why don't you just take a few steps back and leave before I have you thrown out on your . . . on your . . . on your ass!"

I gasped when I heard Elizabeth curse. My father was as stunned as I, but what happened next I was pretty sure neither of us was expecting.

Pushing Elizabeth out of the way, he said, "Get out of my way, you bitch." Elizabeth spun around and stepped back in front of him and punched him square in the jaw.

Not being able to hold the scream back, the doors opened and Father Tim came rushing out as Janet shut the doors and walked over to me. Father Tim quickly walked up to Elizabeth and pulled her close to him.

"Elizabeth, are you okay? Did he hurt you?"

She shook her head and took a few steps away from him. "I'm fine, but Father forgive me for I have sinned." They both turned and looked at my father holding his chin.

"She hit me! She called me an ass and then hit me!"

Father Tim took my dad by the arm and pulled him toward the door. I quickly turned to Elizabeth.

"Where in the heck did you learn to punch like that?"

She shrugged and said, "I took a class on self-defense."

Janet attempted to cover her mouth to keep from laughing.

Letting out a gasp, I took her hand in mine. "It's swelling up."

She brushed it off like it was nothing. "Don't worry, I'll take care of it after the wedding."

Father Tim walked up to us and blew out a breath. "Okay, let's try this again. Let me head back down and let your worried fiancé know everything is okay. Once the music starts, please open the door and let's pick up where we left off."

My heart was still pounding, but everyone else acted like what had just happened wasn't that big of a deal as my eyes bounced between them all.

A few moments later, the music started, the doors opened and I my eyes were pierced by the bluest of blue. "Malcolm," I whispered as I let my gaze move across his body. He was dressed in a black suit and a white tie.

"He looks amazing," I said with a wide smile.

Elizabeth replied, "He certainly does."

I tried to pull my eyes from him to smile at our guests, but I couldn't. I was in a trance and I never wanted him to stop looking at me like he was that very moment.

When we finally made it to him I heard nothing but the sound of his breathing and mine. "Is everything okay?" he asked in a hushed voice.

"Everything is perfect," I responded.

After Elizabeth placed my hand in Malcolm's, we turned and made our way to the altar. The next forty minutes was a total blur. The moment Father Tim announced us as Mr. and Mrs. Malcolm Wallace, I couldn't contain my tears. Pressing his lips to mine, I lost myself in Malcolm's kiss as the entire church erupted in cheers.

When we started down the aisle, I smiled and waved to friends and family, as well as complete strangers who knew Malcolm either from racing or were distant relatives. The thought of meeting all those people at the reception seemed daunting.

Walking out the door of the church, I sucked in a breath when I saw the Rolls Royce Phantom car parked out front. After quickly searching for my father, I breathed a sigh of relief when we finally slipped into the car and drove off.

My head was spinning from the two different emotions swimming in my head. Happiness and shear fear that my father would be waiting outside the church for us.

Leaning my head back, I closed my eyes and calmed my breathing down.

"Are you going to tell me what happened back there at the church so I don't wonder for the rest of my life if you had second thoughts about marrying me?"

I snapped my head up and looked into Malcolm's eyes. "I've never once had second thoughts. It wasn't anything like that."

He let out the breath he had been holding as I took his hand in mine.

Knowing he was going to be angry, I braced myself for his response.

"My father was at the church. He tried to bribe me into giving him money, but it didn't work and he was removed from the church."

I'd never seen Malcolm look so angry.

Pulling out his phone, he hit a number. "You have some explaining to do. He showed up at the church."

My mouth fell open as I sucked in a breath.

What in the hell was going on, and who in the hell was Malcolm talking to?

Forty three

MALCOLM

I COULD SEE PAISLIE STARING at me from the corner of my eye as I lit into Kathleen.

"I want you to find out how he slipped by and make sure it doesn't happen at the reception. Yes, there will be security. Don't worry; I'll make sure they know."

Hitting End, I pushed my phone into my pants and took in a deep breath. I could feel her eyes burning into my body.

"You had my father followed? Why?"

Trying to calm myself down, I took a few more breaths and turned to her. "For this very reason. I didn't want him showing up asking you for money. I figured as soon as he found out you were marrying me, he'd start trying to contact you. I never dreamed he would actually show up at the church."

She frowned and I braced for her to lay into me. "Well he did, so whoever you were paying did a shitty job tracking him. Did I mention Elizabeth punched him?"

"Wait, you're not mad at me?"

Paislie let out a snicker. "Why in the world would I be mad at you? I think it's sweet you were looking out for me like that. You'll never know what it felt like to hear his voice when I was moments away from walking down the aisle."

"I swear to you, Paislie, I'll never let him near you again."

Her smile was soft and sweet. "I appreciate you wanting to protect me, but I've handled my father my whole life. There was one moment I was caught off guard and that moment was today. It will never happen again."

I shook my head. "What if he keeps trying to get money from you? I mean, if he tried to bribe you today, who's to say he won't try again."

"Oh he will; I'm sure of it. I'm guessing he is already trying to sell the story of how you married a poor girl from Dallas whose father was a drug addict and dumped her off at an orphanage."

Anger built up in my veins as I balled my fists together thinking about how her father would do something like that to her. Paislie placed her hand on my arm and gave me a gentle squeeze. "Malcolm, I'm not ashamed of where I come from. It made me who I am today. I have nothing to hide so I don't care what he tries to do. As long as I know you'll be by my side, there isn't anything I can't handle."

Her soft expression left me breathless. Paislie was the strongest, most forgiving woman I'd ever met. "Do you know how amazing you are?" I asked as I put my hand around her neck and pulled her closer to me.

"I think you may have to show me."

A low growl came from the back of my throat. "Baby, if I showed you your hair would be a mess, your dress wrinkled and you'd have my cum running down your leg as we greeted our guest at our reception."

With wide eyes, Paislie moved about in her seat. The desire I felt for her was uncontrollable.

"I'm willing to take the risk." Leaning over closer to me, she whispered, "Besides, I'm not wearing any panties."

My mouth snapped shut and my cock throbbed. "You want to kill me before our wedding night?"

Opening her mouth, she bit down on her finger and slowly nodded her head before saying, "I just want a preview . . . that's all."

My eyes looked over to the driver. "Phil, we need to make a quick stop before we head to the reception."

Nodding his head, he asked, "Where to, sir?"

"It's my wedding day and my wife wants a preview."

Peeking over to Paislie, her face flushed.

"The Ritz please, Phil."

"Yes, sir."

The damn console separating us was driving me insane as I pictured Paislie soaking wet under that dress.

"The Ritz-Carlton, sir. Shall I . . . um . . . wait?"

The doorman opened the door and helped Paislie out as she dropped her bouquet in the seat.

"Yes, we won't be long."

With a naughty smile, Paislie pressed her lips together as I grabbed her hand and lead her into the lobby. People smiled at us as we passed them by, each one congratulating us.

"Hello! Are you staying with us for your honeymoon?" the young blonde at the check in desk asked.

"No, I just need a room."

Her smile faded some as her eyes glanced back and forth between us. "Oh, okay. Only for tonight?"

With a smile and a wink, I replied, "For about an hour."

With wide eyes, she typed on her keyboard as Paislie pinched my arm.

"I'll just need an I.D. and credit card, please."

I handed her both as I peeked at Paislie who was taking the lobby in. I knew she wasn't used to this life style, but I wanted to spoil her every chance I got.

"Here ya go, Mr. Wallace. You're on the fourth floor, room four twenty. I hope you both enjoy . . . well . . . ah . . . I mean um . . . I hope you enjoy your stay with us."

Taking the card keys from her hand, I pulled Paislie closer to me. "Trust me, we're going to enjoy ourselves."

The young girl blushed as Paislie slapped me on the chest. "Malcolm!"

It didn't take me long to get us in the elevator and up to our room. When the door opened, I swept Paislie up into my arms and carried her into the room.

"Wow, it's beautiful in here," she gushed.

If she thought this was beautiful, wait until she saw the cabin I rented in Colorado for our honeymoon. Adaline had picked Paislie's brain for me about some of the places she had always wanted to visit. Colorado was one of them. She had dreamed of renting a cabin and doing nothing but relaxing and reading. I was about to make her wish come true with a two-week stay at a rustic log cabin outside of Winter Park.

Paislie walked up to the window and looked out over the city. She looked so damn beautiful, I almost hated to touch her.

My lips gently moved across her neck as she let out a soft moan. When my hands came up to unbutton her gown, goose bumps raised on her skin. I loved how my touch affected her.

"Malcolm."

The sound of my name off her lips had my nerve endings tingling. I needed to feel her up against me.

Once all the buttons were undone, I held her hand as she carefully stepped out of her dress.

My cell phone went off in my pocket, but I chose to ignore it. It was either Emmit or Janet trying to figure out where we were.

My heart stopped in my chest as I looked at my wife standing before me. She was dressed in a strapless lace bra, a garter belt, and stockings. Topping it all off were the shoes I bought her for the wedding.

"My God. You're absolutely breathtaking. I'm the luckiest man on earth."

Her cheeks turned red as she stood before me. Everything about her was perfect.

With a crooked smile, I ran my fingers along her cleavage, down her stomach and made my way between her legs. "You naughty little girl, not wearing any panties to your own wedding."

Fire danced in her eyes as she sucked in a breath when I cupped her mound. "Please touch me. I'm going to explode if you don't."

Pulling my hand away from her, I lifted her up while she wrapped her legs around me. "Tonight, I plan to strip you completely naked and take my time doing it, but for now, I'm going to give you that preview you wanted."

She wrapped her legs around me tighter as I carried her over to the desk and sat her down. "Spread your legs, baby. I want to taste you."

Her chest heaved as I dropped to my knees. Pushing two fingers inside of her, I let out a contented sigh. "Oh, Paislie." I moved my fingers in and out as she grabbed onto my hair and moaned.

"Baby, you're so wet."

Paislie mumbled something incoherently while I pulled my fingers out and lowered my face. "Oh God, yes!" she exclaimed as I flicked her clit with my tongue. It wasn't going to take her long to come.

Her hand pushed my face closer to her as she pumped her hips. My greedy little girl wanted more.

Less than a minute later and Paislie was calling out my name as her legs trembled and she came on my tongue. Nothing was more of a turn on and my cock was throbbing.

Standing, I unzipped my pants as Paislie's eyes widened in anticipation.

Pulling her up, I lowered her onto my cock as she wrapped her legs around me. I didn't want to mess her hair up, so I carefully set her back down on the desk and slowly moved in and out of her warm body.

"Faster. Malcolm. Please."

Doing as she asked, I pumped faster and harder as I felt my balls pull up. It wasn't going to take me long before I poured my cum into her.

Her eyes burned with lust as I felt myself grow bigger. "Paislie. Oh God."

With each thrust into her, I felt something I'd never thought possible. Each time I made love to her, it was better than the last. Something about knowing this woman was my wife, my forever, made the moment even better.

Burying my face into her neck, I breathed heavily as she wrapped her arms around me.

"That was amazing. It felt so—"

"Different," we both said at once. Pulling my head back, I looked into her eyes.

"I can't wait to make love to you tonight and take my time."

Her eyes lit up. "Me too."

My cell phone rang and I reached into my pocket to get it. I was still buried inside of Paislie as I felt my cock twitching.

"Hello?"

"Where in the fuck are you? If you tell me you stopped somewhere, I swear to God I'm going to pound your face in."

Holding back my laughter, I asked, "Why would you do that?"

"Because I'd have done the same thing with Addie! Any chance to have sex without one of our kids in the room and I'm going to take it."

Paislie covered her mouth in an attempt to hide her chuckling.

"I needed something to eat after that long-ass ceremony."

Her hands dropped to her sides as she gave me a dirty look. "That long-ass beautiful ceremony."

"You son-of-a-bitch. Get your ass here everyone is waiting on you."

"We're on our way now," I said as I kissed Paislie quickly on the lips.

I was about to hang up when Emmit yelled, "Bring me some fries!"

Dropping my phone back into my pocket, I pulled out of my wife and headed to the bathroom where I wet a washcloth with warm water. After cleaning myself, I wet it again and headed back into the room and gently cleaned her.

"Mmm . . . that feels good."

Pulling her off the table, I gave her a stern look. "No more until tonight."

With a pout, she mumbled, "Party pooper."

We carefully put her dress back on and Paislie checked her hair before we headed back down to the car. As we walked by the check in desk, I stole a glance at the young woman who checked us in. She failed at keeping her smile in as she turned and started talking to a co-worker.

Phil was still parked out front and was talking to one of the bellhops. The moment he saw us, he quickly opened the back door as I helped Paislie gather her dress up before she sat in the seat. Walking over to the other side, he held my door open and asked, "To the reception now, sir?"

"If we must!"

He held back his smile and nodded his head.

Ten minutes later we were pulling up to the Brookhaven Country Club. Phil got out quickly and made his way to Paislie's side of the car. Janet glared at me as I walked around the back of the car and up to her. With a quick shrug, I winked at her.

Rolling her eyes, she shook her head. "The photographer is waiting. We'll get a few pictures before you greet your guests."

Emmit came walking up searching for a bag of fries. "Where's my fries?"

Ignoring him, I held my hand out for Paislie as she stepped out of the car. Janet reached for the bouquet and handed it to her.

"Follow me for pictures, everyone!" Janet called out.

Emmit glared at me and then leaned in closer. "You bastard! You had sex."

"I don't know what you're talking about."

Adaline and Annie each took Paislie by the arm and pulled her ahead as they quickly got lost in conversation.

Emmit huffed. "Do you have any idea how much I hate you right now?"

With a dry laugh, I stopped and looked at him. "How about this. I arrange for both of your children to be occupied for at least thirty minutes. I'm sure you and Adaline can find somewhere to sneak away."

"Forty-five. It's been a while. I want to enjoy myself."

I acted like I was frustrated while blowing out a deep breath. "Fine. Forty-five minutes. After we greet all the guests, I'll make it happen."

Emmit slapped me on the back. "Dude, have I told you how much I love you?"

"Ugh. Don't make me throw up, you pansy ass."

Pictures were taken, greetings were done and I was making arrangements for Emmit's kids. It wasn't hard. Who wouldn't want to hold a two-month old sleeping baby, or take an almost two year old on an adventure walk?

Walking up to Emmit, I slapped him on the back and said, "Your time starts now."

His eyes scanned the room for Adaline. "I owe you."

I watched as he practically dragged her out of the room. Shaking my head, I chuckled to myself.

"Where are they going?" Paislie asked.

"To have sex."

She sucked in a breath as I turned to her and pulled her to me. "You, Mrs. Wallace, will have to be patient."

I dipped her as I pressed my lips to hers. When I pulled her up, she appeared to be dizzy.

"Are you okay?"

With a smile like I'd never seen before, she wrapped her arms around my neck and looked into my eyes. There will never come a time when I wouldn't get lost in those big, beautiful emerald eyes. "I've never been better. Say it again."

Tilting my head, I wrinkled my forehead and asked, "Say what again?"

"I want to hear you call me Mrs. Wallace again."

My heart skipped a beat as I cupped her face with my hands. Her lips parted as I gently kissed her forehead. "I love you, Mrs. Wallace."

Moving my lips to her nose, I whispered again, "I love you, Mrs.

Wallace."

Gently kissing her lips, I softly spoke against them. "I love you, Mrs. Wallace."

Her eyes were closed as I stared at her beautiful face. I knew what I was about to say could go either way, but it was on my heart and I wanted to say it now. After all, Paislie always said honesty was an enduring trait.

My thumb moved across her lips as she opened her eyes and caught my stare.

"Mrs. Wallace, will you do me the honor of carrying my child?"

Her breath stalled as her eyes lit up like I'd never seen before.

"W-what are you saying?"

My hand moved to her cheek as she leaned into it. "I want to try for a baby whenever you're ready."

A single tear rolled down her cheek as I kissed it away.

"Is that a yes?" I asked with a grin. My heart was racing as I waited for her response.

"Yes! And if trying for a baby is like anything else you set out to do, I'm betting on a January baby."

I threw my head back and laughed. "Now that right there was the biggest adrenaline rush I've ever experienced."

Pulling me out onto the dance floor, Paislie wiggled her eyebrows and said, "Wait until tonight, Mr. Wallace."

With a quick spin and a dip in my arms, I looked into her eyes and replied, "Who says we have to wait until tonight?"

PAISLIE

SEVEN YEARS LATER

"EMME, YOU BE CAREFUL UP on that horse!" I called out.

"I'm a racehorse driver, Momma!" Emmerson squealed.

My heart dropped as I watched my six-year-old daughter fearlessly trot around on the new paint horse Malcolm bought her.

"Did you hear that? Racehorse driver?" My hands went to my hips as I glared at Malcolm.

"I have no idea where she would have gotten that from, baby." He held up his hand and gave me an innocent smile. "I swear." My heart felt as if it would burst as I stared at my handsome husband. He and Emmerson were two peas in a pod and she was for sure a daddy's girl.

"Uh-huh," I replied with a roll of my eyes. "Malcolm, my nerves can't take her trotting, please tell her to walk."

Malcolm turned and called out, "Emme, let's walk Rascal before we take him out full throttle."

Promptly doing what her daddy said, Emmerson brought the horse down to a walk.

"Ugh! Malcolm, she's six. Stop talking to her like she is part of a pit crew!"

With a laugh, he pulled me closer to him and rested his hand on my swollen belly. "How's our son doing today?"

"Active. I have a feeling he's going to be an adrenaline junky like his father." I rubbed my stomach and felt our baby kick. Hard. "See!" I snickered.

"Four more weeks, baby."

I sighed and placed my hand on my lower back. "Thank goodness. This baby is killing my back."

Emmerson rode her horse up to us and stopped right on a dime. Her brown pigtails bounced around as she flashed her sweet little smile. "Daddy, can we go on our picnic now?"

Reaching up for her, Malcolm took her off the horse and held her in his strong arms. Malcolm motioned for one of the stable hands to come and take Rascal back to the stables. "It's up to your momma."

My body was aching and my lower back was killing me, but when her little blue eyes pleaded with me, there was no way I could say no. "Of course we can. Let's go see if Clarisse has the basket ready to go."

With huge grin, Emmerson fought to get down so she could run ahead of us. "I'm gonna invite Landon too! Y'all know we're gonna get married someday!"

"Damn it all to hell. Why must she say that all the time?" Malcolm moaned as I wrapped my arm around his waist.

"Did I tell you what Addie told me yesterday? She said Emmit about busted with pride when he found out."

Malcolm gave me a worried look. "Do I really want to know?"

With a shrug, I replied, "Only if you want to know the type of boy your daughter is attracted to."

Malcolm stopped walking and faced me as he drew in a deep breath. "Jesus H. Christ. She's six, what do you mean the type of boy she is attracted to? The only thing she should be attracted to is her horse."

Trying not to smile too big, I looked back at the house as our daughter skipped up the front porch steps.

"Fine. Whatever, I'm ready to hear it."

I peeked back at Malcolm and took his hands in mine. "Emmerson and Landon were walking out of school together holding hands."

His eyes closed and he let out a frustrated moan.

"The principal was walking behind them as they made their way to Addie."

Snapping his eyes open, a horrified look washed over his face. "Oh God. What did they do?"

"I guess yesterday at lunch a little boy in Landon's class said Emmerson was pretty and that he was going to date her some day when she got older."

Malcolm's face turned white as a ghost. "Oh holy hell."

Placing his hands on his knees, he dragged in a few breaths. "God is paying me back for all my sins. That's why he gave me a girl."

My hand covered my mouth as I let out a giggle.

Dropping my hand, I went on. "So anyway, this little boy declared he was going to date Emmerson. Landon wasn't having anything to do with that and told the little boy if he so much as looked at Emmerson the wrong way, he would . . . he would . . ."

"He would what?!" Malcolm shouted.

Trying to keep the laughter in, I shook my head and held up my hand. "Hold on! Need . . . one . . . second."

Malcolm waited not so patiently while I got myself under control. "He said he would bust his nuts and kick his ass."

His mouth dropped as I busted out laughing harder.

"Holy shit. Landon said that?"

Nodding my head, I said, "Yep! Addie said she was horrified, but Emmit puffed his chest out and proudly declared himself father of the year, then said Hailey was moving to an all-girl school because little boys were horny and not allowed around his daughter."

Malcolm let out a chuckle as we started back to the house.

"Damn. Who would have thought ten years ago that my daughter and Emmit's son would be crushing on each other?"

I stopped and looked at my handsome, clueless husband. "It's cute now, but you better prepare yourself."

"For what?"

Emerging from the front door, Emmerson and Landon came walking out. When Landon leaned over and kissed her on the cheek, Malcolm gasped beside me.

"For that . . . fast forward ten years."

Malcolm stared at them as they started our way. Landon, taking the basket from Emmerson, like the perfect little gentleman he was.

Turning to face me, Malcolm looked scared to death. "What was the name of that all-girls school Emmit was talking about?"

THE END

About the Author

KELLY ELLIOTT IS A NEW York Times and USA Today bestselling contemporary romance author. Since finishing her bestselling Wanted series, Kelly continues to spread her wings while remaining true to her roots and giving readers stories rich with hot protective men, strong women and beautiful surroundings.

Kelly lives in central Texas with her husband, daughter, and two pups. When she's not writing, Kelly enjoys reading and spending time with her family.

To find out more about Kelly and her books, you can find her through her website.

www.kellyelliottauthor.com

Acknowledgements

THANK YOU TO EVERYONE WHO picked up Ignite and Adrenaline and took a chance on this series! It means more to me than you will ever know.

Nichole and Christine—I could never really ever thank y'all enough for everything you do for me. You truly are both the best!

Laura Hansen—You are truly amazing. Thank you for always making time to read my stuff before anyone else puts their eyes on it. Love you to the moon and back!

Nikki—Thank you for being the last set of eyes on everything. The fact that you always make time when I send you a message out of the blue always fills my heart with gratitude!

Lauren—I love you and don't ever forget it. I've been so blessed with such an amazing daughter. If only you would clean your room . . . you would be perfect!

Texas Motor Speedway—Thank you for letting me make your track my home for a whole day. Your hospitality was beyond amazing.

The Wranglers—As always, ladies, thank you for everything you do for me. Your continued support means the world to me.

Kelly's Krew (Formally known as Kelly's Chasers)—Thank you for your continued support and for making our group such a positive and fun loving group. Thank you to all my admins for helping me!

Playlist

Selena Gomez—"Body Heat"
Malcolm and Paislie meet for the first time

Chelsea Kankes—"Ghost"
Malcolm and Paislie at track

Kelly Clarkson—"Let Your Tears Fall"
Paislie leaving Malcolm's house and parked at the end of the driveway

Carrie Underwood—"Heartbeat"
Malcolm and Paislie horseback riding

Rascal Flatts—"Riot"
Malcolm after Paislie leaves him

Justin Bieber—"The Feeling"
Emmit talking to Malcolm about Paislie

Wiz Khalife—"See You Again"
Malcolm at Casey's grave

Selena Gomez—"Nobody"
Malcolm and Paislie at the vineyard cottage

Justin Bieber—"Purpose"
Malcolm watching Paislie dancing with Landon

Rascal Flatts—"Bless the Broken Road"
Malcolm, Paislie, and Elizabeth in restaurant

Johann Sebastian Bach—"Jesu, Joy of Man's Desiring"
Malcolm and Paislie's wedding

CPSIA information can be obtained
at www.ICGtesting.com
Printed in the USA
LVOW04s1946011116

511197LV00013B/963/P

9 781943 633036